Books of Merit

THE FALL OF GRAVITY

ALSO BY LEON ROOKE

NOVELS

Fat Woman
Shakespeare's Dog
A Good Baby
Who Goes There
The Magician in Love

SHORT STORY COLLECTIONS

Last One Home Sleeps in the Yellow Bed
Vault
The Love Parlour
The Broad Back of the Angel
Cry Evil
Death Suite
The Birth Control King of the Upper Volta
Sing Me No Love Songs and I'll Say You No Prayers
A Bolt of White Cloth
How I Saved the Province
The Happiness of Others
Who Do You Love
Muffins
Arte
Oh! Twenty-seven Stories

PLAYS

Sword/Play
Krokodile
Ms. America
A Good Baby
Shakespeare's Dog

LEON ROOKE

THE FALL OF GRAVITY

A NOVEL

Thomas Allen Publishers
Toronto

Canadian Cataloguing in Publication Data

Rooke, Leon
The fall of gravity : a novel

ISBN 0-919028-36-5

I. Title.

PS8585.064F34 2000 C813'.54 C00-931495-4
PR9199.3.R66F34 2000

Portions of this novel have appeared in *Border Crossings* and *Exile*.

Text design: Gordon Robertson
Editor: Patrick Crean
Jacket photographs: Ann Giordano, Kamil Vojnar/Photonica
Author photograph: William Eakin

Published by Thomas Allen Publishers,
a division of Thomas Allen & Son Limited,
145 Front Street East, Suite 107,
Toronto, Ontario M5A 1E3 Canada

Printed and bound in Canada

whyfore
did you not
hail me,
bright rider?

For the Eden Mills Mud Strumpet Gang,
ever a buoyant crew.

contents

CHAPTER 1: Providence vs. Fate 1

CHAPTER 2: Ghosts 47

CHAPTER 3: Montana 69

CHAPTER 4: Let's Be Forthright About This 91

CHAPTER 5: Where Antelopes Play 109

CHAPTER 6: Oop-edee-doo 121

CHAPTER 7: Caution: Deer Crossing Road Next One Hundred Miles 145

CHAPTER 8: Master, Master, Lend Me Your Horse that I May Ride to Samara 163

CHAPTER 9: Day, Night, Waning Moons 181

CHAPTER 10: Advanced Biogenetics 199

CHAPTER 11: Dakota Secrets 221

CHAPTER 12: Joyel's Other Daughter 241

CHAPTER 13: The New Indian 257

THE FALL OF GRAVITY

1

providence VS. fate

One of the many public meetings the girl's father took her to was that of the priests who had fallen from heaven. This one was in Anne's Ardor, Michigan. The little girl's mother had been spotted in Anne's Ardor and they had shot right down there. Anne's Ardor is what the girl heard when her father told her where they were going. She had torn up the map looking for Anne's Ardor, and her father did not correct her. He was calling Ann Arbor Anne's Ardor also. "I got a feeling this is it," he said. "We are going to find your mother in Anne's Ardor."

"She won't be there. She certainly won't be at any Fall from Heaven meeting."

"You can't assume that. She's turned up in strange places. Why not at an ex-priests' meeting in Anne's Ardor?"

"What's *ardor* anyway? Is that like *sweaty*?

"You're thinking of Anne's Arduous, honey, another famous Michigan city."

At this juncture the girl's mother, the man's wife, had been gone nearly a year. They had that detective named Solly on her case. By Solly's count, Joyel Daggle had been sighted in nine Canadian provinces and twenty-six American states, not to mention south of the border down Mexico way. Occasionally she sent them a memento pillow. *I'm from Skagway*, the pillow might say. Sometimes she sent fruit, flowers, a verse:

I fled my beloved's light
To serve mad discord in the realms of night

The girl said, "No person in her right mind, not called Anne, holes up in a place called Anne's Ardor."

"I bet the place is overrun with Annes," he said. "You take a step, you'll be stepping on another Anne. You'll be knee-deep in all that ardor."

The man's name was Raoul Daggle. He was forty. The girl's name was Juliette Daggle, age eleven. The woman they were going to Anne's Ardor to find was Joyel Daggle, thirty-five. The pillows, the verses, they assumed, were some kind of joke.

Maybe her year on the road was another joke. They were not convinced of this, however. They believed she was running from something or someone, not them.

"Have I told you about my dog?" the girl asked.

"A thousand times," he said. "Let's hear no more about that dog."

She said, "Trash was my dog's name."

He said, "Please don't tell me again about that dog."

The girl tapped a foot, looking out at the Michigan landscape with smoldering eyes. "You like me, then you like my dog," she said.

He said, "That isn't in the rules. There isn't anything in our contract that makes me have to listen to a dumb dog story."

This was in the all-new Infiniti 130 for the year 2000, a spacious, elegant environment, a machine that mirrors, nay, keeps ahead of its driver's aspirations, own one and you'll understand. The Infiniti they were in was in scrubland outside a burg called Hell, Michigan, near Unadillia, Anne's Ardor about two hours southeast.

"Well, Hell wasn't much, was it?" the girl said.

One day back home, standing at the open kitchen window, she was telling her dog story to a bird up in the branches. The bird was one of those gray doves that awful neighbor, Vern, who raised doves, had let escape. They were friendly doves, though skittish. They didn't know what to do with themselves in the wild. Sometimes they would hop right up on the windowsill and ask you what they were supposed to do with themselves out there.

"Trash committed suicide," she had told the dove that one day back then. "At the beach this was. Oh, years ago. One of your ancestors might have seen him." Just as she was telling her father now, in the Infiniti on the road away from Hell. "Trash ran out into the waves. He kept swimming. Then he stopped and sank to the bottom. He never even came up once. Dear father tried to claim a shark, something like that, got him. But I said no, you and I both know perfectly well Trash committed suicide. Despondency, a sense of the futility of life, was always a part of his character. It was something he got from us. You can't deny it. Don't even bother. So he just said the hell with it and swam out beyond the reef and said adios."

"Adios, god of the third realm above heaven, son and sister of—"

"Don't interrupt. You were always letting Trash down. You hardly ever said a good word about Trash. You complained about the food he ate and about his barking. You even complained about how he chased sticks. He knew you hated him. He knew the senselessness of the poor, pathetic kid's love he was saddled with. He could give only so much loyalty to people like us. So he said, I'll show them. I'll kill myself. That's what he did, Daddy. Be truthful for once. See things for how they are. No syrup this time, okay?"

"Okay," Daddy said. "You're right. I stand corrected. Now what?"

Today they had seen a dog lying on the pavement outside Hell Café as they were going in for lunch. People thought the dog had been struck by a car or was sick or was dead; they were having to walk around it and hold their noses and say to each other, Look at that sorry dog.

Juliette said, "Trash?"

And the dog got up. It looked at her with incredible longing; it licked her hand and sniffed her crotch, transformed in the instant from an old and dying dog into a young and robust animal with not the smallest reason to tarry outside in the sun when a beautiful girl stood in the doorway beckoning. Food plus friendship, the dog might have thought, what a winning combination.

When they buried Trash they had buried a symbolic dog, actually an old pair of red high-heel shoes belonging to Joyel Daggle. They buried algae and seaweed with the symbolic dog.

"Trash didn't mind," she told her father, on the road, bound for Anne's Ardor. "He was an algae kind of dog."

"Goddammit!" her father said, pounding the steering wheel. "Goddammit!"

"What! What! What!" cried the girl.

"How old are you?" the daughter asks her father.

"Oh, I've been around."

"How old? Had dirigibles been invented? Were there telephones?"

"Hard to say."

"Were you always a son of a bitch?"

"Now wait a minute, young lady. You mean 'son of a gun.'"

"I specifically do not mean 'son of a gun.' Were you?"

"Okay. Yeah. From the beginning, I was a son of a bitch."

"Good. So long as I know who my riding companion is."

Zooming along on North Territorial Road, Anne's Ardor nearing, Raoul Daggle says to his daughter, "For your first birthday we baked you a cake so big you could swim in it. We sat you right down inside that cake. You almost choked."

"What else?"

"Trash was barking. Trash was having a great time. He was tied to a wrought-iron table leg. This was out by the pool. Trash pulled that table right over to the cake, leaving us at the table high and dry. We thought Trash was after the cake but in fact it was Trash saved your life. He pulled you out of the cake by your little bootie. We had that bootie bronzed and on the mantel all the time you were growing up. People would revel at the tooth marks. That's probably why you have your cute limp."

"Were all of you drunk?"

"All? No. Just the part that was brain-dead."

"You left me to die in a cake?"

"That's the sum of it. Afterwards, though, we had a good time washing cake off you with the hose. I think that was about the best time your mother and I ever had. It was a day of radiant sunlight. I can still hear how our hearts were beating."

"You can soft-soap me all you want," the girl said, "but I am not going to any meeting of ex-priests who have fallen from heaven."

"What limp?" asked the girl minutes later. "What are you talking about? Why are you always confusing me?"

Back at the café in Hell, Michigan, a carload of fallen priests bound for the Anne's Ardor meeting had come in all black-suited, jibbering and jabbering, their faith refurbished, their spirit lifted, if you can credit this, by dining in Hell, Michigan. One old priest with purplish veins streaking his face, a purple nose that betrayed a lifelong relationship with drink, no disrespect to drinkers intended, had plopped down at their table. "Thanks," he said to Juliette, "it says 'Welcome' right there on your placemat." He had fallen hard from heaven, he said, and, yes, he was still falling, since a thing like that, a thing that coarsened your life, set awry your expectations, did not occur overnight.

Raoul was away in the kitchen, getting bones for the dog, he'd said, but probably back there flirting, he was never a papa available when needed.

"Doubt," the old priest said, "it sweeps you up like a whirlwind."

That he was saying this to an astonished child, her face sour with disapproval, did not strike the old man as inappropriate. We all fall in one way or another, was his thinking, and this child will fall also, perhaps the sooner the better, since obviously a child has not so far to fall that the descent will kill her, as to his mind it had him. These thoughts introduced to the old man's mind the broader policies of death, and he wished he had the time and inclination to sit the girl down upon his knee, that he might inform her of matters so much more grave, more at issue, than her platform shoes, her straight hair, pimples, this smelly dog panting at her ankles. "Sit here," he said, patting a knee, becoming cross when the child shook her head, shook it violently, saying, "If you put a hand on me, mister, my daddy will kill you."

Which threat only kicked onto a higher plane the old priest's incentive. He would take the time. Here was ignorance and ignorance must be combatted. "I think about death all the time," he tells the child, "and you owe it to your creator to do the same. The loss of faith is like a shriveled plum that hangs from a black limb through untold winters."

"Come away, Father," some of the other priests are shouting to the old man. "Come back to your own table."

But the old priest is as stuck to his spot as the dog, as Juliette, as the waitress back in the kitchen rustling up a bone for the dog, are to theirs. Beneath the table, the dog growls out of habit, it licks crumbs from the floor, no doubt thinking, This isn't the feast I had hoped for. Nor is the old priest's droning voice anymore to his liking. The dog would sink his teeth into those pink, swollen ankles, but what's the use, the fallen soul already has sufficient pain.

"People who are about to die," the old man says, "who are approaching death but must await the Reaper's vengeance—oh, they are cunning, those Reapers, there's so much theatricality in the enterprise—receive visitors by the score, a long succession of sojourners from the dark plain, people who themselves are dead. They mean to give you solace, but it's all handstands, it's all hollow rhetoric, they speak platitudes in your ear, drivel, just as do the living."

Now the entire complement of priests fallen from heaven ring the girl's shoulders, young and old, their voices intermingling. "He's got it bad," one says. "He needs spaying," another saying. "Come on, Father, don't worry the youngster, we've got chicken dumplings coming, you'll love them."

Oh, Papa, where are you?

"They sit with you," mutters the old man, "drinking Earl Grey tea, biscuit crumbs littering their laps, they say, 'Oh, you'll find death isn't so bad, it's nothing really, you'll hardly notice the difference.' The dead see the present from a vast distance, from a totally altered perspective, that's the biggest change and one that takes time to get accustomed to, I'm telling you."

The old priest is indeed so telling her, or would be, if the child were listening. When did the young ever listen? No, her hands are up covering those ears, mouth and eyes and clamped tight. All the same, there's leakage from those eyes, the chin quivers, her little canary heart is palpitating at great speed, her fanny twitches on the hard seat, her breath means to run away with her, Mother, Mother, why are you not here to save me?

"I'm telling you this," the old priest tells her, "for your own good."

Where has she heard this before?

"Those ex-priests," Raoul says to her later, "they miss the confessional, all those stories. It was those stories of another's sin that propped them up, just as it's our own stories that keep us going, because if we have none, what's the point in continuing?"

Juliette is only partially attending to her father's nonsense, she's punching the smart Infiniti radio buttons in search of some little spark of happiness. She feels weighted down by the old priest's words, also she misses the dear dog and wishes this minute he was between her feet, panting and licking and growling, such pathetic growls. Now the dog will be missing her as he licks his bone and dreams of the time a young girl said *Trash?* In the dog's mind, no doubt, today's event is seen as one transpiring a long time ago, perhaps in the dog's youth, and one the dog will likely play out a hundred times in his future, since unlike ourselves a dog wisely does not divide time into the three quadrants of past, present, and future but instead summons all three into the living present, for how else could a dog persevere?

Ah, but let us now relax, for Juliette has found on the Infiniti radio dial at 91.7 a station calling itself the Happiness Station. Here they fill the airways with music of bygone epochs, mostly polkas, waltzes, aeolian chants, interspersing these inane tunes with reports on happy events in the immediate locale and beyond. So-and-so was married today at Waddling Saints Meadow, so-and-so today in celebration of their sixtieth anniversary took off for fourteen carefree days at Jethro's luxurious Beverly Hillbillies Mansion and Casino in Reno, here is more news from home. So-and-so have given birth to nine-pound darling baby Cassandra at Waddling Saints General Hospital, firefighters this morning rescued a tabby named Theodore from the well it fell into nine days ago, glory, glory. A man in Gypsy Falls is giving away all his money, updates on this later, folks. In the meantime put this date on your calendar, the great Waddling Saints County Fair opens next week, now a word from our sponsers.

Segue to this now; an invited guest is on 91.7 speaking of the Black Hills massacres of 1876, Chief Crazy Horse's battle at Powder River, the Chief's defeat of General George Crook on the Rosebud River, March 17, 1876, and of George Armstrong Custer at Little Big Horn three months later, skirmishes in which, unhappily, many perished, but, happily, palefaces and redskins alike now sit side by side in heaven, the historian said, proving again that happiness resides with the beholder, a truth repeated so often it tortures us to hear it repeated, but such is life, Raoul Daggle is thinking, pardon me if I have a little swig of gin.

"I don't have to be Joyel Daggle's kid," the girl said. "I could be any berserk mother's kid who abandons her one and only child."

"No, you couldn't," said the father, patting her knee. "You have to be Joyel Daggle's kid."

"I could be *that* woman's kid or *that* one's."

"No," said the father. "You're Joyel's kid."

This was on Joy Road, outside Dexter, the Infiniti crawling along, the road bumpy. A dozen or so women outside a Joy Road bingo hall were shouting and waving their arms.

"I could be the prize. One of those women yell 'Bingo!' and out I pop."

"These Joy Road people don't want you," Raoul said. "These women want cash."

When she was two and they had moved to a smaller house in a smaller city in an extremely small-minded province her father had painted a false window in her room that lacked a real one. He'd stand by the foot of the bed looking out the bogus window. "Look," he'd say, "there's old Jack Splat eating his fat. There's old Jake Crumb eating his thumb."

"You would fly to the window. You would scream, '*Where? Where?*'"

In that Hell Café, all black plastic, under wash of red lights, anquished shrieks from the walls, the little girl says to the waitress, "My tastes are refined but simple."

The waitress takes a frightened step backwards, hopping like a bird. She had thought this older man and his little daughter would be nice. She perceives now that they have made of her the enemy. What has given them the right to refuse their menus? If they can't trouble themselves to read a menu, let them go to the burger joint across the street. Let them walk over there and be run down by the traffic.

The man is beating out a tune on the table. Originally with his speared martini olives, now with his and the child's fork. What one must put up with for a mere five twenty-five an hour.

"Write this down," the girl says to the nervous waitress. "I'll have your *sopa de dia*. Hurry up, Papa. You know we have business."

The waitress is appalled. She has never seen such a rude child. She has no idea in the world what this *sopa de dia* is. All she knows is that the kitchen will not have it. Ten o'clock will never come. Her shift has just begun. At ten o'clock her boyfriend will be picking her up. This will never happen. The hours are too far off. She cannot imagine any future that takes so long to get where it is supposed to be going.

"What is your *sopa de dia*?" the man is asking.

The waitress knew it. She could see it coming.

She flings up her arms, screeches, flies from the room. Let's admit it, not all waitresses are stable.

For her eighth birthday, the girl's father brought home a foot-high replica of Michelangelo's David. The girl looked at the white sculpture and vowed she would marry an Italian.

"Now," he said, "for your art lesson."

He disrobed and stood naked on the kitchen table.

"Consider this. Size of the whole is often relative to the power of the whole. But don't be sappy about it. When you grow up into a beautiful woman you'll find that the mate who attracts you isn't anything like this David. They are more like me. That is one of the mysteries: why we settle for, even are excited by, the second rate. Perfection scares everyone away."

"I want to stand on that table," the girl said. "Call Trash. Call Joyel Daggle. Let's all stand naked on the table."

Her father was a great reader. According to her mother, the reason her father was so fond of books was strictly on account of his alcoholism. Whenever he read the words *liquor* or *drink* or *refreshment* or any word directly or abstractly related to what he loved best in the world he could taste it on his tongue. Like a shot, he was up and pouring. Then back to his book, until the next occurrence.

"He liked his booze and his women and his poetry," Joyel Daggle one day said. "It's right there on his tombstone."

"Did he die? And I wasn't told?" asked the daughter.

"Many times, dear. Many times."

"That is unmitigated falsehood," Raoul told his daughter. "The only time I ever have a drink is when you drive me to it."

Such a lame joke, the girl thinks, it deserves no response, and thus for the next miles she keeps her lips tightly clamped, a witless father is such a pain in the butt and the miles so dreary.

One of the little girl's many recurring dreams is of Trash sitting up, paws folded, begging for food. He has eyes like those starving children in the posters.

So she began leaving kibble on a plate by the side of her bed and at night as she herself slept the dog came. He comes. In her dreams Trash licks her feet, wags his tail, sleeps beside her on a pink pillow. In the mornings, she goes running to her daddy, the real bowl hoisted high, crying, "Daddy, Daddy, the bowl is empty."

"My goodness. Just imagine."

Long, long ago, Papa was in a coma. A horse had kicked him. He came out of it saying, "Use the eight-inch pan. Bake at three fifty."

In summer Raoul Daggle helped the little girl catch tadpoles in a white net. The tadpoles were for her aquarium. The tadpoles that were not eaten got bigger. Frogs were hopping all over her room and into the hallway and onto every ledge; they sat on chairs like gentlemen and ladies. You had to watch where you walked and sat. All night long the frogs played Mozart, not very well.

"The black ones were into rap," the father said. "They drove your mother crazy."

This was in a place called Barton Hills, while gassing up the Infiniti 130 for the year 2000. Anne's Ardor was right around the corner.

"Why do those priests have to have meetings?" asked the girl. "Why did they leave the church if all they want is to attend another meeting? Who created the heavens and the earth, anyway?"

"Your mother," said the father. "It was a slow night. Not much was happening."

It hurts us to confess to this but the truth is that what has not been reported on in this journey, nonevents, if we may refer to them that way, are every bit as important as that which has found print. What we are presented with and see before our own eyes is merely a fragment of the whole, in the same sense that our own lives are smaller particles belonging to a grander spectacle. In one café, that greasy spoon in Hell, Michigan, our travelers wanted soup, in another before that they wanted breakfast, no insurmountable objective, you might think, yet the obstacles were many. We don't serve breakfast after ten, right there you can see the sign. That was one hurdle. Well, what is another, asked Raoul, "Are you out of eggs?" "I like bacon," Juliette said, "and toast if you use real butter," a comment that only served to make matters worse, since the waitress then said, "What after all is wrong with our blue-plate special, chicken dumplings, we get a lot of praise for those dumplings." "I don't eat chicken," the girl said, there she goes again, making more trouble, small wonder her mother has elected to be out there in the world all by her lonesome. But is this breakfast business important? You may ask. Do I need to know this? And the answer is No you don't, perhaps you should have skipped over this portion just as others would skip the entire narrative, let's face it, not everyone can be satisfied. Juliette and her father, for instance, who only want breakfast, or the old priest who only wanted a new ear into which he could pour his troubles, or the waitress who had a headache, chapped hands, sore feet, and would have preferred to be at home in a warm soft bed, or her husband who at the precise minute the squabble occurred was atop an earth-breaking machine also wanting to be at home in the same warm soft bed. Or the other diners, what was it they wanted or would have preferred. To repeat, not everyone can be satisfied with chicken dumplings and many can never be satisfied with anything, heap a thousand blessings upon them and still they will be complaining. Maybe that's why Joyel Daggle abandoned the family nest, I wouldn't put it past her. What do we know about this woman anyway, and why should we care, *goddammit! goddammit!* Now I'm mad, I'm not reading anymore of this nonsense, comma splices be damned, I hate fused sentences, I can't make heads nor tails of this madness, no sex, no fun, no *nada*, I'm withdrawing from this maze, I may never read another book as long as I live.

The decision is yours, a view those of us in the print world are powerless to oppose, although it's a pity in a way, because just a few miles down the road, in Anne's Ardor, actually, the old alky priest we have so much detested will soon be looking a long time at the handful of pills dispersed into his scaly palm, bursitis, you know, shingles as well, God help him, he will swallow these pills six or seven at a time and gag as often, he follows this swallowing each time with a sip of watered bourbon, no ice, he has never been one who finds pill-taking easy, he's a dying man anyway so why not empty the bottle, he's pretty sure, too, that this coward's way out will guarantee perpetual damnation, though what's the dif, haven't recent years been just that?

There, the last batch, now he ought to stretch out, remove his shoes, hide the bourbon bottle under the mattress, pity the poor maid who will discover his corpse here in the morning. Goodbye everyone, I wasn't so bad as you think, I did more than one-person good, I never passed wind in public, I honored the downtrodden.

Goodbye.

And will you, dear reader, will Juliette ever learn that this old man also is an orphan, deserted by both parents, truly a baby left on a doorstep, a ready solution in those olden days when doorsteps were more plentiful, then raised by the School of Our Boys of St. Paul, but that was a long time ago and is mentioned here not to forge a link, dubious at best, between a vile old ex-priest and an innocent young girl but mentioned because the old fellow will go on thinking until his last breath that betrayal of those crafty buggers who reared him, spanked him whether he was a good or bad boy, yanked him this way or that and a thousand times said, Bend over, yet for all of that still remained true to their Savior, never veered from the tenets of divine faith, always there to hoist the chalice, what would they think of him now, our Lord God casts these burdens upon you only that you may be made fit to enter paradise, that's the one bit of guilt the old priest can no longer live with, granted his thinking is muddled.

So there he goes, will he die or survive another day? This isn't the first time, and he has many friends among those who have fallen, surely one of them will enter and find him, those who have fallen prowl the motel corridors midnight till morning knocking on each other's door, one or another now and again even climbing into the old alky priest's bed, it isn't an unforgivable sin whatever higher authority avers, let us pray, let us close that door.

"We used to ride you around like this when you were a baby," Raoul Daggle told Juliette. "We'd change your diapers under sour apple trees, beside running brooks. We always wanted to climb Pike's Peak and change you up there. We'd dress you in about six sweaters, until you looked like a fat pig. Tie a cap under your chin. In those days all baby clothes were either pink or blue, and your mother and I fought every minute over these colors. We'd ride you around in these white booties, one foot in a pink sock, the other in blue. It took about three hours to dress you. You looked gorgeous, until you dribbled all over yourself, like a sewer."

"I've seen the pictures," said the girl. "In every one, I've got snot hanging from my nose or food caked around my mouth."

"When you were a baby, while everyone else was getting rich, we'd pull our chairs up to your crib and watch you sleep. 'We made that,' we'd say. Then we'd say, 'Which of us do you think *most* made her? How much of her do you think she made herself?' This dialogue went on for hours. For weeks on end, that's all we did. It was one of the best times we ever had. We were always having to get up and wipe drool from your mouth. 'You made the part of her that makes her cry,' your mother would say, 'I made her smile. I made the space in between her toes.' 'Be quiet,' I'd say. 'I'm making her teeth. I'm working on the dimples in her cheeks.' 'You didn't make anything,' she'd say. 'All you did was put your roger inside me.'

"'Roger?'"

"Un-huh. Your 'Roy Roger' Joyel sometimes called it. Or 'Roy Acuff.' She was awfully keen on those Roys in those days. She was cute. She could get away with anything."

"Sounds sappy to me."

"You have to be sappy when you have a baby around. There's something in nature that drives parents to be as brainless as the baby is. Innocence is a great equalizer. It was when you took up the violin, not two years old, that matters got serious."

"I never took up the violin."

"In our minds you did. We wanted a prodigy, you see. Every other parent we knew had one. We wanted one, too."

"I was a terrible disappointment to you. That's probably why Joyel is on the lam."

"No it isn't. Once we drove you up to that water place, what's it called?"

"Niagara something."

"That's right, Niagara Something. We went out on that boat, *Misty Maiden*."

"'Maiden', no, *Maid of the Mist*."

"Something. They gave us bright yellow slickers to wear. We all got drenched. You cried. You thought we had gone there to drown Trash. I bought you a little boat the exact image of *Misty Maiden*, down to the little play people in yellow slickers on the deck. You gnawed that boat into nothing. Paint flakes all over your chin."

"I was toothing. Teething. I remember every detail."

"You do not."

"I remember even before that. I remember the moment your seed and Joyel connected. *Boom!* they went. I remember saying, '*Hooray!*' but the two of you were so wrapped up in each other you couldn't hear a word."

"I don't doubt it. Your mother said to me, 'It's time to declare bankruptcy. We're going to have a child.' But that time at Niagara Something, we tied our wet clothes to the radio aerial, like the flags of nations. We let the tin cans just stay there tied to the bumper. You were an illegal alien, you see, an immigrant who had sneaked in while lust was blinding us. We were gone a long time on that trip. Three months."

"I remember what Joyel wore," said Juliette. "She wore a yellow tank top, a tight yellow skirt, yellow shoes, yellow socks. A wide-brimmed hat, that same yellow. She was one big yellow blob."

"Miss Neon. She did like bright clothes. She wore them so that we could find her when she got lost."

"She pulled that hat down over my eyes. She said, 'Look at the falls through my hat. Save the real sight for when you're older, a young woman in love. You're too young for such riches now. The falls won't thrill you the way they do me and your papa. To you, all that splashing water, all that mist and foam, will just be humdrum and natural. You'll think, why are they making such a fuss? You can have the same experience standing under a shower, without being miserably cold and deprived.' In the meantime, you were dangling poor Trash over the side. I saw you."

"You're an inventive child, your imagination runs away with you."

"All this is a lie, mine wasn't an illigitimate birth, I wasn't adopted, either."

"You're right. I'll never forget that yellow tank top of your mother's, sexy as the dickens."

In the motel room in Niagara Falls she—the girl, the infant—had flicked the lights on and off. Four lights, in lamps at either side of the bed, an upright in the corner, another overhead.

"Stop that," her mother said.

Stop that stop that stop that!

Her father had lunged naked from the bed and got Joyel in a bear hug from the rear. He lifted Joyel up and down, up and down. "No spats," he said.

Next, there had been a big pillow fight, which broke the bed. The three of them had slept that way, on a tilt. "This is how mountain climbers sleep," Raoul said. "Without knowing which way is up. Let's dial room service. Let's order the mountain climber's pack. Who wants to go over the falls in a barrel? Can we procure a barrel big enough for the three of us?"

"The four of us."

"What?"

"You're always forgetting Trash."

"You were too young to remember, but you had another dog before Trash."

"I did not."

"That dog was devoted to a neighbor, a little girl with buck teeth named Kristan, Kristan Shanty. That dog was forever playing with Kristan and never with you. We would find you sitting in your wading pool, your sandbox, deserted, cying out your eyes. So I shot that dog."

"You didn't!"

"No, Joyel and I gave that dog to Kristan, who was equally besotted. You cried for days. Your mother said, 'she will never forgive us,' and she was right, you haven't."

"No, I will never forgive you. Both of you did hundreds of things I don't even know about, that's why I can't forgive you."

"There are so many sorrows. You can pick and choose them at will, like apples you'd pluck from a tree. That was your first sorrow, losing that dog that didn't love you, though you can't remember the heartbreak now. Sorrows are like that sometimes, they get buried and forgotten, that's the one good thing about them."

"What was your first sorrow, Daddy?"

"Wide feet. I walked like a duck. My mother said I'd look good on the table, *duck à l'orange*."

"Please, Papa. Be serious."

"I can't be serious. Serious, I'd wring your mother's neck."

"Me, too. I want to wring her neck."

"Good. That's how serious we both are."

In Anne's Ardor Raoul and Juliette found the Fall from Heaven meeting scheduled for two p.m. at the Best Western had been canceled. A dozen ex-priests patrolled the lobby, saying, "Who canceled the meeting? Well, Jesus Christ!" Juliette tugs at her father's arm. "Look," she says, "there's that old guy with the purple nose." "What guy?" Raoul asks. "You know," she says, "that old fuckhead priest from Café Hell."

There he is indeed, unshaven, paunchy-eyed, disheveled, but otherwise in fine mettle, now assailing a youthful bellhop with his tales of the social practices of the dead. Unknown to him his fallen brothers have tampered with his sleeping pills. The movement would be lost without this venerable old son of a bitch to remind them of the horrors of their fall, the hot flames awaiting them in the beyond. "How many popes have been doomed to hell?" he asks the terrified bellhop. "Take a wild guess."

So that all would not be lost, Raoul Daggle took the little girl to a meeting of the Widowhood Gulag. Membership was composed entirely of women whose husbands had died prematurely.

"This is what awaits you," he said. "The format is always the same. It comforts them. Let's sit right up front."

A svelte woman named Polly White gave an inspiring talk. Then there was coffee and cookies baked by a team of widows comfortable in the kitchen. Before the cookies and after the talk there was a discussion period.

"Mine used only his finger," one said.

"I hope to God I never have to hear the words 'six-pack' again," said another.

Polly White's lecture was called "Cutting Corners" and involved numerous demonstrations. She demonstrated how to "four-corner" a sheet in three seconds flat. She argued against old women like themselves having pets underfoot. "Better a python snake," she said, "than a cat or dog. How many of you have broken bones?"

Hands went up all around the room. Those who hadn't suffered in this regard lowered their heads in shame.

"Get rid of your pets," Polly White said. "Push them out in the street. Don't feed them. They'll quickly take up with some other dotty old lady."

Polly White received big applause at the conclusion of her speech. The widows loved the scorn she heaped on them. "You're a sorry-looking bunch," she had said, such rage, "all those pinched mouths, your blue hair, your big bottoms. Small wonder your children want you in old age homes." Polly White was perspiring, she was red-faced and breathing fast, her blouse had slipped free of its skirt, her brassiere was catty-cornered on her heaving bosom which was like one enormous boulder cleaved into perfect halves.

The little girl and her father were among those clapping. They were on fire with enthusiasm. "She gets one hundred dollars for her speech," he said. "She gets honorary lifetime membership in The Widowhood Gulag."

Polly White had been spearing looks at her father throughout her oration. She had been winking. When finished, she made a beeline for him, shoving herself straight up under his face, laying a demure hand softly upon his chest.

"I've been betrayed," she said. "They assured me no men would be present."

She batted her eyes, swiveled her hips. Her ringed fingers were as busy as a yard rake. This was how Polly White flirted.

"Who's the little twerp standing beside you?" Polly White asked.

"I'm indoctrinating my daughter in the ways of life," the little girl's father explained. "I'm preparing her for the ordeal."

"Last week he took me to the court house," the girl told Polly White. "A man was on trial for selling horse meat in a butcher shop in Racine, Wisconsin."

"One twenty-nine a pound," said Raoul.

"It was his finger on the scale that got everybody mad."

Women of the Gulag were snatching at Polly White's elbows. They were insisting she try their cakes and sit in their best chair. Several were wanting to know where Polly White had got her red shoes.

"These old biddies make me sick," Polly White said. "Let's go out and get something real to drink."

So Juliette and her papa hopped into the Infiniti and followed Polly White's red mini to a tavern with a blue door.

"Get rid of the little girl," Polly White said before they were seated. "Make her wait in your car."

Instead, Papa seated her in his lap. "Hark, what light. Sit right here," he said. He spread her legs wide of his, pulled down her skirt, patted her kneecaps, and kissed her neck.

"We go everywhere together," the girl told Polly White. "Papa is my guide through reality. He says there are two vicious watchdogs guarding the Gates of Hades, and that is the one place we can't go."

"Yeah," said Polly White. "I go there every night. It isn't any place special, let me tell you."

It did seem to the little girl that Polly White and her papa knew each other. They were touching toes under the table. More than once they touched fingertips. They touched noses. Polly White often spoke in a whisper so low one was compelled to lean close. You could look down upon her wonderful breasts, leaning close. You could look into her eyes. You could breathe her sweet breath and be imprisoned forever within a field of rapture.

They had five drinks each, Papa letting Juliette sip his. That way he always had a good reason for ordering another.

Then Polly White said she had to go to work. At five p.m. sharp she was showing a house to a pair of nitwits from Duluth. It was a starter home, she wouldn't make a nickel.

Her papa looked like he was galloping towards some terrible calamity.

He wanted to buy this house away from the nitwits, he said. For his little girl. "A starter home is just what a eleven-year old girl needs. When she's thirteen, she can move up. Maybe a condo."

"What is your present residence?" asked Polly the realtor.

"We're gated."

"Pardon me?"

"We live in a gated community."

"Ugh," said Polly White. "You must have brains the size of a Barbie doll's."

"For senior citizens. Well, we don't actually live *in* it because of the moat Papa invented. He's made millions on that place, two hundred acres, and doesn't have to work ever again if he doesn't want to."

"My goodness," said Polly White, fluttering her eyes as she kissed Raoul's hand.

"That's why we can spend all our time chasing down my lost mama."

"Well, you're a very grown up little vixen, aren't you?" Polly White said.

"Juliette has already hit puberty," explained Raoul. "Each generation moves a notch closer. Pretty soon birth and puberty will occur simultaneously."

"I've never got over mine," Polly White said. Her hands clawed the table. She crunched her ice. "It knocked me loopy."

She blinked wet eyes at her drink. Her hands were splotchy, the nails chewed way down. Tears trickled down her cheeks and no one at the table, least of all Polly, knew why.

There, there.

"Nothing's real anymore," she wept. "I don't believe in anything."

"Another ex-priest," said Raoul, perhaps because at that very moment a gang of these people had made a noisy entrance and were now stalking the aisles in search of a good table.

"Sex and starter homes, sex in starter homes, kept me going a long time. But now."

"That's very sad," said Juliette.

"I never got the least pleasure from it," cried Polly White.

"That's so, so sad," said Juliette.

Polly White said, "What the Sam Hill do you know?" She turned and said the same thing to Raoul.

"Not squat-all," he said.

Polly White took off her red high heels, placing them side by side on the table in front of her, then placing her hands inside the shoes and walking them over the tabletop.

"There I go," she said, after a pause. "Walking the last mile."

"Mama says drink's a depressant," remarked Juliette. "She's opposed to alcohol taken in quantity."

Polly White raked the ceiling with her eyes. "Snooty beady-eyed, pimply-faced children make me gag," she said. Her eyes settled on the child momentarily, with every appearance of loathing, then they went on to smolder over Raoul.

The priests who had fallen from heaven were still not yet seated, winding about as though tethered by one long rope, among them the old alky with the purple nose who now sights Juliette and shouts, "Looky, there's my sweetheart. Marry me, darlin'!"—as he's whisked away by his brothers.

Juliette slides low in her seat, thinking, Everyone's looking at me. They are looking at my little pimples Dot, Spot, and Pecan Praline. Oh, hide me, she thinks.

"I took you for, like, cool," Polly White is saying to Raoul, her apparent loathing now including him. "A divorced with-it guy. Now I see the error of my ways."

"We really do have a moat," said the child. "My father inherited this huge chunk of land. He parceled off that land and made a killing. He calls it Daggle's Adult Lifestyle Estate, because Daggle is our name. My mother is every bit as beautiful as you are."

"Listen, kid," Polly White began. But she couldn't go on. She couldn't keep her eyes inside her head. Her eyes were swirly and she'd already knocked over her shoes and drink. She laboriously extracted goods from her purse and patted pancake makeup over her face. She snatched up Raoul's drink and gurgled it to the bottom.

"You're a shit," she told Raoul Daggle, getting up to leave, tucking the red shoes inside her purse. She was wobbly and Juliette thought for a second Polly White meant squishing her. But Polly White was being sisterly now, whispering in the little girl's ear. The little girl thought Polly White said, "They're all shits. But don't let it worry you."

The little girl wasn't sure.

It was like having a seashell at your ear. It wasn't like anything, except that it tickled.

She and her father stayed on for his sixth drink. "Make that a double," he told the waiter.

"We've upset poor Polly White," said the girl. "Poor Polly White needs a seeing-eye dog."

They watched through the plate-glass window Polly White mincing in her stocking feet across the parking lot, the red purse dragging the pebbles—Polly there, talking to herself, giving the finger to a shuffle of fallen priests who leap from her path in the nick of time.

"There goes your happiness," Juliette told her papa.

The little girl sits in the booth playing with the little pansies on her dress. Some are purple, others yellow. The purple pansies want ice cream. But the yellow pansies are in charge. They are the big bosses. The big bosses are telling the purple pansies they can't have ice cream. They can never have any more ice cream. "Look at you," the yellow pansies are saying. "You purple pansies are fat, fat, fat! It hurts my eyes to look at you. *Shame, shame, shame!*" The purple pansies start blubbering. That's all they can do, is blubber. Life is so unfair.

Juliette Daggle, eleven years old, is on the side of the yellow pansies. The purple pansies are ridiculous creatures. They are ludicrous. They would eat ice cream every minute of every day if they didn't have someone like her to order them around.

Thank goodness she has her father to look after her. She has Polly White to instruct her in the four-cornered sheet in three seconds flat. She has decided Polly White is very beautiful. Polly White drinks like a fish, but she is an admirable person. She's so much more admirable, for instance, than Joyel. Juliette wishes her own name was Polly White. She watches Polly White out in the parking lot, unable to get in her car. The key won't fit into the lock. She's there cursing, flinging her red bag against the window.

"Papa, you must go out and help that woman."

"Must I?"

"Polly White is a damsel in distress. You have no choice in the matter."

Raoul goes. In another minute Juliette sees Polly White leaning against her father. Her arms are up around his neck. Her head rests upon his shoulder. Her eyes are closed. Her body is shaking and her makeup smeared. The handbag has burst open, its contents litter the pavement. Polly White is such a wreck. Poor Polly cannot handle alcohol. Raoul now has the door open. Polly White is in his arms; he is lifting her up, kicking the door wide open with a foot, settling her onto the seat. Juliette's own face is pasted against the tavern glass. There is something very beautiful about this. Her papa is on his knees, searching for Polly White's possessions among the pebbles. He is tucking these possessions inside the red purse. He is taking the red shoes from the red purse and now he is placing these shoes on Polly White's white feet. He is first brushing the dirt from her soles. Juliette finds this so beautiful, so touching, she wants to cry. Her papa is such a hero. Polly White's face and shoulders hang over the wheel. Her skirt has risen high on her hips and, plain to see, Raoul Daggle does not know what to do about that. He turns, looks at Juliette's face pasted against the window. He grimaces, shrugs. Juliette also shrugs. She does not know what to do about that. The world seems to be filled with nothing except Polly White's long naked legs. But her papa, Raoul Daggle, is not defeated. He has one arm around poor Polly's waist; he is lifting her fanny off the seat. He is tugging down that tight skirt. He is covering those beautiful, naked legs. Juliette, face at the window, can see her papa's lips moving. He is talking to himself. He is saying, "There. Now you are decent, my love." He is fitting Polly White's backside against the seat. He is shifting hair away from her face. Folding Polly White's hands onto poor Polly

White's lap. Placing her red purse on the empty seat. Now stepping back, closing the door.

Here he comes. What a guy. He's hardly even staggering.

Exhausted, slicking down his hair, stuffing in his shirt. He's nobody's fool, her lovely papa. You've got to get up early to get the jump on him.

"Now are you satisfied?" she says to the stuffed purple pansies. "Now are you happy?"

She eyes with suspicion the priests who have fallen from heaven. Their martyrdom to the lost cause imparts to the group generally, and to each individually, a certain slothfulness of character: a listless demeanor, sagging shoulders, pasty faces that have never seen sunshine. They wear baggy pants, suit coats that need pressing, they have dirty shoes, some of them ought to go away and shave. They have fallen from heaven because they are mean people. Or maybe they are good people made bitter by a destiny which will forever find them huddled near God's doorstep. A church is for the faithless; if you believe, then what need have you for a church? They have fat stomachs, too, the loss of faith hasn't affected their appetite.

Their eyes are closed, are they praying?

Juliette likes how that line of a moment ago must have sounded on Polly White's tongue. That "They are all shits." The satisfaction those words must have given her. It helps when you know inside yourself that you are superior to all that surrounds you. The struggle is made worthwhile. *They are all shits*, the little girl thinks, is a motto you can take with you into battle. You can rout the enemy. You can prevail, and everyone knows that if you prevail, you are made whole again. *I'm not pushing this mop another minute*. That is what her mother liked to say before she ran away. It's how she swings into battle.

Now for the potatoes, her mother says.

Her mother strides from one thing to another. She never rests.

Raoul Daggle slides into the booth.

"Let's let her sleep a while," he says. "A little sleep and Polly White will rise from the ashes."

"I was thinking of Joyel," the girl says. "I was wondering whether she's changed or is the same old Joyel. What do we do now, Papa?"

She shudders. The priest with the bulbous, purplish nose has one eye open, he's boring a hole into her.

"I think I'll hire Polly White as my new estate manager. She has all the assets, including venom. Poor Polly is wasted in Anne's Ardor."

"You like women around you, don't you, Papa? There's a special place in your heart for female warriors."

"Polly White will manage hell out of that place. She's aces, is our Polly. She's like that Xena on TV that you like so much. Those old gated fuckers won't know what's hit them."

"What do we do now, Papa?"

"Let's go join the faithless," Raoul says, nodding his head towards the ex-priest's table. "Their disenchantment with the church, their utter belief in the futility of existence without it, peps me up. Just sight of someone worse off than I am gives me a buoyancy of heart."

On the road out of Anne's Ardor, Raoul singing *No sugar, no sugar,* his own creation, Juliette says, some tension in her voice, "Papa?"

No sugar, no sugar, sings Raoul, thumping the wheel, *I had sugar, now my sugar has gone*, he's always wanted to be black and miserable, in and out of jail, singing a bluesy song, *No sugar, no sugar, won't somebody tell me where my sugar has gone.*

"I want to revise our contract, Papa."

"To what end?"

"No more drinking before six o'clock."

"Why's that, sugar?"

"We could have an accident, die, and never see Joyel again."

No sugar, no sugar, Raoul sings, *my sugar has left me, she's bereft me, my sugar has gone.*

They are on the wrong road out of Anne's Ardor because here's the same cloverleaf, the same strip of gas stations, quickie food stops, there are all those downtown buildings coming into sight yet a third time.

"How about noon?"

"Noon what."

"We stay dry until noon."

"No, it's six or nothing, no sneaking, either. I want all secret flasks surrendered."

"Okay, partner. Because you're my sugar, sugar, *at last I got me some sugar*, is it six yet?"

"Oh, Papa!"

Raoul Daggle's body drapes over the wheel. "We're adrift," he says, "we've got to get back to the basics. We've lost the moral imperative. Frankly, I think the collapse started with . . . with I don't know who. No one has any initiative, no one cares, we all hate each other."

"I don't hate anyone, Papa. I love everyone. I even love the man in the moon."

"Yeah, well, you're different. You're the one different person on the whole face of this earth. That's because you're my daughter."

"I know it, Papa. I'm your *only* daughter."

"I wouldn't be too sure of that. No, honey, you can never be too sure of that."

"Oh, Papa!"

She smacks his hand. Radiohead are playing softly on the car stereo. Raoul has been searching the dial in vain for the Spice Girls, he loves the Spice Girls, he says, he's grief-stricken at their demise, "You could be a regular little child prodigy if only you shared my love for the Spice Girls. "Juliette's full enthusiam, however, is reserved for that ten-year-old way-cool Spanish kid Juan José, who can hit more notes than Placido Domingo, and hold them longer."

"I want to stop and eat. Let's fill our guts with junk food."

"We can't eat at a time like this, it's an emergency, no time to think of food, we've got to unearth your mother."

"Let's stop at the next place, okay?"

"I have been anchor to the secret griefs of numberless wild, frenetic, scatty, scantily clad women. Even among the thousands in a domed stadium, these women could scent me out. They were as relentless in this as the Second Coming. Before I was married to your mother and we had you these multitudes of weird companions helped me make it through the night. The strangest one of all was a twenty-three-year-old Scientologist from Winnipeg, Manitoba, what a city! Do you know that woman's name?"

"Jane Doe."

"That's right, how did you know? I was ready for anything, after Jane Doe. Jane Doe was something else. She was—what do call those machines that break up concrete?"

"Sledgehammers, pneumatic drills."

"Right. Dead-on. That was Jane Doe."

"She drilled you, she shook you up."

"'Oil my feet,' she would say. She was into those oils, my Jane Doe. All those Scientology women are."

"Was she nice?"

"Who wanted nice?"

"Pretty?"

"No, honey, she was perfectly anonymous, my Jane, a true Jane Doe. That anonymity of hers, it was a powerful attraction, a magnet. Jane's father was Jimmy Doe, Jimmie worked at the St. Boniface Tool and Dye. Her mother was Jackie Doe, she clerked at PriceChopper Foods. Jane had a brother named Danny Doe, who sang country and western and rode in the Calgary Stampede. They were all Scientologists. It's a known fact, Scientologists make the best rodeo people. Boy, did I ever love Jane Doe! I was smitten with the entire family and through them found my anchor in the expanding universe."

"Calm down, Daddy. You know how easily I can be upset. There's another place, 'family dining,' it says, let's stop there."

"No time, honey, and we're only an abbreviated family, not allowed in an establishment of that description."

"You're insufferable."

"I knew that if I stayed on with Jane Doe I could never have you. So I went on through other strange partnerships until I met your mother. This was when your mother was a bareback rider in the Ringling Brothers Circus."

"Oh, Daddy."

"I was crowing with vigor in those days. She wasn't a Scientologist, your mother, but I forgave her. The FBI, you know, will never let up on their crusade against the Scientologists. They are a fated match, the FBI and the Scientologists. They have the same beliefs."

"Papa, Papa, Papa."

"Especially as regards the Sci's E-meter, which tells whether a person is honest."

"You're babbling, Papa."

"I know. Yeah. Sorry. I read about Jane Doe in the paper not long ago."

"Don't tell me about it. Please let me keep my innocence until I'm in my teens."

"Faint chance, darling. A thirteen-year-old these days is as old as my mother. Anyway, while sleeping, Jane Doe, who was a big woman, rolled over and smothered her Scientologist baby. That would have been you, had I stayed with Jane Doe."

"No, Trash would have saved me."

"She's in prison now, Jane Doe. They said it was intentional. They said she didn't want a Scientology baby. Frankly, I blame L. Ron Hubbard."

"I would want any kind of baby. I love babies."

"Me three. Ours is a family crazy about any kind of baby. Our house must be full of a thousand baby pictures. Everywhere you look, there's another baby picture. But whose babies are they? I ask you. We ought to be stopping at some of these other gated communities, pick up ideas, see how they run things. There's one down in Coral Gables—that's in Florida—sentries patrol the walls with shotguns, bayonets, they even have mortar emplacements, bunkers. Look. There's a boy hitchhiking. Let's give that boy a ride. Maybe the two of you will fall in love and have babies."

"Why did she leave us, Papa?"

"She wanted a better husband, honey. She has lofty goals, your mother, she wants perfection."

"That's not so bad."

"The lure of the road is its potential for the miraculous conversion, I'm sure you noticed that. All these people we're meeting, they're pumping me up, I'm getting better and better and soon will be perfect, I'm sure the same is happening to her. That Polly White, for instance, what a—"

"Put a lid on it, Papa."

"Those Fall from Heaven people were a morose bunch," said Juliette. "The only time I liked them was when they agreed dogs have souls."

"But not tadpoles. They put their foot down, when it came to tadpoles, and I don't blame them. A frog has a soul, I'm prepared to admit that, but not a tadpole. But back to Ringling Brothers and your mother. She was called Joyette in those days. Joyette rode a white-speckled horse round and round the ring, standing on its hind quarters, that one arm above her head shaking a castanet. She was dressed in this beautiful skimpy carny suit. Net stockings, high boots, a whip. Man, did that whip sting!"

"What was the horse's name?"

"A horse called Beethoven because it could sound out the 'Hallelujah' chorus through its nostrils as it pranced the ring, it could dance the polka on its hind legs."

You can hang up the phone, I'm not listening to you.

That was Joyel's line, among her last monitored words the night she left, that evening during which there were numerous anonymous telephone calls, ring-ring, you pick up the phone, you say hello and there's no reply, ring-ring, there it goes again, hello, and someone is breathing in your ear, slam down the phone, ring-ring, there it goes again, a man's voice this time, what is he saying? Oh, you're sick, sick, do you know that, how long has this been going on, why are you letting it upset you so, ring-ring, there it goes again, pick up the phone, he's back again, *I'm going to wipe out your entire family, you last, and there's nothing you can do to stop it short of vanishing from the earth, gated, you understand, don't mean shit to me*, ring-ring, there he is again, what can you do, you can scream into the mouthpiece *I'm not listening to you.*

Who was she not listening to? Why not unplug the phone, dial the police, confer with family and friends, put sharpshooters on the walls. Who will cast the first stone?

They have pulled into a highway roadstop because the little girl has to visit the washroom. A thousand cars and trucks are whizzing by. They are in Wisconsin, I believe, up past ritzy Grosse Pointe Woods and all those other Grosse Pointes, following a hunch. Up past St. Clair Shores and Mt. Clemens and New Baltimore. "I've got a hunch," Raoul said, "Joyel is in one of these points." They can't seem to find a highway going into Canada, for all that free border business getting into the great northern woods is a nightmare.

The girl's mother is speaking to Juliette over the phone. They have called home and discovered on the answering machine a number to call.

"Forget those points," she says. "You need a new plan if you are to find me," her mother is saying. "Tell your father his old plan isn't working."

"Where are you, Mama?"

"I can't tell you that, honey pie."

"Give us a rough idea."

"Earth, darling."

"Oh, Joyel."

"I'm in my motel room in a burg called Cut Bank. That's in Wyoming. I love you, Juliette Daggle."

"I know you do, Mama. I love you, too. I love you to pieces."

"That's lovely, darling. All my pieces are going to cry now. Give me a minute."

Away there in Cut Bank, planet Earth, Joyel Daggle cries.

"I learned about four-cornering sheets today, Mama."

"What a waste. Fitted sheets are more the Daggle style."

"We got a woman drunk today, then she cried, Daddy had to fold her inside a car. I think he likes her, Mama, they were like old friends."

"Don't tattle, darling, it isn't nice."

"We're dying for you, Joyel, please come home."

"I'm mending, honey. It's been a long recovery, but I'm getting myself together."

"I know you are, Mama. Here's papa, he's chomping at the bit."

Raoul Daggle snatches up the phone and Joyel says, "Hello, you handsome devil. Are you hot on my trail?"

"You won't fool us forever," Raoul says. "We've got your number." Then he says, "Kiss-kiss," Joyel says the same back, and they smooch and whisper for a time.

"When are you two weary travelers returning to the nest?" Joyel eventually asks.

"We see your smoke, Joyel. No rest until we find you. No portion of earth unturned."

The girl and her father are watching a man in jogging clothes trying to get into the women's toilet. But the women already in there apparently are holding the door.

"Come on out, Lucille," the man pleads. "I told you I was sorry."

"*Go away!*" cry the women in there.

Then her mother is talking to Juliette again. "Your grandfather chewed tobacco," she says. "He had black spit around his mouth, sunrise to sunset. That's how I see you and your father when I am feeling discouraged. How far have you got today? I can't imagine why you were in Anne's Ardor, Michigan. It was six months ago I was in Anne's Ardor. All those Anne's, all that ardor. I loved those Spartans. I went to their homecoming game and cheered myself hoarse. It was like every pass thrown I was catching myself."

"You hate football, Mama."

"Not anymore. I've branched out. My seat was in the M section, midfield. When the Spartan marching band performed at halftime I nearly wet my pants with excitement."

"Hold on, Mama."

The man whose wife is locked inside the public washroom is trying to break down the door. He is banging on the knob with a metal pipe. "You come out this minute, Lucille!" he's saying. "This minute, so help me!"

The women in there are shouting at him. They are daring him to come inside. "*Come in here and you are dead meat!*" they are saying.

"Papa, you've got to do something," Juliette says to Raoul. "Mama, wait a sec," she says into the phone.

"Okay, honeybunch."

Raoul Daggle approaches the man wielding the pipe. He places a hand over the man's left shoulder. "Hi there," he says. "How're you doing? What say we negotiate."

The man in the jogging suit bursts into tears.

"I love her," he says. "She's got to come out. She's got to forgive me."

The women behind the door have fallen silent. Who is this stranger interfering with them? The doorknob is down on the ground between the man's running shoes. The knuckles on one hand are bloody. The pipe has rebounded and struck him a good one.

"*What's going on out there,*" the women inside are now saying. They are screeching that out.

Juliette Daggle has the phone at her ear.

"Go ahead, Mom," she says.

Joyel Daggle has been speaking all the while. What can she know about this incident transpiring around a far-off roadway toilet door?

"I wish I could be home to greet you when you get home. Has your father cleared new ground, sold more lots? How high are the walls now? If I were home, I'd have dinner waiting for the two of you. Maybe a potroast. I know how my little honey-bears love their potroast."

"Daddy's hiring a new manager, Polly White. She's got breasts that . . . well, he says they're boulders cut into perfect halves."

"Don't worry, love."

"He hates the place, too, Mama. It's just that he's trapped by greed and wants to leave us a big nest egg. He's in bad shape, Mama."

"I know, but aren't we all?"

Mama, Mama, Mama.

The jogging man and his Lucille are reunited. They stand by a yellow trash barrel shaped in the form of a wolverine, embracing each other.

"It wasn't your fault," Lucille is saying. She is kissing the jogging man all over his blubbering face. "God did it to us."

A gaggle of women hover nearby, uneasy with the fate of such rapture in the unfolding universe, snacking on pasties, northern Michigan's contribution to global cuisine. They are all in jogging clothes, wearing identical orange shoes. They are "Save Our Wetlands" women, jogging from the Sunshine State to the Last Frontier in a hair-brained scheme that already has raised a million dollars. The man receiving Lucille's kisses is the poor creep driving the medical van.

"Your mother sounded in good spirits, didn't you think?"

"You're a bush-beater, Daddy," Juliette Daggle says, on the road. "You beat the bushes, but you do not talk to me."

"That's exactly what Joyel said. She claims that when it comes to certain matters, like marriage, I have an absent manner that can only improve with death."

"Good grief."

Beyond this simple remark Juliette is keeping her thoughts to herself, surely there are times when this should be allowed, privacy in this instance being the one thing she craves, since it is her mother there preying on her mind. I ask you, How can they be kept out? The womb is such a gigantic abode, a shadow looming over our lives larger than any cloud, motherhood has tentacles that make octopuses blush. Here Joyel is, in her daughter's thoughts bundling the girl up for school, a cold winter day, every window icy, the wind whistling, pavement slippery, icicles long as spears, every tree limb scraping the earth, it's a whiteout out there, she ventures outside surely she will die, *Oh, Mama, I'm sick, do I really have to go? Yes, don't try that on me, young lady. Lift your arms, put on this coat, let me zipper you up, quit wriggling, these boots, toboggan, muffler, gloves, stand still, please, oh you abominable child.* Joyel there on her knees kissing her cheeks, a last pull of the muffler, last clamping down of collars, belts, socks to yank, *Turn around*, more kisses, embraces, *And eat your lunch*, a hard shove through the door into heaping muck and freezing cold. Now we are cosy and warm and like a good girl can troop ourselves off to school where we can learn our ABCs and make Mommy proud.

This scene, one among so many, sufficiently etched into Juliette's memory, tender and beautiful, yet so painful in its reenactment that we must override all our desires to witness intimately this child's anquish in her bucket seat, let's do as the Infiniti is itself doing, let the child alone, pay no attention to her wet eyes, the streaming tears, the dabbing hands, the trembling shoulders, the slumping head, now knuckles between her teeth to obscure her cries, we are so much better behaved in this instance than the obtuse parent, let us applaud ourselves and condemn him, for he's chiming in now with these truly repulsive words, *Why are you sniveling, get hold of yourself.* Fathers, what do they know, how can they time and time again be such insensitive brutes as to make our own eyes moisten, storms and hurricanes, earthquakes, these have as their cause God's breathing of the native breath, quick, douse the light, some truths, a child's grief, are self-evident, in case you were unaware of this.

The father tells this to his eleven-year-old daughter, Juliette Daggle:

> I carried around an ache inside me big as a melon. All that red meat, all those black seeds, that rind which was always leaking its juices. I was tacky to the touch, an invitation to starving insects and to stray dogs who wanted to run away and bury my bones. Such a torch I carried for your mother, that torch a bleak, black thing filling my every footstep with black ash fine as the finest powder. Take a rock and thousands of years, the rock shrinking under the sun's heat, expanding with the night's cold, thus this ash, this black ash, covered my body whenever I saw or talked to or even thought of your mother. I was lonely every minute and every minute the air, the very wires of the air, hummed your mother's name. It was only this raw air, my primitive lust, which kept me going. I would call her up, I would say, "Let me hold you, let me look at you, let me smell you." She would say, "Oh, it must be my tormentor idiot calling me. Hello, idiot." "Let me see you naked. Let me see your naked feet, I must hold you. Let me, let me."
>
> I stood each day, rain or shine, beneath her dark window, begging for an audience with her, the same way that you can't just see the Pope but can only have audience with him because of all the weighty issues the Pope represents. Your mother, the Pope, represented all those millions of women I could never have. They were all incarnate in her sexy flesh.

I bayed like a dog, I whimpered like a puppy. If she showed herself for a single instant, passing a window, I turned into jelly. Her shadow on a wall pitched me into spasms of ecstasy. I wore my Arrow shirt with the no-wrinkle collar, ironed fresh each day by my own hand, that shirt carrying the imprint of a thousand hot irons. "This is what you're doing to me," that shirt said, "you're burning me alive." I wore a belt buckle wide as the Assiniboine, as the Missouri, with her name emblazoned on it in a high shine blinding to my enemies. I polished my Dak shoes, wingtips, six and seven times a day. I killed a thousand trees, carving our names into the trunks so deep we would be there together through eternity. I dressed a hired man in sandwich boards to patrol her street, I had batontwirlers, gymnasts, tumbling on her lawn, I had helicopters parachute red roses into the trees about her house. I sent perfumes in burlap sacks, shoes of every description from Theodore's Foot Emporium, I sent sacks of Belgium chocolates, fresh lettuce, peaches, cucumbers, from the A&P. Thermal underwear, coat hangers, frozen fish—whatever I could get my hands on. I endlessly called up radio request shows under a variety of pseudonymns, please play "Love Keeps Me High", play "Play Me For A Fool", play "Love For Sale", play "Anytime You Want Me", the downhome blues, "No Sugar", play them all for glorious Joyel Moffit of number two Foot Street, this great city, what a miracle that it has produced both of us, play them because I love her into delirium's madness, never mind the redundancy, I hear in my sleep her every heartbeat. The deejay was amenable, friendly to my cause, he too was smitten with this angel residing at number two Foot Street. But his adoration was feeble, love for him was an abstract entity only vaguely attached to the human body, a sometime thing, whereas I was the Arctic explorer aslant in howling gale, Napoleon aslosh in bitter ice and mud outside St. Petersburg. I poured over secret Persian recipes guaranteed to produce magical cures for my heartbreak, I scrutinized Einstein's incredible formula for bomb-making techniques useful to my purpose, I ransacked through dusty histories to unravel Cleopatra's mystery, Omar Khayyam nightly transformed me into a river of tears. "*Idiot, idiot,*" was all she said. "*I loathe thee, idiot.*" The ground over which I walked showed no fruit, and I thought to the withers of my flesh. What shall I do, Lord, because I have no room wherein to bestow my love and no one to receive my fruits and must I pull down my barns and build greater?

"Please, Papa. Get control of yourself."

Then one day she caught my eye as I lay retching my heartbreak in a gutter, she strode up and placed a foot upon my backside, saying, "Are you the fool who has made my name a commonplace upon the airways? Are you the very same fool who has plagued my every shadow, now there in harmony with this gutter, stinking and dehydrated and shaking like a lizard?" "I'm the one," I said. "I stand convicted." "Well, then," she said, "I shall have pity on thee, dear fool, as thou art still a man and therefore carved to your craven particulars. So rise up and kiss me and I shall restore thee to thy ignorant folly, and forevermore through the whole of your life's span shall you track behind me, shouting your adoration every instant."

"Joyel doesn't talk like that. That doesn't sound the least bit like her."

"She is a woman of many voices."

"She doesn't love us, Papa. Let's turn back."

"She loves us, darling. But could be she loves the chase more."

Juliette Daggle has on the floor at her feet a box of oranges from Indian River, Florida. She is eating one of these oranges, the peel in a napkin on her lap, she's such a tidy child. Lucille and the man in the jogging suit back at the roadside washroom have pressed this fruit upon them. "You have brought me to my senses," the jogging man had said to Lucille, "you have made me see the light," to which Lucille said, "Oh, honey, you *are* the light," a statement prompting cheers from the gawkers, Juliette and Raoul included, sometimes love's little dramas can be so powerfully moving.

"Your mother is *my* light," Raoul is now telling the child, "she's my salvation, but I don't deserve her, she's lost faith and will never recover. I hereby nominate her as president and roving ambassador of that divine and mystical Order of Priests Who Have Fallen from Heaven for the year 2000. Time for a drink, I think. Let's call up Polly White and all have martinis."

Juliette sucks three fingers in her mouth. Juice dribbles down the child's pale hand. Ignore the gnawed fingernails, the flaking paint on those nails. Highway light illuminates the golden hair growing on the nape of her neck and her golden hair is itself a whirling star of radiance along Highway 19 up near Goodells, elevation six hundred feet—up past Brockway, Yale, Peck, Sandusky, and all these other drably elevated podunksky, forgive me, cities, towns, villages, outposts, fishing shacks, and hunting lodges which unite to keep this part of the Great Lakes State from sliding off into the vast waters of Lake Michigan.

"Want some, Papa? Or is it just to be that martini? Keep your eyes on the road, please."

"Now don't get preachy, young lady."

Her own pipestem legs straddle the fruit in its box on the Infiniti floorboards. They are little growing planets down there. They have no orbiting moon, but they are planets all the same. They are worlds unto themselves. There's the planet Ng and the planet Ang and there's the planet Rang. Juliette Daggle, age eleven and motherless, is the one moon these planets have, what light that reaches them must come from her, she's their little girl god. They are down there praying to her now, she can hear them, Give us back our tree, they are saying. How long, oh Little Girl God, before our tree returns to bring us salvation?

"These are seedless oranges, Pop," she says.

"'Pop?' Who says I'm a *Pop*?"

"Pop goes the weasel, pop goes Pop." Juliette sings this out. She has talked to Mama, to oranges, she's witnessed the powerful force of love at a roadway washroom, she's been purged by an avalanche of tears and in this second feels on top of the world.

"Eat this," she says. "Eat this in one gulp the way Trash would." She places a juicy unbroken wedge between Raoul Daggle's welcoming lips.

He gulps it down, "Woof-woof," he says.

There they fly, the miles open ahead. The big sky is dropping down snowflakes the size of mothballs, all the little mothballs that have gone to heaven are coming down.

The Little Girl God's godless mother in godless Cut Bank, president and roving ambassador of the divine and mystical Order of Priests Who Have Fallen from Heaven, is this minute in her motel room away yonder in godless Wyoming looking out a window at this same falling snow. *Ooo-ooo*, Joyel is saying, like a ghost, *that snow looks like mothballs*, her voice ensnared within the wind howling by her daughter's ear as the white Infiniti cuts down the highway, a ghost crying, *Find me, save me, I never left you, only my body did.*

The white Infiniti sweeps along, in the past year it has gone through burning sun, rain and wind, over roads bad and good, over hill and dale, now this driving snow, what can this Infiniti tell us of this unseasonable snow, which so much resembles mothballs, except to say it's very beautiful, it's cool and feels good to my bonnet, it's honey to my tires, no worry, baby, come snow I'm up to the task, I'm a metallic warrior determined to get you where you're going, look out, Joyel Daggle, I've got your scent, how my engine, my very crankshaft, loves these country roads, thank goodness for that purebred oil so warming to my purring heart, this cruise control is a wonder, such a relief from those urban settings when I must of necessity be endlessly shifting gears, stopping and starting, what a headache those red lights are, oh my aching brakes, but now I'm cool and have found my stride, you big trucks, you gas guzzlers, you old rattling heaps destined for the junkyard, well, suck my exhaust, expect no pity from the king of the road, really I despair of these lesser specimens of automotive genius, it's automotive malpractice, if you ask me, I can spot a lemon a mile away and can't see how some of these wrecks can have been legitimately tagged, frequently their occupants no better, still it's a democracy, they've as much right to the byways of city and dale as I have, oh, I suppose, but where did my little vixen MGB get to, a vintage chariot circa 1957, *sugar, sugar, where has my sugar gone*, I don't mind telling you lately I've been having this nice little courtship with her, such a beauty, her skin a highly polished British Racing Green, what taste, I always fall for those sexy roadsters, her bumpers alone make my pistons ping, these road romances, you know, they're great fun, though at the end of the day you and I both realize all too well that nothing will have come of them, a fellow like me, Infiniti 130 for the year 2000, for all my classy talk I lack the resolve, the grit, the gumption, the all-out git up and go of, let me spell it out, that gin mill Raoul at my wheel.

2

GHOSTS

In the world we live in, where one knows so little about why a person has done this or said that, and when the person herself would likely decline any offer made that she put into speech some little honest effort at presenting herself, or if she were to do so would very probably produce a string of words whose every syllable is intended to serve as a shield hiding away her real thoughts, motivations, acts . . . faced with this, then, for God's sake, what harm is there in simply dropping down and motoring along, so to speak, with the party in question, accepting with some degree of tolerance, as a gratuity of sorts, since all else is denied us, those rare moments when the woman's guard is dropped, the revealing remark falls—and we are thus allowed to walk a while in the alien shoes. It is clear by this time, or should be, even to the most dense among us, that Raoul Daggle and his overly precocious (some will say ludicrously so, well there you have it) daughter Juliette, have not the smallest clue why Joyel Daggle has abandoned the family nest and shot off into the night—if, indeed, it was night when she left. I, for one, cannot remember whether I, or we, have been told this, and would proclaim in my defense—in yours as well—that it can scarcely matter at this juncture whether she left by night or by day, and will have to hope that some surround in explication of her actions, her present whereabouts, her state of mind, will shortly manifest itself, the veil be lifted, that at least a modicum of pleasure may be granted us. At the moment a small curiosity exists, though even this in precious little quantity. It is perhaps useful to remind ourselves that flight from the nest is, of itself, not an unusual act in these times. After all, I need not, I hope, remind you, you who are alive in the same world as I am, that a child or parent is fleeing the family nest each day by the thousands, and home—home sweet home—is hardly the succoring, vital, ideal place it was in our grandmother's hallowed time, when antimacassars and the like spelled the matter out onto the armrests of untold sofas and chairs in countless rooms around our earth, *Mi dulce hogar*, as the Mexicans say, implicit in this lovely term a concept embarrassing to our own, inasmuch as those of the richer visage require God's blessings on the home and all within it, not to exclude yourself the minute you enter the gate.

Back to the subject, we read of these runaways in the daily press, do we not, and read there as well where normally it is these disappearing parties often go (to large cities) and how it is they account for themselves upon arrival in these evil centers. Drugs, prostitution, squeegees on every thoroughfare, endless strings of riffraff cadging our quarters—life on the street, I mean to say. This is, you will admit, well documented. I myself, who have not the remotest to do with this narrative—a document under construction, if I may be so bold, and thus subject to worrisome architectural laws, bad wiring and the like—have seen them, as has anyone else with eyes of the seeing variety. You only have to look at your milk cartons or at, as I recall, the faces imprinted on the envelopes containing your telephone bills, your banking statements—or it could be that I am recalling those poisonous missives that come our way monthly through the social conscience of a large department store, *Sir, Madame, please remit, your payment is overdue*—to satisfy yourself that people have gone, and every day do go, missing. My reference above, of course, is specifically to missing children, a child one parent has kidnapped from the other, a situation which fortunately has nothing to do with ours beyond their being, as the phrase goes, in the same ballpark.

Crimes occur. So far as I know, no crime has, or has yet, occurred with regard to the missing Joyel Daggle—unless, that is, you happen to be Raoul and Juliette, or Joyel herself, then you might very well, and with reason, on the personal level claim otherwise. Knowing so little in this particular regard (why Joyel left, how she has been conducting herself in the interval), we can hardly ascertain with any assurance that Joyel Daggle is not or has not been party to any or all of these more or less common resorts of the runaway. Not, I am advised quickly to point out, that we have the smallest iota of evidence in support of such a contention. It is fair to say, I think, that not even her worst enemies back in the gated community of Daggle Estates, can envision Joyel as a serious druggie or prossie, and the idea that she might be making ends meet by working a squeegee over their windshield as they pause at this or that traffic light, is one that can ignite whooping gales of laughter—that is, if these enemies are the whooping sort, which I can tell you with some authority is not the case.

All the same, a runaway Joyel Daggle certainly appears to be, although hardly, if you'll forgive the expression, the garden variety. She's mobile, she sends pillow mementoes from time to time, likely has not ignored birthdays, has access to telephones, appears to have a certain means. We know that much. All else coming our way from the mouths of her husband and child many among us will be moved to discount. More than once have I thrown a disbelieving hand up to my own open mouth, as those two chatterboxes nattered away. Their very syntax, the tone employed, the ceaseless bantering, the absence of realistic description (*North Territorial Road*, are they kidding me?) is awfully *suspect*, that being not the strongest word I could offer, either. Do I have time, if you are me, you will be saying, for disquieting rubbish of this ilk?

"For this crap?"—you will be saying.

We may even hear a second party, a party in the presence of this perturbed first speaker, from her position within the shadows of this space they together occupy, saying, "What is upsetting you now, dear? You don't like your book?" And that party in the next second will be sorry she asked, since her ears are now being filled with vile expletive, vituperation, the voiced remonstrances of her partner explaining to her something of the dreck, *The Fall of Gravity* indeed, with which he has been foolishly wasting his time. It is well known, isn't it, that women make the best readers, are more tolerant, more receptive to a work's extremes, as indeed they are with all of life's traffic, its cumbersome details, the plodding weight of years refusing inspiration, renewal, affection's grander stuff, while men are better off left working with their hands, spending their time with tools more natural to the male instinct, let's say a stick. Better they be left alone to put up storm windows, unplug a drain, fix up little engines, hose the car, slap meat on the barbecue, everybody knows this, knows that women are champagne while men are flat beer, mugs, nothing much to speak of, everybody knows this.

"It says here," the man is saying, "that these three people and their suicidal dog went to this Niagara place—"

"Niagara Falls, do you mean, dear?"

"'Niagara Something,' the one loathsome figure says, and the four of them went out on a boat, the *Misty Maiden*—"

"Then that settles it, darling, because the boat is called *Maid of the Mist* and it certainly plies those waters around Niagara Falls."

"Will you please hush up? I am trying to tell about this tripe that deigns to—"

"I'm hushed, love. What is it that you dislike? The boat's name, Niagara Something, that the dog was—or is—suicidal, that dogs, suicidal or otherwise, are not allowed out on those tourist boats in the first place? Kindly go on with what you were saying."

Now, of course, if we were to pursue this exchange in the realistic mode nearly everyone prefers, even women, even women with a poet's blood flooding their veins, it would be to find that first speaker more incensed yet, for up has jumped the devil into his mouth, as folks used to say, turning his anger away from *The Fall of Gravity* towards an attack, say, on the integrity of the person sharing his roof and sleeping in his bed . . . though my point surely already ought to have been made, so I for one am content to let these two voices disappear forever, inasmuch as they are surely tangential to the document in our keeping. No, I say let's bid this pair adieu, let's get on with it—the *it* herein being the trail, none other, of that elusive and unobliging individual, Joyel Daggle.

Joyel Daggle, we may say again, has not been exactly panting to get her two bits onto the page. Quite the contrary. She has been running from us, we might say, as she has been on the lam from her husband and child. Should we shine our torch suddenly on her, we might fully expect her to duck and run, resort to disguises, remove herself to some foreign corner of the globe, hide herself away in yet another place unreachable by us with our limited means. (I have done the same myself—avoided the spotlight, although never for a year—and can admit it, why can't you?) During this year on the lam Joyel Daggle has learned more than one way to avoid detection, that's obvious. She has got street smart, or highway smart, if the matter might be put that way. She has been seen, naturally she has been seen, she is not, after all, invisible, insofar as we yet know, which of us is? She has been last heard from in Cut Bank, a startlingly boastful city down the line from Blackfoot and Santa Rita, in upper Montana, you understand, *not* in Wyoming, as you have been told. Who can be trusted these days? These being Joyel's own words to her one and only child, which cartography at least provides us with a starting point. Cut Bank, yes. One has only to draw ever-widening circles on a road map with a compass (mind, don't prick the finger, as Raoul did), with Cut Bank at the center, to arrive at an understanding of where she conceivably might now, this very minute, be found. She could be at or near any one of the four quadrants or thirty-two points of the compass, naturally enough, on any one of hundreds of roads, or in any one of a thousand cities, small towns, in a place, for that matter, too insignificant even to have a name. Plus, there are all those mountains, all that desert or prairie, all that wilderness, even in an area so small as that which our compass has designated. Two thousand miles separate our parties, ah me.

Why not give up? Why not go home?

These last, if I may say so, are good questions, and even as we pause to reflect on them, even as we are shutting the book, convinced that no good will come of this search for the lost wife and mother, help arrives. We see it—hazily, but it's there, a small town, black night, a road, a dusty vehicle whipping through a red light—and wouldn't you know it, there seconds later, somehow in a rearview mirror that oddly enough appears momentarily to be our own, suddenly intrudes the whirling red lights of a police car.

"*Jesus,*" someone says, "*just what I need, a cop on my tail!*"

Hold on a minute, I ask you, was that Joyel Daggle's voice?

Engine noises, the crunch of tires on gravel, first one vehicle, then the other, halting by the side of the black road, no moon, such a night. A pale light comes on, as when one is inside a vehicle opening the door, the vault opens, and there in that dimness is a figure, a beautiful hand settling upon a door handle, a face briefly in the rearview mirror. Then the door closes, the light is extinguished, and some of us must ask, Was that Joyel Daggle's hand, her face? Did you see those dashlights, was it a woman, a woman in that car? But others, old friends, perhaps, perhaps Raoul Daggle and the woman's child, are instantly popping up. They can be heard excitedly proclaiming, maddened by our density, our stupidity, our bad eyesight, not to mention our cavalier and uncaring manner—"You fools! What is the matter with you? Open your eyes. That was *our* Joyel Daggle, most certainly it was. Shake a leg, please. Find her, because we cannot do this job alone, we need divine intervention, magic, the conscription of stars, if ever this family is to be reunited as one."

"She's lost weight," comments a voice out of the blue, "I don't know," murmurs another, "the little ninny could always slide through a keyhole."

Where are they, these voices? That's an easy one: here are people talking to us from away up yonder behind the high walls of the afore-referenced gated community, that infamous polyester enclave known as Daggle Shores.

"She looks tired. Older."

"She ought to do something about that hair."

"I will say this about Joyel Daggle. She was never one to get food to the table on time, even to get it there at all, sometimes. But she kept a clean house, she didn't economize on the living-room curtains, I would frankly kill for her kitchen, and she didn't allow that kid to run loose at night the way that husband of hers does. She didn't put on airs, her child is tidy, whatever else her flaws. So, what I'm saying, she's a mixed bag, in my book."

"Well, your 'mixed bag' never gave me the time of day. She was the airy opinionated sort, just like him. I never liked her. Any mother who would desert her child, I say—"

"She'd water the grass, weed, mow the lawn wearing practically nothing. I miss that."

"Did anyone ask you? Did they?"

There they are, gone, these voices out of the blue. Why make so much of the improbable when all the evidence suggests it is the improbable that makes so little of us, why make exaggerated claims for mystical presences when the perfectly ordinary is so mysterious as to make us dizzy with wonder. No one is aghast when confronted with the sworn truth of an immaculate conception or grows pale at the thought of a dead man resurrected or is affronted by the tale of Moses at the Red Sea copycatting the miracle of Isis at the river Phaedrus, lo, the voices were there, they spoke, let's go on, oh, come all ye faithless.

As we have heard all our lives, one thing leads to another, a car door opens, in the dim light a face is glimpsed, Joyel Daggle's face. We scan it as we might a snapshot, catch a wayward movement in the corner of the eye, a shadow lunges, and that suddenly some old life, an old memory, is revived. Here I am. It takes so little, we might be prepared to admit, for a person all at once, and with no accounting for this at the time, to enter our lives. When I met so-and-so . . . is a line we've heard all our lives, and repeated ourselves, a thousand times. The globe tilts, a door opens, someone walks into a room, crests a hill, shares a table, asks the time, requires change for a meter—answers the unspoken summons, I am saying, and thus are our lives, for better or worse, forever altered.

Thank goodness, I say, thank goodness and glory, glory, for otherwise would only cockroaches and the like, beasts of the wild, have reign.

Well, I'll be a horned toad, here we are back again onto our favored subject, Joyel Daggle, truly by now a missing person, damn her eyes, for we are faced all at once with unexpected choices: Do we tune into that chorus of garrisoned voices offering privileged assessment of the inexplicable Joyel, or do we plunge headfirst into chaos, seek to join the woman herself, poor Joyel Daggle, that waif and stray, that child deserter, that—dare I use these words?—lonely heart, on a highway at night some distance out of arrogant Cut Bank, a cop car on her tail?

Here's the bulletin, just in: Ladies and gentlemen, a woman carrying the ID of one Jane Dearborne, thirty-six, of no fixed address, was this evening, at or about eleven p.m., stopped by police for running a red light in a small town in—where was it? Biddle, Ekalaka, Ismay, Alzada?—southeastern Montana.

She "had a dazed manner," according to informed sources.

The woman who gave her name as Jane Dearborne and produced documents to that effect was not Jane Dearborne. Events soon to unfold lead us to believe the woman in question is none other than Joyel Daggle.

There.

As for Jane Dearborne, she is as yet a nonentity and must await her turn, not to say that this makes her any less real, her blood flows as does yours and mine, the IRS knows where she is, her social security file is on record with the Department of Labor, hers isn't a happy life but she struggles on.

I will use my womanly wiles to get out of this jam.

Surely Joyel Daggle must have said or thought something like that. It's in our nature to claim innocence however much we are guilty, to use our God-given wiles to escape gross and insufferable penalty for an infraction so trifling. Frankly, I forgive her.

Before this, as night fell, to jar loose the momentum, bestir the inertia to which she had succumbed, the boredom, the stark blackness of the grinding road, Joyel Daggle had been practicing an old trick picked up from her husband. In her head she had been telling herself a story. For the trick to work, the story being invented along with the droning miles had to be one far removed, that is, light years away, from the teller's own particulars, since in no otherwise could the miles be defeated and consciousness of a meaningful sort assert itself.

A man (Joyel Daggle had been telling herself) had come to this woman's door, and this man had said to the woman, "Mine enemies have intention of wounding me. You must come with me now and together we will slay them before their evil can be done." And she said to the man who had come to her door, a man dressed in the unfamiliar apparel of another country, "Thine enemies are not mine enemies and I do not know them or thee, so why should I join you in this combat when the outcome might well be that my own life shall be forfeited, and not only my own life but the lives of my loved ones as well." And the man at the woman's door, sorely affronted, waved his burning torch about, enraged beyond the point of solace, the temperate mind, then saying, "Harlot, by your speech have you betrayed your allegiances, for, besooth, if you are not with me, then you are against me, in secret consort with mine enemies, conspirators who this minute likely as not are seated at your table, weaving their plots to undo me even as they forge their weaponry." To which Joyel replied, speaking into the wind at her open car window, "Sire, no one sits at my table. I sit at my table alone and have done so for much of the past year, and who are you in any event to threaten me and speak so uncivilly of 'your friends' and 'your enemies' when I have never once set eyes upon you until this minute?" Whereupon the man bellowed with a rage untoward to the moment, hurling threats as unpredictable as any our heroine could imagine, in the meanwhile swirling his torch and pacing the earth at her door, beside himself with fury so that one could not so much as get a word in edgewise. Lo, in the instant he had set fire to the grassy roof of the woman's hovel and now his torch was at her skirts. "Neither thee nor any of mine enemies shall escape me," he shouted. "Let the bitch perish!" Sparks flew and flames roared, and to Joyel's utter astonishment a massive horde of people, men and women, children, all unfamiliarly garbed in the raiment of another country, swept from her table and surged as one through the burning door, screaming, "Fire! Fire!" as they bolted, in their frenzy trampling the surprised enemy with his torch until his body lay inert upon the ground. These people, so many of them, swarming up from what presumably was her table, an unending chain, many still carrying the fruits of her alleged table, a chicken leg, a ham hock, roast beef, pasties, gnawing this and that as they leapt in flames through the burning window, jammed the fiery doorway, then to streak as ribbons of fire across the fields, and the man with the torch now supine at her feet, raising baleful eyes to her countenance as he too burnt to his slow death. "God and fate have mercy upon thee, wicked sister," he was saying. "Upon thy shoulders alone rides my death and the disharmony of all my loved ones resides at your door. Be assured, revenge shall fly swiftly as an arrow and before this day ends shall you join me in hell."

Then, then, Joyel Daggle then alone under the charred roof as night fell and a coldness gripped her flesh, such an uncommonly cold night for that time of the year, flaming bodies still striding the hills, loons shrieking, a man cloaked in the scorched rags of another country, the face disfigured, lying dead in her doorway, such a horror this is, though no child seems to have perished in the conflagration, thank God.

Joyel haunched over the car wheel, her shoulders stiff, intoning to the road's black surface, "I tell you I do not know who these people were or where they came from. They were neither friend nor foe nor were they seated at any table that rightly could be called mine. What hovel, where? Why me? I tell you I am only an innocent party found venturing upon the road, who happened to be nearest the door when that insane man's fists shook the house."

Oh, Joyel Daggle, such was not what we sought. I for one wanted modern talk.

You have only heaped upon our heads more trouble, for who speaks that way these days, did anyone ever, when did we last hear such talk on the late show, for instance, or at the movie house or speaking to us from the newspaper or stage or radio, within any kitchen or bedspace I have frequented? Joyel Daggle would say the same, *miffed* she'd be and is, which is one of her favorite words. "I'm miffed," I can hear her saying, "talking like that . . . but oh my friends," she might add, "exercise forbearance, I beg thee, I am only trying to exorcise the boredom of these miles until I get home, assuming home is where I am bound." But she is still locked within the domed agony of this olden wooden parlance, is she not, since what modern woman is it these days who would mouth "forbearance" or "I beg thee" even when on the road, middle of the night, by herself?

Not many, we may be sure. The water deepens therefore, becomes more troublesome, swirly, if this narrative may be thought of as water, which of course it is not, far from it, I say, even if the case might be argued that words are a liquidly or watery thing and often run like a swollen river. Such tales, if they are to be told at all, should be reserved for the early morning release, the evening spray, as with the watering of lawns, such a waste if executed in the heat of day. I am myself altogether in alliance with the man who, pages back, raised strong (if unsolicited) objection to this business of "Niagara Something," whatever it was, and can find no excuse for what is transpiring here. There are people I know, know for a fact, for whom the straightforward realistic approach is the sole satisfying model. I must confess that I am on the side of this majority totally; I say, amen, I say, being one who has arrived on this earth with but niggardly capacity for the romantic, the dreamer, for those weak sisters and brothers under enslavement of magic potions by which witches ride their brooms, though thank God none of these are in government, they are all number crunchers there, stemming the tide of dollars ransacked from the public purse, I'm with them, call me neo this or that as much as you please. How such inane, soft-headed fodder has found its way already onto Joyel Daggle's pages altogether eclipses my understanding. It is not her fault, I leap to affirm that, this despite her having brought that loathsome relic of olden days to her door, these people adorned in their unfamiliar garments, indeed! How trite, we might say, how droll, how quaint, but why should I care, why insult me, is the relevant question, never minding the improbable content of the story flung at us. How often does a man, however costumed, arrive at a stranger's door demanding that we drop what we are doing in order to hurry out and help him slay his enemies? Surely such a tale, in this day and time, is rather silly, bearing no application to the trials and tribulations a citizenry daily, hourly, endures from a wicked world, a divorced and often crooked, vain, and implacable government, an unworkable city without adequate parking, what you pop into your belly has been genetically altered, Fidel still rules Cuba, immigrant mystery ships ply our polluted waters, TV's the pits, art's gone to hell, the poles are melting, the ozone thinning, our kids shoot up, our parents have retreated into imbecility, the gods have abandoned us without mercy and black night is upon us.

But I am on guard. I beseech thee, have faith, I stand on guard for thee, I guard my home and native land, I sing *O say can you see* with gusto, I sing "Rule Britannia" in a high falsetto. This, I mean, shall end molestation of these pages, no further intruder will capture the sentence, the overzealous paragraph is hereby outlawed, not a single word shall be cloaked in the wordy idiom of antiquity, if a lunatic thinks to supplant me at the helm, with your assistance I shall tell him where to go. Patience and faith shall walk hand in hand like the good lovers they are, including in this those many who possess neither, stay cool, hang tough, let there be light.

The calm approach, we are told, reaps big rewards, to walk beside stilled waters restoreth the soul, another reason the red Indian did not attack our wagons moving westward at nighttime. I move we follow the Indian's calm example. Time, then, perhaps, for review, analysis, contemplation, compromise.

A face in a car mirror, a hand on the door handle, the gristly tale of a house gone up in flames, but where has that got us?

In Montana, yes. But, to be realistic, to consider the issue objectively, to a person living remote from Montana as I and most of you do, Montana means nothing, in truth it hardly exists. It lodges no more in our minds than does Liverpool, England, or Hobart, Australia, or most of New England, the Atlantic provinces, even Texas, Guam, Rangoon, the Aleutian Islands, the Solomon Islands, the forty-seven square miles of gull dung known as Saint Helena in the South Atlantic Ocean twelve hundred miles west of Africa, Assyria, Babylonia, the Elysian Plain, the Bay of No Regret, Min River, Fuzhou harbor, Funian province, China, from which all those rusted boats packed with immigrants bound for our shores are daily departing, yikes!

Montana is so far removed, contributes so little to the national good, is such an indifferent and unrefined habitat, as to mean zilch to me and the average reader. Not for nothing does the Continental Divide slice through the area, never mind the state's unparalleled beauty, its untamed wilderness and vast grazing lands, the rugged individuality of its people, the production limitless in quantity of copper, zinc, lead, manganese, tungsten, uranium, vermiculite, chromite, ammolite, gastrite, fukrite, fluorspar, phosphate, sand and gravel—"Such a wealth!" you might exclaim—but unless we are miners, importers with such needs, we remain unmoved. On our globe not one in fifty million ever has heard of the place, what a shame, what a disappointment that our heroine has been found in such an unarresting environment, why in heaven's name could she not be in New York City, in romantic San Francisco, perhaps down with the Kennedys on Martha's Vineyard or seen as a face in the crowd at Wimbleton, having tea with the Queen at Balmoral, hiking the Swiss Alps with a handsome novelist or musician such as John Irving or Elton John, in a bikini walking the beach at Acapulco with Ralph Fiennes, at Monte Carlo or Vegas playing the tables with Willie Mandella. Don't try telling me those are not possibilities offering far more promise.

But here she is, in Montana, at least *crossing* Montana, so she shall soon be free of this dreadful setting, Idaho or the Dakotas looming, things are looking up.

"Any mother who abandons her child, abandons a good and loving husband, deserves, I say, to be shot. Just look at that island oasis of theirs, the grass this high, the trees unpruned, the moat scummy, dog doo everywhere, a thousand newspapers littering the steps! God did not put women on this earth to—"

Unforeseen demands are being placed upon us again, lower your guard one second and here comes the riffraff, for some minutes now newcomers sounding suspiciously like property owners ensconced behind the gated walls of Daggle Senior Citizens Estates, sounding suspiciously like those magpies a few pages back who have had one drink too many, have been insisting upon their divinely inspired rights to the page. Why not, let them have their moment, what's the harm, God gave us a mouth that it might be used and free and unfettered speech for the elite wealthy is a fact of life long with us.

"So you say. If God had meant women to give birth and stay at home, he would have made houses. He did not make houses. He only made two people, saps both of them, and left them naked in a garden, with no thought given to pending inclement weather or that day when voyeurs would be out with binoculars."

"Stop this. Both of you, put a shoe in it. I care not a hoot about Montana, as the man said. But if it is a choice between Montana and listening to your anti-Christian rot, then I choose sorcery, I choose to listen even to that imbecile runaway, Joyel Daggle, in godless Montana."

"Joyel's not talking. A fucking traffic light, a cop on her tail, I tell you the broad's not only a dingbat, she's a mute."

May flesh be implanted upon invisible bone? Can the disembodied voice be made to walk, can it be induced to sing? May it at least be made visible? Let us try. The man who has just now spoken of rot and sorcery stands by a window looking out into the night. He wears khaki shorts, which reach below his knobby knees, and a pink polo shirt, which rides over a ballooning paunch and has a rabbit insignia stitched by the manufacturer into the pocket above his heart. He is seventy-two, now retired, formerly in management, assistant CEO at St. Boniface Tool and Dye, if you can believe him, in good health, his doctor has declared, vigorous as a magician, though his blood count is high, prostate problems loom, cataract operations, gall bladder surgery, are down the line. Of his character, a brusque individual, he would assert, a plain speaker who has never taken shit from anyone and doesn't mean to start now, witness that business at the Tool and Dye when shopworkers struck for "extended vacation benefits," didn't he ream their asses, closed the plant, locked out the fuckers, an honest wage is one thing, benefits another.

Eyes close together, nose bulgy, complexion ruddy, made so by this gated community's incessantly sunny days, weight 235, much of it dropping, feet—in the sandals he's now seen wearing—plainly calloused, size twelve, fat toes, thick nails, although, as it happens, earlier today the toenails were clipped by the wife, one foot and then the next up in Doodoo's lap, not a chore she requisitioned, I'm telling you. A liked-enough kind of guy, frequently hearty, not tight-assed like some, as well-fixed financially as a man can be when the goddam pussy-whipped liberal-heart socialist government tries to take your every dime. Nothing to complain about, that's old Vern, except when he is to be heard saying that it has all gone to the dogs out there, welfare creeps, immigrants, guys with women's scarves tied around their noggins, queers and transvestites under every bush, rapper black guys, picaninnies, on every street corner, boozers, loonies they are now calling the homeless, dope addicts, shootings, stabbings, you can't walk down the street someone's not coming at you with an ice pick, yet I see on TV our gutless leaders calling for a reduction of the nation's arms, pussies picketing the National Rifle Association, I say thank God for Charlton Heston and my fellow like-minded gun enthusiasts, anyone comes at me over that wall they'll have their guts splattered into next week.

That's how it is out there.

Which, in a nutshell, is why Vern, like the others domiciled at Daggle Estates, has signed the dotted line and slapped down his dough-ray-me into that prick sharpie Raoul's money-sucking hand. Protection, security, a mecca into which vacuum cleaner salesmen, Avon ladies, thieves and jackals, the world's losers, the ethnic hordes, may not penetrate save they attack from the air, storm the gate with armored car. "Fucker is making millions, believe you me, but I don't regret mine and Doodoo's decision one minute, life behind these walls is A-okay!"

A-okay, they are all like-minded citizens at the Daggle. With the rare exception, if an argument flares up at the Daggle, it isn't going to be because one party says to another, "But what about the plight of the homeless, those dreary deadbeats." No, any argument Vern or anyone else gets into at the Daggle is likely to be over what's for supper tonight, "Did you take off your muddy shoes," shit like that.

Old Vern is one of eight souls, four civic-spirited couples, attending a dinner party at one of the eighty-seven houses comprising the Daggle Senior Citizens Adult Lifestyles Sheltered Community, Daggle Estates or Daggle Shores, the Daggle, for short. And the dinner, such as it was—antipasto shit this, antipasto shit that, fish sticks in the fucking microwave, runny cheese 'n' nibbles, black olives, *dip*, that fucking dog food the women call, what is it, *humis, hoomis*, I can't even spell the fucker—is long-since over. Bridge has been played, not to everyone's enjoyment, because the men as usual have drank too much. Our man at the window speaking of rot, old Vern, this week trying out a mustache, hair a fine buzz cut, seen this minute yanking up his white tennis socks, wishing he had thought to wear his red suspenders, give the women something to hang on to, is among those who has drank too much, when ever is that not the case.

Indeed, at this very minute he holds in his hand a glass filled to the brim with fine vintage scotch, no ice, are you kidding? Those Scots, the whole damned country, can sink into the sea for all Vern cares, but first let's rescue the single malts. He has come to the window out of multiple desires: one, to get a close-up look at Lucy Devonshire's tits and maybe cop a feel, but scratch that, the little cockteaser has scooted away; two, to take a gander at Raoul Daggle's fucking moat, to see if maybe the heartbroken pisser is back yet from his sojurn into infinity for the koo-koo wife. No such luck, however, no car, no lights, the same fucking garbage litters the yard. Vern wonders again why those Daggles seem to be immune from the corporation's contract, bylaws, and constitution, how is it their place gets to feel so separated, so disconnected, from the other eighty-six homes, when the whole idea behind this place is that you're supposed to be One Happy Family with roughly the same set of moral values, the same general level of income, the same high regard for the earned reward, the luxuries of life, the same appreciation, by God, of what it was built this country in the first place and what now is decaying into a habitat for Asia and the Third World.

Why does that fucker get to have a moat? Vern asks himself, not for the first time. If we all had moats, we'd be like fucking Venice without the rot, not a bad idea, good though a place is, it can always be improved, this being a philosophy served him in good stead at St. Boniface Tool and Dye, although admittedly it has been less effective with Doodoo. What was it she said today when he said, "How about we cut my toenails," can you believe it, she said, "Why don't you get Lucy Devonshire to cut your toenails, anybody can see you got the hots for her."

Ducks waddle about in the Daggle moat, it's a goddam outrage.

Still, there's been talk the fucker Raoul is going to sell out, that's good news, everyone knows the entire crazy family hates this compound, they think they're too fucking good for us, that Raoul may be a goddam millionaire but if you dug to the bottom of him you'd certainly find a rat, they're all socialist sob-artists at heart, if I ever see that Joyel again in her bikini mowing the grass I may just have to introduce her to the family jewels, get my jollies off.

Doodoo stands nearby, observing this polo-shirted man with mild wonder, as ostensibly she attends to the conversation of those chattering behind her. All that can be said in Vern's behalf, completely against the estate's rules, is his keeping of doves, his fascination with raising, nurturing, these fragile sensitive birds. What a puddle of contradictions people are. Doves, a dove in his hands he's like a child, such a sweetheart, it was what attracted Doodoo to him way back when; when he's speaking of these gentle creatures, relating a noble history that stretches all the way back to Aphrodite for whom they were sacred, of long-extinct relatives such as the dodo, the solitaire, when he's feeding a sickly baby a paste of ground nuts off a finger or caressing the soft feathers, his eyes water, the bird dies and he will mourn it for days. Otherwise, he's crude, gross, an animal. Now there's that meek bird, Lucy Devonshire, in the kitchen crying out her eyes because Vern has trailed her all evening, pinching her fanny, whispering obscenities in her ear.

"What are you looking at?" he says.

The topic tonight remains those Daggles, which is not unusual, such a showcase of the bizarre those Daggles are. Families in this friendly enclave are ever assessing these strange, those impossible and unruly, these frenetic and peculiar Daggles. These Daggles are not much liked around here, as someone in this group is attesting yet again this very second, the speaker being that same party, our host, who earlier declared that shooting, for moms abandoning a child, is a just punishment, biblically directed, and a modest enough one at that.

"Abortionists, grave robbers, pickpockets, cop killers, pedophiles, lunatics, terrorists, Greenpeacers, all that pro-this-and-that bunch, they should all be shot."

Someone is singing in the entertainment center in the hosts' gaming room, a rinky-dink piano, the CD stuck, a mistake that CD is, borrowed from Daggle and never returned—a black woman, black as the ace of spades, blacker than the blackest pit, backed by the Echoes of Eden of St. Paul Baptist Church circa early forties, Central Avenue, Los Angeles, so long ago, Etta James a child, five years old, the lady bad and squawling and messy, moaning over and over, *Not enough sugar to make my cream my cream not enough sugar to make my dream.*

Yeah, yeah, yeah.

A normal evening, then, in this gated enclave of senior citizens, early and late retirees, close enough to the ocean, they will say, that you can scent the water, feel the salty breeze.

"Why don't you go home?" Vern tells Doodoo.

"Why don't you go to hell?" Doodoo replies.

Vern regards this woman, his wife, with a twitching, bewildered eye. Why is she dressed so outlandishly? Who else in this conforming community would garb herself up in the costume of—what place is it tonight?—Africa, Iran, Afghanistan? The constitution should have a regulation about this.

"Doodoo, you know, Doodoo, I've said it before: You just don't fit in around here."

You lack the gated mentality.

He's right, old Vern. Of all those 174 people residing in the eighty-seven houses within these secured walls—no children allowed, exempting the Daggles, no pets allowed, exempting budgies, canaries, and Vern's doves—aside from the Daggles, Doodoo alone despises and would incinerate the place. A thousand times has Doodoo wished she had the courage to do what Joyel Daggle, that wisest of women, has done. Scram, hit the road, *eat my dust, Vern.*

I wonder where she is, Doodoo thinks. What I would give to be in her shoes.

Here, Doodoo. Here she is. Turn the page.

3

montana

TIME PASSES, who knows why. Why doesn't it stand still, even go backwards? These are not questions put to you by a child. One day Joyel is old and weary, next door to death, the next day her bones don't ache, the next, she's spiry, the next, mature, soon she's in love, gamboling in a field, time flies and soon she's a child, then she's not yet born, she's her mother old and weary, *Would Mrs. Moffit like her tea*, the next day her bones don't ache, the next, she's spiry, the next, mature, how time flies, for soon she's in love, gamboling in a field . . . on and on, until she's old and weary in primordial sludge, now here she is in a green valley romping with gazelles, a furry, all but four-footed creature crests a hill . . . run, woman, run like crazy.

This is how a modern woman on the road at night alone amuses herself. Passes the time.

Oh, here I am coming into Alzada, how nice.

Joyel was stopped for running a red light on the outskirts of a small town in Montana, near the South Dakota border. She was trying to get out of Montana as fast as she could, having never met such strange people. Especially the women, whom she considered strange primarily because they put up with, and often seemed to love, very peculiar men. The wife of one of these men, was it in Missoula, had said to Joyel, "Love defeats me." The woman's husband had said, "You've got to grab it the way I do a rodeo heifer. Whump it down, rope the legs. Takes about five seconds."

The policeman says to Joyel, "Why didn't you stop for the light?"

Joyel says, "What light?"

She thinks, Here's another one.

Cops are taught in whatever training school they attend to look directly into a miscreant's eyes. If the miscreant squirms, slap on the cuffs. Joyel is holding her hands tight to the wheel. She isn't going to look this one in the face unless she has to.

Joyel thinks that this helpless feeling must have been incubating since infancy. She imagines crying for hours out of hunger, pins stabbing her skin, suffering a crazy rash, and no one arriving to take care of her.

She would like to cry, though not in Montana. Montana is already populated with too many weeping women that no one attends.

The policeman has followed her through the whole of the one-horse town. She spotted him on a side street before he pulled in behind her. She counted one, two, three, aloud, and on four, there he was. She has always been what might be termed an erratic driver, hapless, or so Raoul, who has no feelings and speaks what he thinks, who divines pleasure from seeing a woman squirm, so he claims. But why is she thinking of him now? More to the point, how has she missed the light? It could be that it was some kind of trick light, there and not there like the beating of her heart.

Joyel is frantically looking for Jane Dearborne's driver's license, the ownership certificate, the insurance form, she hasn't yet got her feet back inside her shoes, should she turn off the engine, cut the lights? She is doubly upset now, suddenly certain someone, she knows who, if not his name, has been rifling through her car. Jane Dearborne's car, she means, it's so hard to keep these matters straight. Someone, oh yes, bet your titty she knows who, has gone at the glove compartment with a screwdriver or knife, look at those scratches on the lock. Dammit, she thinks, now doesn't that take the cake. A big policeman is standing beside her, no time yet to be afraid, to throw up her arms and screech as she wants to, as she would if alone, That son of a bitch has found me, how? The son of a bitch is on my tail, why? The goddam son of a bitch has been on my butt a year, won't he ever leave me alone?

A flashlight is in there that she has never seen before, the ashtray, full of butts, is another clue. She does not herself smoke, nor does Jane Dearborne. That certain someone, the son of a bitch, has sat in her car, smoking Camels, how many, five, no, there are two more down at her feet. And why hasn't she put on her shoes? Surely it must be illegal in this day and age, when everything is, to be driving with naked feet.

"Excuse me," she says to the waiting officer, such a big man, "I'm a bit rattled."

"Take your time, miss, this isn't a hanging offense."

Miss, am I a *miss*, has it come to that? In the old days, herself a child, a smoker would walk a mile for a Camel, people did a lot more walking, generally, in those days, before the cigarettes killed them. Camels with their bumps were strange to her then, she imagines—well, she would if she had the time—they still are. She has actually met, not in Montana, an expert in cell structure who crossed a camel with a llama, no humps, the size of a pony.

The cell expert told her future generations were in for a good many surprises; in the laboratory now any living creature may be matched with any other living creature, this, he said, is capitalism's new frontier, forget microchips, forget oil, sink your money in Newlife stock, it's a rocketship. She wants this for herself, not the matching but a new frontier, a new life without so many humps. Her new frontier would embrace the old one, Joyel Daggle back in the family bosom: husband and child, the same and not the same, better, perfection, a Raoul who has seen the light, she gets a horny feeling just thinking of that. But is she back now where she was a year ago, with no option but to *run, bitch, run*? Hell, she thought that certain someone, who had rifled her car, the son of bitch, was dead. Hadn't she seen his body sink down through the mud in Orick, California? What is going on here?

"Shake a leg," the policeman says.

Joyel wants to tell the policeman that she comes from good stock, she is a victim of circumstance, of stars gone awry, for instance, that red light.

She wants to say, This isn't my car.

That would not be a wise thing to say.

She'd best be squinting, put a sneer on her lips the way Jane Dearborne did when they snapped this ugly photo for Jane's driver's license.

"I'm hurrying, officer."

The son of a bitch sitting in her car smoking Camels has also left a note; she recognizes the scrawl: *Yet she must die, else she will betray more me.*

Othello, somewhere near the end.

More me doesn't sound right. And what's this, more writing on the back: *It's about time you came to your senses, you can't escape me, I'm yours, you are mine, nothing can change this, not the law, not your husband, not God, not anyone.*

"Turn off your engine," the policeman says.

"Yes sir."

Finally she's found them, the documents, she thinks that's what this bundle must be, too bad she and Jane hadn't taken the time, hadn't had the foresight, to think through the perils of this car-swapping idea. "Here, you sort it out," she says, and passes over to the policeman wads of stuff, the license, registration, crumpled napkins, get-two-pizzas-for-one coupons, ticket stubs, hairpins, whatever was in there.

Now wait. Take deep breaths. Don't think of that son of a bitch who's been chasing me, has sat here smoking his filthy weed, just when I thought I'd given him the slip, the son of a bitch, but he still hasn't found me, he's only found the car.

She looks around, up and down the dark road, suddenly terrified, her hands shake, she's got the jitters, tears spring to her eyes, the road's deserted, thank the Lord, not a soul out here but her and the policeman who is now backing up a step, watching her closely, likely thinking something's not right here. Although what he says is, "Here now, don't cry, what's got you so squirmy, you never run a red light before?"

"Hyperventilation," she manages with a squeak, "hyperpnea also, they run in the family." Isn't that the truth.

"Jane Dearborne. That's you?

"Yes."

"You don't look like your picture."

Joyel contemplates telling him it has been a hard year. What she says is, "I've cut my hair." What she thinks is, I've cut my bangs, I've lost weight, gone off the deep end, please don't slap me in jail.

"It says here, *brown* eyes, yours are blue."

"Contacts."

"Height five-two, it says here. What, were you squatting?"

He's on to her, in a minute he's going to slap on the cuffs—would it help if I showed a little cleavage, practiced my wiles? She doesn't have any wiles, she's never had any, ipso facto she has none now, and precious little cleavage, too, as Raoul says she's an Aunt Jemima pancake down there, all buttermilk and cream, just the way I like it, ma'am. But the lawman is now giving her what could be a smile, he's softening his tone, these Montana savages can be gentle after all.

"You're far from home, Ms. Dearborne. Enjoying Montana?"

"Not at the moment."

The policeman has her grandfather's same wide jaw, the same intelligent eyes. In the one photograph Joyel has of her grandfather he is standing in a muddy field, in hipwaders, his legs spread, holding a white horse over his head. A cowboy hat rides low over his brow, there is a look of fierce concentration, purpose, on his face.

The policeman returns to his cruiser. He will be running the plate. Jane Dearborne is scatty, she has doodle for brains, but surely her car plates are good, the state of California has no warrant out for her arrest, Joyel is almost certain of this. She drums her fingers on Jane Dearborne's steering wheel, fidgets with the radio. Jane's aerial won't pick up any stations out here. A man at a gas station in Conrad, way back there, had attached a clothes hanger, probably that sucker has worked loose.

In the background of this photograph of her grandfather was a very fat little girl who might have been Joyel's mother. The photo is blurred, however; it might be that the fat little girl was a bush. To Joyel's mind, this is clearly a trick photograph, though her mother insists Grandfather always lifted horses over his head, as an entertainment for Sunday visitors. She can hear her mother saying, "Well, we were circus people, you know. If you look closely, you can see that what you call a bush has an apple in her mouth. Look more closely and you'll see the tree."

Joyel scrutinizes the flashlight, the butts, the scrawl. The flashlight's batteries are low, it's a keychain, actually. *The key to home*, it says on the disc, that son of a bitch Camel man's little joke, she supposes. She's feeling less frightened now, at least there isn't any immediate danger, not unless the cop is that son of a bitch in disguise. But wait a minute, let's not go off half-cocked, let's not lose our wig. Self-control in a situation like this is paramount, be still, my beating heart.

"Some SOB broke into my car," she hears herself saying to the policeman, who is back again. "It must have happened back in Cut Bank."

The policeman nods, he's oldish, but he must have been quite a dish at one time. "Patience is a long, thin line," he says, how strange of him. "People go too far, or not far enough. Yes, I'd say that describes it." What kind of policeman is this? His voice is quiet, deep as a bass fiddle, as though the sound is coming up through his body from mysterious sources within the earth. The sound is coming up so far from within the earth that Joyel can't locate a point of reference for the words he speaks. Has she said anything to him about patience, about extremes?

Joyel's window is down scarcely an inch, a cold wind blows, the night is dark. The window was that way when she got the car, the turn handle gone, the windshield has a crack in it from top to bottom. So much of this heap is broken, rusting, it's a claptrap, Jane Dearborne got the best of this deal, maybe for the first time in her life, she's a casebook of misfortune, old Jane. The policeman's fingers curl over the glass, what's he going to do next? He bites his nails, she observes, just the way little Juliette does hers. He's slim or slimmish, no gut, a tired face, a body she would describe as sinewy if ever she had to.

They are alone in the dark night, near the bewitching hour, you can hear frogs croaking their woes, no moon. Joyel is not absolutely certain she is on the right road, although she can't imagine how she could have got onto a wrong one since her map shows just one road through this southeastern corner.

Alzada is a town so teensy she's astonished they can afford a lawman.

She can see the traffic light in the rearview mirror, now on red again, bold as can be, she must have been dreaming to have passed right through it. It occurs to her that she's hungry, she hasn't eaten in a long time. A raw potato is an infant, she thinks, a baked potato is a senior citizen. But then you split the potato open, lather on the butter, and it goes back to being a potato. Whereas new potatoes in an orange mesh bag have the faces of little imprisoned children, you can hear their screams as you plop them into boiling water.

She closes her eyes. You've got to stop this, she tells herself.

"Get out, please," the policeman says, is he still here? "Wait in my vehicle."

"Why? Am I under arrest?"

"What for? For having no purpose in life?"

"Pardon me?"

"I need to search this automobile for contraband."

Contraband. She loves that word.

"I am not getting in your car," Joyel says, her voice high and strained, hardly hers at all. "Be sensible. What kind of contraband?"

Joyel stands by the side of the road probing a toe into Montana's roadwork while the sinewy policeman searches Jane Dearborne's car. She understands that this is a cursory search, performed on impulse, that this policeman's life is as lonely, as desperate, as her own.

"Why is all this mud caked in the floorboards?" he asks. "This is truly a filthy vehicle."

He pulls from beneath the driver's seat a satin shoe, spaghetti straps, open toe. "I might have to bag this shoe. Evidence. A shoe like this, it tells a story."

Lucky Jane Dearborne, someone is going to tell her story, high time someone did, don't forget to put in how her estranged husband likes nothing better than to beat the hell out of her. The satin pump is stained and misshapen, mud is wedged inside, it's missing a heel. Joyel can hear herself saying to Jane Dearborne tomorrow on the phone, We found your satin pump, Jane will say, How's it going, love? and they will have a long confab about their lives in a pernicious world in which the sublime knows no home while the ridiculous is everywhere.

"About size four, I'd estimate. That your size, Ms. Dearlove?"

"Dearborne."

"One shoe. Of itself, suspicious. What's with all the pillows?"

Joyel clams up. She knows her rights. There is no law against riding about with a thousand pillows. She doesn't have a thousand yet—only, if she remembers correctly, thirty-four, minus those she sent home.

"They are a record of my achievement," she says. Then relents as the cop plants his feet, rakes her with accusing eyes, hands hitched onto his belt, a lefty, she notes, the holstered pistol riding low, secured by rawhide string to the long leg, shades of the Old West.

"Souvenirs, sir."

The policeman holds up the Wyoming pillow, right there on top. The state name is spelled in glitzy green, the *W* just about gone. Soon it will be her Yoming pillow, a brand new state, on the velveteen cover an old cartoonish wheezer rattling a miner's pan in a rocky woodland stream and from his expression you know that pan has never seen a single nugget of gold.

And then the policeman does such a strange thing. He does such a strange and unpredictable thing that the heart goes pitter-pat, the breath holds, his statement comes so unheralded, so much without warning, which in this case is what unheralded means, that one is compelled to ask, Who *are* these people inhabiting our globe? How come? one asks. Certainly Joyel Daggle did. What brought this on? she asked herself.

That the old miner's pan was empty, is it that simple? That here in this gold-rush country, the continent expanding, Horace Greeley's cry "Go West, young man" resounding in the breast of every man, woman, and child, whatever their ages, every man and his brother heeding the call, buffalo being shot right and left, not to mention women and children, the native brethren with their backs against the wall, gold there for the pickings in every field and stream, what happened? Gold barons exercising the might of dominion over each butte, stream, and gully, men, women, and children being shot, knifed, hung, garroted, or scalped every which way you looked, and for most of these heroics the hero with his pan empty, these heroes of the West being shot, knifed, hung, garroted, or scalped, often the deeds to transpire concurrently, and the Indian, his back to the wall, his pan nonexistent, is it this history peculiar to the state of rugged individuality that explains Joyel Daggle's policeman's extraordinary, unheralded remarks, remarks beguiling to the mind inasmuch as the measure they take of human relations, 130 words for the year 2000, taking their measure of how far we've become removed from each other in the present apostatized age, namely the year 2000, remarks that are so much to the point that the heart pounds, and not merely that empty organ the heart, an organ merely performing its accustomed duty, a stake driven through it, and through the mind also, through the mind most particularly, that we must—in a moment, let's allow ourselves a moment—analyze and make adjustment and come to grips with the situation postulated by, or soon to be postulated by, our strange policeman. Even the puzzled reader must do so, pardon our shifting the burden to you, but, yes, you and most particularly you, must consider what this oddest of policemen at this junction in the narration going by the title *The Fall of Gravity*, let's try and be polite about it, said.

And pause to give reconsideration to the strange man's character, the policeman's, I mean, even to revise our previous sentencing of the proud state of Montana into some limbo-land where no speech of much significance has ever, or rarely, been uttered, unless these utterances issued from the mouth of the victim years ago just as he, he or she, was about to be shot, knifed, hung, garroted, or scalped, or as each of these injustices was being executed upon his defenseless person simultaneously, a reaction which is certainly within the bounds of possibility, since a person with his back against the wall, nowhere to run, is apt to mouth any avalanche of words in postponement of his fate, including the most plebian cry for mercy, a plea that in his case there are extenuating circumstances, *please don't do it.*

Bear with me.

The remarks made, the story told by the policeman, in all innocence I must assure you, was as follows:

"When it was suggested to a gold baron in Virginia City, circa 1860s, that the rich should share their wealth, the baron replied, 'Let the poor share their poverty since they have so much of it. Let the old and the young enjoy equal portions of adversity. The little children shall be made happy that they have not been forgotten, and the newborn who sups at his mother's bosom may do so with the full awareness that he, too, and his sister in the bargain, may likewise anticipate a lifetime of equalized squalor. When the poor do this, then, and only then, shall I empty my pockets and share with these wastrels my daily bread."

Joyel Daggle, however, wasn't blown away.

"Let's begin another conversation," she said, "or get back to the old one. I don't believe I like where this one is leading. I must say, though, that it is exactly the sort of thing my husband might say, especially back at home when he's in a shouting match with that creep Vern."

"What's your husband's name?"

"Raoul Daggle."

"So Dearborne is your maiden name?"

"No. My name is Daggle also, I'm traveling under a pseudonym, actually that of my friend Jane Dearborne. We've swapped cars and ID because there is a son of a bitch out there, I don't know why, who is out to get me, maybe even kill me."

"Oh. Well, that clarifies matters."

"You're a nice man, and should anything terrible happen to me, should you read about my murder in the paper, I didn't want you to think I had misled you."

"I'm honored. Thank you, Ms. Daggle."

It's uncanny how well she and this policeman are getting along.

At the same time that she thinks this, she admits also that a lot has been left unsaid.

"It's the midnight of my soul, and I don't know which way to turn."

The policemen gives her shoulder a squeeze.

"You'll pull through," he says. "My bet's on you."

Oh, Raoul, she thinks. The touch of this understanding man's hand has made her want to squeeze right up next to him. It's as if up in the dark sky a thousand people have been listening and all their hearts have come home to lodge in the heart of this strangest of all breeds, an empathetic policeman.

"I want to show you something," the policeman says. He has whipped the cruiser about, driven one block, taken the alley behind an abandoned factory. They are barreling up this alley now and to Joyel's eye much in this town seems abandoned. A cop is abducting her, wonder why? The alley empties into a lane, they are rising into a bleak, dark surround. Snow abounds. It's foggy up here, arriving in drifts that somehow stabilize the mind. Black creatures of imprecise dimension and intent dart about in the headlight's glare, eyes glint at her, she sucks in her breath, a little nervous but nothing she can't control. Eyes reflected in the headlights, what's that?

"Raccoons," the policeman explains.

"Raccoons will dip their food in water before eating," Joyel replies. "Should they have the choice. The exact reason for this practice is a raccoon mystery."

"Me, too. In water."

The policeman's name, she's learned, is Horace Yew.

"Yoo like yoo-hoo," she asked, "like the ram and the ewe, like y-o-u?"

"No, Yew like the yew tree, known in these parts as ground hemlock. Maybe I don't look it but I'm part Chinese."

"Isn't that strange," says Joyel, "what a coincidence, I've always felt I was myself part Chinese, but the other parts, well, those parts feel so foreign I can't even imagine what array of people in the many countries might have given birth to them."

How mysterious.

Joyel finds her mood shifting to one of quiet exhilaration. It's having company, she thinks, it's having a gentle soul to talk to, although neither she nor her policeman friend Yew is saying much, saying nothing, really, with a friend you don't have to speak your every syllable, that's a well-established fact, too bad such long silences are deadening to a narrative such as this one, but if we had everything, it's unlikely we'd be reaching for a book, whereas if one has nothing, a book is still useful for propping up a wobbly table. Silence in such instances as the present constitutes a third agreeable party, finally silence has got a chance to strut its colors, the occasional grunt in illustration of the fact that we are still alive doesn't despoil the atmosphere, it's pleasant to have a little time to let your mind rove, who knows where it's going next, all those gaps it jumps, those murky dwellings it ventures into, really the mind is like a bird flitting from twig to twig with no one twig more advantageous than the other, not even the bird would claim otherwise, it just tweets and flies elsewhere, frequently out of sight, which, again, is a mirror of the roving mind. Joyel recalls a husband trait, Raoul saying *Come to me, object of my desire* when he wanted the two of them to do something they both wanted to do together, which is a something she has been yearning for with some desperation lately. He was, is, such a good and sexy husband, dynamite in bed, thank goodness she has no complaints in that area. True, he's hard to nail down, strange how a motormouth can remain such a private secret being, *enigmatic*, that's the word. Raoul has yet to acknowlege his true capacity, dear Raoul, and possibly never will, he surrenders to the same black holes astronomers bicker about, which prevents him from shooting for the stars, he's male and can't help it, the roots diseased, his love cup is rarely filled, a jigger here, a jigger there. *Life is a Picasso*, Raoul used to say in explanation of his moods, when mopey, he'd say, "I'm in my blue period," he'd say it whether mopey or not, if only to boggle the mind of that reprobate, Vern, who spent a lot of time trying to figure us out, how strange it is that all those passionately heartless gated people at Daggle Shores, the Daggle, have available to their eyes the same moon and sundry stars, the same Milky Way and Little and Big Dippers, not to mention satellites, that Yew and I have here, or would have here if this beautiful mist was not all around us.

Scattered house lights, dogs barking, raccoons plundering, animal life abounds in Montana. In fact, for all the squeeze being put on them, Joyel Daggle, alias Jane Dearborne, would maintain animal life abounds in each of the thirty-four states, seven provinces, and Latino-land she's passed through, maybe South Dakota will be the exception.

"Where are we going?" she asks Yew.

"Hold your horses," the policeman says.

In the year Joyel has been on the road, which she is inclined to think of as her period of recovery, she had unleashed all the horses, invited any number of strange beings to enter her orbit, some of which have proved refurbishing to her character, others cataclysmic. In pursuit of the wondrous, you find both the magnificent and, alas, the terrible, she's ready and willing to endure whatever Yew has in store for her. He wrenches an arm over the seat, lifts up a six-pack, says, "How about opening us a brew?" The policeman sounds subdued but modestly content, he has put aside all traces of forbidding personality, he isn't sinewy in the least, more than one would say he's still a dish. He has a chiseled, comforting face, gentle watery eyes, a lot of pain there, younger than she first supposed, although you get the feeling he's only a year or two, perhaps a single night, away from being an old man.

He whips into a driveway. The tires make crunching sounds going up a rise, darkness lurks all around, Dracula under a wide cape.

They sit a moment drinking the cold beverage, in surrender to private thoughts denied to this chronicle, then suddenly the entire yard is lit up, the yard, the house before them, is as radiant as a playing field, all yellow and gold, under a wash of drifting fog. A man with an enormous beer belly, in one of those bare-shoulder T-shirts beer drinkers invariably wear, appears in the front doorway, one hand on his hips, the other up shielding his eyes, the screen propped open by one naked foot, how gross, as Juliette would say. On his head is a Davy Crockett coonskin cap, the fur singed, the tail gnawed, wild hair made golden by the yellow light bulb over his head flares about his shoulders, truly he is yellow or golden from head to toe, his whiskers yellow, even his eyes, his teeth, when he calls out, as he does now, "Oh, it's you." Or "Yew," who knows?

Not the warmest of welcomes, lacking much in the social graces, but how much Joyel loves that *you*, for it means that she, a perfect stranger, has been included. Or so she thinks.

Our history is brief. Compared to reptiles, the original horse was hardly larger than a wolf, Joyel thinks, where will that man be, who will breathe his dust, breathe mine and Yew's, for that matter, in a million years? Someone will, perhaps on the moon once water is found, they'll shudder, goose bumps will romp over their flesh, they'll say, Someone just walked over my grave, just as we do on earth, a statement coming close to the truth since the goose bumps will have as their originating source all our molecules out there swarming up from space's dark holes, which in one sense is all space is, space is our escaped molecules out there finally free to dispense with the laws of gravity, the laws of logic and happenstance, in the blind creation of a just environment, too bad so few of us in our present form can make the trip.

"The kids are fine," Freddy calls, again how strange, how incomprehensible, Joyel would think he was speaking of Juliette had he not employed the plural.

Fog comes and goes, frogs croak, crickets sing, mist hangs along the yellow man's roof line, a roof bathed in gold, yellow lights casting a soft halo there. The rickety structure, no more than a shack, might be some kind of underprivileged House of God minus the steeple, minus the cross, unless you want to superimpose over the structure the figure of the man come to the door to greet the unannounced callers, unless you want to impale there his sadsack form and place on his head a crown of thorns. No thank you, not tonight, perhaps another time.

By the door hangs a bouquet of red and green bells, tinsel, ribbons, flowers, all disintegrating, possibly left there on a rusting nail in year-round expectation of Santa Claus.

The man in the doorway waits, now he, too, is guzzling beer from a can, scratching his groin, eyeing them with curiosity but little concern, the way the cat can wait for a timid mouse to emerge from its hole.

"Freddy robbed nine banks before he was sixteen," Yew says. "Then he was fifteen years behind bars. You want weed, Freddy's is the place to come. Freddy grows pretty good Montana weed."

"I don't want weed. I want to get to South Dakota. Are we going inside?"

"Not me. Freddy might shoot us. Freddy doesn't exactly have all his marbles."

There in the headlight beams, in high weeds to the side of the house, is a black iron pot. Fires once burnt beneath that pot, as is clear from the soot. All your imagination has to do is clear away the weeds, look at the pot, the soot, to invent a snaggle-toothed homesteader woman under a sunbonnet here a hundred years ago stirring clothes with a pole, readjusting the child on her hip, snarling at another urchin to behave, the woman here keeping the home fires burning, keeping ahead of the riffraff while her man is off Virginia City way panning for gold or getting shot, stabbed, or hung, getting any of the other harsh punishments God devised long before we crucified His son and His punishments found meaning.

Yew sighs, such heavy sighs, "Let's get these groceries delivered, shall we?"

"I beg your pardon?"

But Yew is already out of the car, he's back there raising the boot-lid. Well, how about that, the man's a shopper, he's been to the Food Lion, look at all of those bags.

They slog through high weeds, tin cans, pots and pails, car tires, strange stacks of rock-like objects heaped into high cone shapes, in the near distance a yellow rusting sidehoe, a plow, my goodness, is that a trailer home up ahead? All back here is cast under the spell of drifting fog and diffused yellow light, entrancing enough visually until one notices, as Joyel now does, that the trailer door is open and inside within a cloud of yellow smoke two teenage boys repine against the far wall. One boy appears to be asleep, the other has a cig stuck between his lips and he's looking back at Joyel with the same intense air of disbelief, of held breath, that might describe herself. Now the boy shifts his glance towards Yew's approaching figure, he slowly gets to his feet, Yew settles his grocery bags by the doorway, he strides between the sleeping boy's outslung legs, and in the next second there are the two of them, Yew and the standing boy, stepping into each other's arms, embracing, holding frozen one to the other through extended minutes, as still as statues whose all available energy has been consumed in getting them to this point.

Father and sons, well kiss my fanny.

Now Joyel has shaken the two boys' limp hands, she's said, "Nice to meet you," the boys have been civil without saying a single word, both are clearly strung out on dope, teenage hauteur, angst, addictive drugs of greater power and consequence than simple weed which undoubtedly grows in profusion here, but now the boys are drifting back into their little trailer house, they are closing the door, let them go, who can say what will become of them, it isn't within our province to decree a fate for everyone entering these pages. It is then that Joyel asks in all innocence, "Why are all these cone-shaped piles of rocks stacked about?" The question clearly is an embarrassment to Yew and Freddy, who stutter and swivel about in indecision as to how they might reply, illustrating once more that men can be reduced to imbecilty with the stroke of a pen, the merest word. Meanwhile, Joyel is drifting towards one of these piles, now suddenly curious when a moment ago she was only making conversation. Yew and Freddy race to intercept her, Yew says, "Don't look, you'll only get upset," a remark which fuels Joyel's determination, these men are treating her just the way men have been taught to treat women, as frail vessels, and no way she can allow that. In the next second she makes the discovery, her hands fly to her face, unknown to her a soundless shriek escapes her lips. These mounds are not composed of stones, they are bones, bleached white bones, human bones, the odd intact skull among them, the odd foot or hand as well. She is instantly overcome with shivers, tremors, tears begin pouring, she's upset but she's also outraged, as can be told by the cry now erupting from her, "What is the meaning of this," a cry whose sound soars across the range, hits the tree line over there, and comes echoing back in all their ears, "What is the meaning of *this this this*?" Yew the policeman and Freddy the bank robber are beside her, each scrunching her shoulders, each mumbling, "There, there," mumbling, "It was a long time ago," mumbling, "It's just bones, don't let it bother you," without question foolish nonsensical words, but when one is overcome by tears the content of the words from those offering solace is not under investigation by linquistic experts, in fact these experts in similar situations resort to the same banalities. So give us a break, why not, let's not be among those who would cast stones.

"I guess you could say collecting those bones was Freddy's old man's hobby, one he got into as a young man, one he believed would put Alzada on the map. He hunted, he fished, he and Lakmé and the kids squeezed out a life together, but on weekends, whenever they had a free minute, the whole family would throw tools into the pickup, they'd pile in and head off to the ghost towns, the old mines and shantytowns, any of those known Montana sites where a panner in the old days staked a claim. They'd dig here and there, load up the booty, I mean, these bones, and come on home. The old man's idea was to use the bones as a tourist lure, they'd charge admission, and Lakmé and the kids would sell fresh fish and the like, birds and hares and opossums and such, and they'd get rich and Alzada be famous. But over time the idea went the way of many such grand schemes: Lakmé took sick and died, Freddy went off to prison for robbing banks, the other sons and daughters skidooed and skedaddled, and all that remained were these leftover bones of our historic gold-rush days."

"We got one bank robber/weed grower here," Yew tells Joyel on the way back to her car, "one kleptomaniac, a pickpocket, no ladies of the night, two suspicious beings driving Harleys. Otherwise, it's the usual husbands-and-wives story."

"Maybe I'll move," Joyel says. She's dead-tired, her mind drifting, having been on the road from Cut Bank since daybreak, eighteen hours ago.

"Coldest spot in the nation, Cut Bank. Did you see Cut Bank's penguin?"

"Penguin?"

"A hundred feet high. It can prophesy the future, that penguin."

"Maybe I'll go back."

"Special penguin-constructed eyes. You look out through the penguin's eyes and all you see are other penguins."

Joyel and her policeman sit in the cruiser looking up into the cold Montana sky. There's Jane Dearborne's car in front of them, looking saggy and bereft, you'd swear it has gone its last mile, though Joyel hopes not, she's raring to go, never mind she can hardly keep her eyes open.

"What did you think of my two boys?"

"They seemed real nice."

"I've tried everything short of shooting them. I don't hassle Freddy about the weed and in return he keeps them happy."

"Where's their mother?"

"Gone."

"Ran off?"

"Fast as heels can fly. Reason I stopped you, you had that same look."

He opens Jane's car door, pats Joyel's shoulder as she slides in.

A dog standing in darkness by the side of the road looks at them piningly as the policeman gives directions to South Dakota.

"Straight ahead, you can't miss it."

"Where have I heard that before?"

Is that you, Trash? Joyel thinks to ask. But before the words can be spoken the dog has crossed the road and jumped in, scrambling over Joyel's lap, taken licks at her face, sniffed here and there, then spun and scrambled to secure its seat.

"Looks like you've got yourself a dog."

The dog sits on his hindquarters on the passenger side, sneezing, licking his chops, displaying a yearning gaze for the open road. Not Trash, she sees now, but a reddish-hued mongrel nearly hip-high, long haired, long in the nose, floppy ears, white paws, an ancient sojourner's melancholy eyes. The dog's fur glistens, soft and beautiful, with a fine lustre. Someone has been looking after this dog better than Joyel Daggle has been caring for herself, her own hair feels like that nesting stuff candy makers put in the bottom of Easter egg baskets. She's likely smelling a bit ripe as well, though not so bad policeman Yew seems in any hurry to leave her side. He wears a woeful expression, as though he's thinking, Here's another one could be mother to my boys, but I guess lightning didn't strike. So long, Ms. Daggle, I'll think of you.

He says, "In bed at night, I hear a heartbeat through my pillow and I don't know whose heartbeat it is. Is it the same with you?"

"Yes."

There he goes.

Here I go, too, fate be kind, may our lives prosper, may our ship come in, hello, dog.

4

Let's Be forthright About This

GOOD MORNING, citizens of the world, and hello, God. Dear Almighty, what tortures and favors have you in mind for us today?

How might we help this story along? Episodes are invented, arranged and rearranged as would a charwoman dust propelled by her broom, voices come and go as does the wind. Meanwhile, our players in the drama entitled *The Fall of Gravity* are like people boarding a packed train, irritated that they can find no seats, the train is ever late arriving and departing, new characters, phantoms, constantly boarding, and it is such a daunting journey, no end in sight, the route suspicious, the night darkening, who can have faith in such an author.

"*What, what, what!*" cries Juliette.

Wind stirs anew, the Infiniti soldiers on, here is Raoul obligingly nodding, although not to us or to any remark his pissed-off daughter has uttered, he is talking on the cellphone to his detective investigator, Solly by name, a man away yonder in Seattle, Washington, who presumably one day soon will be properly introduced to these pages. The girl petulantly appraises her father's wrinkling brow, his narrowing gin-soaked mouth, his despairing tone, as that mouth says to Solly, "What dead man?"

It turns out a dead man has showed up in a wash of mud in a place called Orick, California, a hamlet where Joyel Daggle over recent weeks, every indication points to this, Solly reports, has been hanging out.

"She wasn't in Anne's Ardor, after all?"

"No, sorry about that."

"But she's in Cut Bank? That's confirmed?"

"She was yesterday."

"Okay, tell me about this dead man."

Juliette, at the conclusion of this dialogue to strike up her own, "What does this dead man have to do with my mother?" she asks, her tone whip-like, strident with outrage. "My mother wouldn't have anything to do with anything like that, you wash out your mouth!"

"She left me for dead" is her father's intemperate response. "What makes you think she wouldn't do the same to another poor son of a bitch?"

"In my true mind," Raoul tells his daughter, motoring along, goodbye Epoulette, hello Knickknack, "convenes a massive army from the Palace of Despair."

Darkness, men in big boots, in humongous overcoats vast as the imagination may contain them, scour the earth in the eradication of the world's beauty. Nightly they are there, overcoated and booted, eradicating as fast as they can what's essential to humanity's breath. Need we reminders, need we names, let's not honor these evil merchants even by entering their identities onto the scrolls, for ultimately banishment awaits them, we have only to endure another billion years and they will be no more.

"If I ran away, would you follow me?"

"Absolutely."

"You'd be on my tail every mile, the way we are on Joyel's?"

"Don't use that word."

"'Tail'?"

"Yes."

"Would you?"

"No question."

"You got a phone call in the middle of the night, here you'd come after my tail?"

"Yes."

"Middle of a drink?"

"Yes."

Miles and miles and miles, so many miles, there went Engadine, Corrine, and Blaney Park, here comes Manistique. "Oh, Daddy, look at all those deer crossing the road, where are they going?"

"If I went missing tomorrow, would you take off after me or keep on Joyel's tail?"

"Please don't run away. Don't even talk about it."

"Did Joyel talk about it?"

"No."

"Why can't I talk about it?"

"If I lost you, too, it would break my heart. I would crack up. I would die."

"Are you being straight with me?"

"Yes."

The girl looks at her papa and sees that he means what he says. His eyes have misted over and now tears pool beneath his eyes, the tears roll, a good time to press her advantage.

"I might do it anyway. How come my allowance is so piddly?"

"I wouldn't be able to live without at least one of you. It's so hard with the one gone that I can hardly live with that. It's like gravity itself has come undone."

"I don't understand this gravity business. I think it's all made up."

"It is all made up but that doesn't lessen my pain."

The girl frees herself of the seat belt, snuggles against his chest.

"Is that why you drink so much? Because of the pain of missing Joyel?"

"Yes."

"Liar. You always drank. You drank like a horse even before she left."

"I did? Are you sure?"

"Yes."

"Like a horse?"

"Joyel said so. You're a horse with his head in a bucket."

"She said that!"

"Absolutely. Do you want to drop the subject?"

"Yes."

"Okay, it's dropped. Ka-*boom!* Did you hear it drop?"

"Yes. No gravity?"

"Can't you stop crying, Papa?"

"No, I can't stop."

"Then I'm going to cry, too. I'm going to do it until I can't stop. Are you crying because I said that about the horse or is it because she left and I might? You'd be alone like a man on Mars, is that—*hic*—why? Now look, we've both got the—*hic*—hiccups."

"Where do you see her now, Papa?"

"Slung over a pool table, showing off her legs."

"Now?"

"Eating chop suey."

"Now?"

"In a river washing clothes against rocks with a bunch of naked women."

"Now?"

"It's your turn. How come you keep skipping your turn?"

"Mine are no fun."

"Try harder. Close your eyes."

"I can't see her at all. I scarcely remember what she looks like."

"She's sent pictures. Maybe she'll send one from Cut Bank."

"I don't care if she doesn't. Let's play something easier, something I can play."

"Wait a minute. I see her bent over a sink washing her hair."

"She's always washing something in your pictures. What's she wearing?"

"Nothing."

"You always have her naked."

"I can't tell whether this one is really your mother. She's got her back to me and she must have cut that hair, got herself a new rinse. She's skinny, though, lost weight, if this party is your mother.

The person I'm seeing could be someone I once saw in a movie, it could be Jane Doe, or maybe it's you all grown up. Wait a sec, no, it's not you, I don't know who it is. I don't think she's ever going to turn around. She's never going to show her face, or speak, or make the smallest gesture. She's going to keep her back turned, just to drive me nuts."

"I don't care who that woman is. I hate Jane Doe. Let's count cows. There's one, there's another. Let's bet money."

"Those were not cows."

"They were, too!"

"They were made-up cows."

"So what? I don't care! They are all made-up, and yours, too, but I don't care! You hear me, I don't care!"

"My gracious. Such a tantrum."

"I don't care, I don't care!"

"Town after shiftless town," moans Raoul, passing along yet another Main Street, eyeing the pedestrians, "warriors," he says, "in lurch from or to the grave, like rumpled specimens upheaved from ancient tombs, remnants from lost civilizations, all as if under spells induced by hordes of inept apothecaries from earlier eons. Look, honey, there's a woman in a yellow hat pushing a pram big as a Russian tank, God, I love this country, let's invite her to have a drink."

"Our preconceived ideas are to be shuffled, to be fanned from time to time as we would a deck of cards, a necessity if change is to have a chance with us. In my opinion, forgive me, much is to be said for—"

"Oh, Daddy, do be quiet," Juliette says.

"Now this is curious, it represents a clear reversal of my expectations," replies Raoul. "Our affairs are out of joint. Which of us know when we rise in the morning full of good cheer, brimming with confidence, that by afternoon, by the next tick of the clock, all will flip over, we will be mired in deepest depression, tired as a dog. Who is that haggard man whose face I caught in the mirror? we may ask ourselves."

"Enough, enough!"

Night has fallen and the road we were on is now a thicket, we are overcome by brush, by granite boulder, only wilderness, high mountains, boiling clouds, rain, and snow stretch ahead. All the same, we are somewhere in North America, we know that, and by the look of things we are to remain in these woods yet a while, up the creek, if you care to put the situation that way. "Are we lost, Daddy?" inquires a voice frail with fatigue and worry. Juliette Daggle speaks, she's wan, a poor little lost thing looking so lanky, so skinny and worn out on the Infiniti's gray leather seat. "Do we know where we're going, Daddy?" What a question from one so young, surely you do not expect me to stop and ask directions, any man will tell you that such is the one sure way of losing your way, losing your grip, even, it's happened to me a thousand times.

"Stop, Daddy, let's ask someone."

"Fine, go ahead, don't let me cramp your style."

So there is Juliette Daggle out by Frosty Morn gas pumps, Divine Judgment Bar and Grill adjacent under a wash of yellow light, play swings painted yellow, a clapboard house. Small white butterflies hop, dart, and flutter in beautiful courtship under the yellow arc, theirs a delicacy of movement so refined, so casually poetic your breath falters. Juliette, on a mission, strides past these beauties with barely a glance, butterflies, please, get a life. There she is now, tugging at a busy man's sleeve. "Excuse me, sir, excuse me." Finally the man takes notice, he winks, his face lights up, he says, "How are you, little lady, what can Gerald Halfsong do for you today. I've got a little girl just like you except she's littler, she spends all her time in her tepee, on the swings, or in that sandbox you see over there, which it happens I've fitted with a thirteen-inch TV fed by satellite. Are you lost?"

"Show him the map," Raoul shouts, and the gas man beams, displays twin lines of ragged teeth, says, "Map? What does a person need with a map? Small wonder your daddy is lost."

I spare you the prolonged description of this sequence, we are all in such haste after all. Let it be merely noted that Juliette decided she was hungry, so here they are now on bar stools at Divine Judgment Bar and Grill, a fat-cheeked native lady asking, "Would you like buffalo meat grilled over hot coals, venison shot just this morning, fox in a bath of ginger with capers, or I've got a nice bear tongue freshly roasted, will that be a diet Pepsi or a regular?"

"I'm going to be sick," Juliette whines, to which the native lady, presumably Mrs. Halfsong, replies, "Honey, if you're going to be sick, you've come to the right place. I've got a daughter right next door is a registered nurse."

Raoul finally speaks up, what a clod he can be when he's in his moods, he says, "I could never make it as a nurse, I would never make much of anything if you want to know the truth," a statement which seems to warm Mrs. Halfsong's heart, for she is laughing a full belly laugh as she lays out paper napkins, silverware, "They're clean, honey, you don't need to look at them like that."

Raoul, we can say, is enjoying his daughter's discomfort, Mrs. Halfsong's belly-jiggling laugh, truly the world is such a friendly place that his heart is a pot of glue that sticks to any benign face, as Joyel would inform us were she available. Raoul loves those parties where everyone says "Hello, how are you?" with a friendly smile, these rituals mean the world to him, ditto insofar as concerns myself, although that's completely wide of the point.

Raoul loves kissing everyone's cheeks, kissing the one cheek once, then the other, then back to the first, and not those inconsequential air kisses either, but kisses in the true Continental tradition, he's very much a Continental-type fellow is Raoul, wearing only Italian shoes, those classy Italian suits, although it must be admitted he's lapsed a good bit since his wife left him, you'd hardly recognize the guy, part hobo he is now, rarely taking the trouble to shave, thinking nothing about the soiled clothes he drags himself into each morning, oh, he's gone to the dogs, you know, love's important to a man, whatever you might think. It has been so long since he embraced a woman, since he could say "I love you" to anyone other than his daughter, who has told him she's tired of it, don't say that anymore, okay? Children can be so cruel, we've heard that, we have only to look back at how cruel we were when we were children, only don't bother, let's stick now to that other point: how much one warm body needs another warm body to say to that body "I love you," realizing it isn't the body we are saying this to but the whole part, which means the body part is certainly included, let's not diminish the importance of that. "I love you," to affirm this over and over because without that other warm body our own body turns cold, our shoulders droop, bitterness drops us into the deep freeze, I won't belabor the point, surely you have been there.

Since Joyel isn't available, much of that rendered above has fallen from the mouth of Raoul himself, a huge embarrassment to Juliette, not to mention this gross business about eating bear tongue, foxes, and the like.

"She's missing her mother," she hears him say, her jaw dropping, "Don't mind her."

There is so much to see, and so few our eyes, ears also, but thank the Lord, Papa has only one mouth, but here they are now walking back to the car, the woman back there was nice and jolly and the food not bad, just a plain hot dog, no mustard, no ketchup, no nothing on it, which is exactly how she likes it, ugh to that other stuff, trimmings indeed, she'd like to trim anyone making her put that gross stuff in her mouth. Truth is, Juliette is still a trifle miffed because why is it must her Daddy always make a scene? Like he can't stop doing this very minute, what, is he drunk? Out here in the parking lot saying "Hark, what light through yonder window breaks, is that my little Juliette?" Saying this nonsense in a loud voice that anyone can hear, and patting the top of her head the way she would Trash's if Trash were alive today. It's crazy letting liquor rule your life just because someone has left you and you're alone, nothing is going to rule my life, never, just let them try it.

Here we go, let's hit the road, she's thinking, although they are going precisely nowhere yet, just sitting in the idling car burning innocent gas. "I love my little Juliette," he's whispering again, her sweet little pouty stub-nosed face, he really must have snitched a bottle from somewhere, maybe from that Mrs. Halfsong, they were alone for a minute when I tripped off to the bathroom. The whisper is all right, though, she can take the whispers, her poor departed lamebrain mom used to say it that way to her as a baby just before she turned off the light, *good night, love*. You heard the words, then knew that in another second you would be inside a darkness where other worlds reigned, but the darkness was all right, really you were no more than a baby whose mother had read you a story and the next second you were in that darkness sleeping while the story went on in your head, you were the three little pigs trembling behind the door while the big bad wolf huffed and puffed. How strange it is that you were never the puffing wolf, always the trembling pigs. Now you are, you are the puffing wolf blowing down the doors of all the houses on these roads and why not since your own house no longer stands.

So here they are anew, once more on the road: "Deuce River is this way," Gerald Halfsong has said, "Wallpepper that way, Dry Socket twenty-six miles to the east, heck, if you gunned it, you could be in Mexico before daybreak. But why not hang around, meet the New Indian, take in the Crazy Horse Days at the county fair, I tell you strange thinks happen when Crazy Horse is on the scene."

Only then Raoul and Juliette notice what a curiosity the speaker is, him there in buckskin, a raccoon hat, leggings, homespun boots ringed in fur, leaning on a musket that must have been a hundred years old, a man who served gas but belonged in the history books.

"It will cure what ails you, our fair will, mark my words."

Heretofore, Juliette has had little inclination to regard the world from another's perspective. As proof, has she ever once attempted entertainment of her own mother's point of view? To be in that woman's mind, how horrible. Now she finds herself thinking, What would it be like to be my mom? If I could truly make the leap into JD's mind, then I would forever know why she abandoned me, mine is the same plight as that of those goofy priests who have fallen from heaven, they can't enter God's mind, He abominates theirs, we can't even enter our own minds is the awful truth, frankly the whole damned business makes my head ache, hello, Raoul, hello, old friends, hello, dear mother away out there in Montana, how are you doing, sweetheart, have anymore dead men popped up out of the mud, are you looking after yourself, have you missed me, can you hear me talking to you?

On the Infiniti radio a man is saying, "You have heard of the famous miracles of our Lord, but do you know of those He wrought as a child, the Miracle of the Three Blind Birds, the Miracle of the Restless Deer, the Miracle of the Talking Dog, the Miracle of the Briar Extracted from the Big Toe? Send for my free booklet, just ten dollars to 'Booklet,' Omaha, Nebraska, that's 'Booklet,' Omaha, Nebraska. Thanks, folks, much appreciated, now onwards into light."

To their front stretches a golden day, along with a strange contraption not so easy to describe. It is motorized and licensed for highway travel, taking up far more than its rightful share of the road. The icy eyes of a massive painted Indian peer down at them from a height all but level with the road wires, the drooping evergreen. Mounted on a long flatbed, the giant Indian advances in a surround of whirling yellow discs, red warning flags at flutter, though fluttering less so than the Indian's befeathered headdress, wig, leather harness, garish appendages, some of which have the look of dancing skulls. A giant tomahawk is poised to strike, when the road dips the weapon dips as though flung and each time Raoul smacks the brakes, throws up a hand in protection of Juliette. At every sway and turn in the road the giant Indian's luminous eyes weigh and accuse him, as does the rig's driver, SEE YOU AT THE FAIR says a sign roped to the rig's rearend, the Infiniti groaning, every second shifting its gears as they ascend a long grade, the two vehicles traveling as though linked by a power greater than either driver possesses, and once they've crested the hill and are descending here where passing lanes are plentiful the Infiniti chooses to remain glued to the flatbed's tail, practically kissing the rear bumper. You would think the Infiniti had fallen in love—call this a car for the year 2000, do you? We must write to the manufacturer about this: "I kept pumping the gas but bedogged if my Infiniti would respond, it just clung there, burping and groaning, pining like a kitten, through, I don't know, another forty miles. Dear Infiniti makers, please explain."

"What, what, what! Daddy, what are you saying?"

And through all of this, well may we ask where has Raoul Daggle's true love got to? Is a dog's company proving sufficient? Let us trust that Joyel is not so sleepy she has run off the road; perhaps she is in a motel room this minute doing something about those awful bags under her eyes—grate a raw potato, secure over eyes, hold for fifteen minutes, repeat daily until improvement noted. If so, please don't forget to reinvigorate tired flesh, tighten pores, with Elegant Egg White Mask—beat egg white till stiff, add sprinkle of lemon juice, any nice scent, spread over face, and poke about in *The Fall of Gravity* until dry, cleanse with water. How are we to account for ourselves when nothing exists above us to keep us faithfully aligned to the path, without which we have God on high or the devil down low and the paths splatter as paint from a bucket, innumerable as imagination or the lack thereof may devise, thus we have the saying "You go your way, I'll go mine," together with "Never the twain shall meet" or "Go the last mile," among other peculiarities.

There is no song in our hearts, we have bedded down with thieves, we are up all night with insomnia or we sleep like angels, an Infiniti for the year 2000 has fallen in love with a flatbed trailer. Zounds! you might say, may the loyal reader be forgiven for drifting off, someone has been asleep at the wheel, Lord forgive him.

"Goddammit!" Raoul Daggle said.

"What!" cried the child. *"What, what, what!"*

"This has gone far enough," said Raoul. "Goddammit, I can't take anymore of this. I'm hanging up the hat, calling it a day. Goddammit, let's pull in."

"It's early, Papa, let's drive our tails on."

"I've got to find someone to blame. Those goddam fallen priests, the Widowhood Gulag, let's blame them. All aboard, those who want to blame the ex-priests, those shits, I can feel in my bones they're the guilty party. Are we agreed, no, you don't have to say a word, let's just hit the hay, call it a day, bury the hatchet, let bygones be bygones, goddammit, godammit!"

"*What? What? What?*"

"Goddammit it all to hell."

"And I can't even say *tail*? My goodness, Papa, such a tantrum."

"Oh, sweet Papa, it's all a mess, isn't it? But tomorrow's another day, I can't wait, can you Papa? Let's sleep and wake up refreshed, go that extra mile and it will all come together, we will find her, I can feel it in my bones, can't you, Papa?"

"No, I cannot."

"But I can, Papa. All is not lost so long as one of us is keeping the faith. Don't turn in to that scruffy old motel, Papa, *let's burn rubber, hit it, Papa, hit the gas, let's haul ass on to Cut Bank!*

From their Best Western room, all rustico, a North Woods Best Western here on Deer Lake by Laughing Fish Pointe by Hiawatha National Forest, Jack and Pearl Buck your friendly proprietors, no conventions currently scheduled, the priests who have fallen from heaven tonight are adrift in impenetrable darkness beyond our ken, but Raoul Daggle is up late as he is every night, on the stroke of midnight, aslosh with gin, he takes to the telephone, finding at home an honorary lifetime member of the

Widowhood Gulag, a woman much on his mind lately, one Polly White by name.

"Hello," he says, "what's cooking?"

"I'm wearing a skimpy chemise." she says, "My nipples are out to here."

All over America, since the intern Monica's aborted affair with the nation's presiding officer, lines have been burning with such phone sex. This is not what Raoul had in mind when he dialed Polly White's number, not to say he isn't impressed but still he's shocked, "Pass me that gin," he tells Juliette, another late-nighter.

"My legs are wide open," Polly White croons, oh, she's so wicked she's cool, there are no flies on Polly.

"I hope your mind is," Raoul says, his businessman's voice, "I'm calling to renew my job offer, CEO, Daggle Estates."

"What's the pay?"

"Bring a valise."

"Pension? Benefits?"

"You hum, I'll play."

"A car?"

"Lamborghini."

They iron out the details, finally Polly White sighs, she says, "Okay," she laughs, her voice becomes sultry, she's dripping honey, before hanging up she says, "Is it big? May I touch it?"

"You were flirting," shouts his daughter at him seconds later with her tiny fists. "What about your wife?"

What wife? Where? Excuse me, do you see a wife anywhere around here?

In the Best Western's Hoosegow Lounge, Jack and Pearl Buck your friendly proprietors, whitefish our specialty, Juliette upstairs moping, the bar walls and ceiling, every nook, strung with fishing net, a scattering of wagon wheels, pickaxes, blunderbusses, stuffed Canadian geese, a bear, grizzled old-timers at wade in mountain streams, Raoul saying to the bartender "Make that a double," a woman who gives her name as Lavender Blue slides gracefully onto the stool next to his own, plants stiletto heels over the brass rail, a glittery metal evening purse hits the counter, she rakes his face with the bluest eyes Raoul has ever seen, she lights up, smiles, picks a tobacco speck from a red lower lip, says to the bartender, "Well, Jack, look what the cat has dragged in." Does she mean herself, or grim Raoul Daggle with his face over the familiar drink? Pretty soon, wouldn't you know it, Raoul is telling the bewitching Lavender Blue his story, once his ends she will tell hers, because they are lonesome troubadours cast to a frigid world ever intent on sapping them of all dignity, eternally dragging them down.

"I know that rig," Lavender says. "That's the New Indian's rig, everybody knows that rig, he and Chief Crazy Horse play the fairs."

"Will that be another double, Miss Blue?"

"Alas, yes. My day? I didn't know what any of those men wanted with me, it wasn't spelled out. I went to the door as I was told to do, three o'clock, the precise minute arranged, but the man answering the door said, 'Madame, you must be mistaken either in the hour or the address or in your apparel because this house has no use for females plying your trade.' Of course it was all part of their game, the butler in his trim waistcoat, two poodles yapping in the hall, the ropes and chains, the master on the stairs in his BVDs shouting, 'Is that my nurse at the door? Come in, come in, can't you see how sick I am?' Then both of them dragging me inside, twittering, sticking their pins in me, it hardly matters which door we call at these days, no one pays us any respect. Sometimes I swear I must give up house calls.

I do make hotel calls, however, might you be interested, Mr. Daggle?"

Is he? A year without sex, it could be, is he wavering, but now the bartender is shouting, "Anybody know a Raoul? Kid on the phone wants him to bring up toothpaste."

A fallen priest drifts in, old and purple-nosed, he's on his way, he alleges, to the annual meeting of the Minnesota chapter this year being held down in Marshall in the state's southwest corner. "Listen," the old priest said, addressing Miss Blue, "when the snake spoke it was not first to Eve. Eve was away in dreamland concocting refinements on her paradise. Drapes for the windows, a down sofa, carpets from Persia. It was her partner around whom the snake entwined. In the first place, the snake said, 'I am not the evil creature I am painted to be. In the second place, by no means assure yourselves that you are the only Eve and Adam, that yours is the lone paradise. In the third place, if you resist the allure of this down sofa, these fancy drapes Eve wants cut to a Frenchman's specifications, you will live to regret it. Here, eat of these apples. In the fourth place, why should you heed a God who himself was invented not more than one week ago and then only as a word—*And the Word was God and the Word was with God*—you see what I'm saying?'"

"Write for my free booklet," a man on the TV behind the bar is saying. "Send ten dollars to 'Booklet,' Omaha, Nebraska. Thanks, folks, now—"

Lavender Blue, the old priest, and Raoul Daggle make a fine threesome on the dance floor. They hold each other up, they sway, glide, shuffle, and stumble. "We go to our graves unmourned, our lives unremarked upon," Lavender Blue is telling them, "nonentities of no more consequence than the shadow a hand momentarily casts upon a blank wall, here and then gone, but in truth all along our life's trails reside a thousand witnesses, accidental collaborators in our sojourn, how breathtaking that is, what a colossal truth, and perhaps enough to make the most insignificant life significant. Would either of you gentlemen like to kiss me?"

Lower your eyes, reader. The child is bathing now, she is up to her chin in hot soapy water. A child, Juliette Daggle, is softly singing, singing to herself alone, and you must not embarrass her by letting her know you are present. Do not allow yourself to think as her father does, entering on tiptoe, that she reminds you of her mother. Say nothing. Quietly close the door. Let the singing voice continue. Let it be there tonight in Raoul's sleep, in yours also, a tenderness to calm us when otherwise we would toss and turn.

5 where antelopes *play*

THE DOG has a kind, open face, one that invites conversation. They are communicating as equals, Joyel feels. She could tell this dog her entire life story and it could tell her his. It's good having a dog again. This dog can be her protection, it can provide company across the lonely nail-chewing miles.

"You're a found poem," she says to the dog.

The dog's eyes close as though in pain.

They are crossing the Little Missouri, *swish* and it's gone.

The dog sniffs the ashtray, looks at her inquiringly: has a Camels smoker been sitting in this car?

Joyel stops directly by the border sign, emptying Camel butts on the Montana side. She says goodbye to the 147,000 grueling miles of Montana. Montana has many remote areas and is a state thinly populated by citizens who take their individualism seriously. The western border has the outline of a man's craggy face, with Missoula as the eye. As Missoula has grown, the proportions have become nearly perfect. But it's not the face of a man you'd want to take into your bed.

Joyel remembers a young girl, Nancy, who often babysat her when she was a child, post-carny days those must have been. The minute her parents left, Nancy stripped off her clothes and fell asleep in the exact middle of Joyel's parents' double bed. "Now you must be very quiet so Nancy can catch her Zs," the babysitter invariably said.

Joyel would kneel by the bed counting all the roads in the sleeping girl's scalp. She would peer up Nancy's nose and into her ears. Then she would go inside her cave, which was papier-mâché painted to resemble a gigantic rock, with an actual room inside. In the room Joyel would snap all her crayons.

A rich uncle one birthday, Joyel six or seven, had found her that cave in a famous New York City store specializing in unique objects; hers was a one-of-a-kind kind of cave, not another like it in the world. Just for you, my darling, so pucker up and give your sweet uncle a big kiss.

Her refuge, that cave. You could crawl in there and lock the door with an actual bolt and lay out the teacups on your diminutive table and ask of your imagined guests, Do you require sugar? Oh, what a shame, for we have no sugar. Will you have ice cream, these nice mosquito cookies I baked myself in my actual oven?

It must have been in Cut Bank that the certain someone, that son of a bitch, broke into her car. She had parked Jane's car in one motel lot, gone by cab to another.

She hoped he was fooled by the North Dakota brochures above the visor. North Dakota is not in her plans. Which is why she took Route 59 South at Jordan. Probably it is too much to hope that he will be fooled, although she means to hold on to the thought all through the Dakota sister state. She further hopes that the son of a bitch following her will comprehend that she is bound for Minneapolis, in the erroneous belief that it is a city large enough for a person to get lost in. Certainly there must be many lost people in Minneapolis; it is not her intention, however, to become one of them.

Olden days, when she said to her daughter, "I love you," Juliette rocked back on her heels, replying petulantly, "When you say that, you sound so much like a child."

"I evol you."

"Now you're cooking."

Good. There's . . .

Wyoming

The Cowboy State will claim Joyel Daggle no more than twenty minutes. It is only such a teensy snip of Yoming she is passing through, like the page of a book one might crimp down. Her route runs parallel to the Belle Fourche River—too distant, too dark, too much another world—for even a glimpse now. Colony, three minutes north on a dead-end road, is likely too small, too much off the beaten track to support a motel, a café open at this hour. "I'm starving," she says, "how about you, dog?" Colony is located at the end of a dead-end road. It would not be wise to be trapped in Colony by that son of a bitch who takes his inspiration from the Moor. Still, it would be nice to see a place that calls itself Colony. Is it an old or a new colony? Is it a lost colony? It is a colony of what and how long has it existed as a colony and why was the one site favored and not another?

Jane back in Orick, California, had told her of a man who had no heart, a phenomenon written up by three Des Moines surgeons in the *Omaha Journal of Bizarre Medicine*, Jane said, and she had the article to prove it, or did have it until she sent it under anonymous wrapper to her asshole husband.

The dog sneezes. It has no interest in aimless chat. It is an *official biographer* kind of dog, no off-the-cuff remarks permitted.

The vibration of the tires can be felt through Jane Dearborne's seat, in the shudder of springs, the steering wheel, the tires' faulty alignment. The odometer has long since clicked over, twice or a third time, with much hemorrhaging along the way. "But it's got two new front tires," Jane had said, "well, newish, it's got new gaskets, frog plugs, new brake linings, shoes, new hoses, a thousand fixed thingamajigs. On cold days, though, you'll have to pull out the choke." Choke? "Little knob up on the dash, just pull it way out, pump it a few times, it spurts gas into the carburator. Don't you know anything about cars?"

Joyel Daggle, motoring through Yoming, wonders how Jane Dearborne is enjoying life in Orick, California, under her new identity.

The dog is getting antsy. His nose presses the glass, his rear-end twitches, he moans. On the whole, another woman would be the preferred company.

"Are you a Montana or a Yoming dog?" Joyel asks. "Did you ever meet a suicidal dog named Trash? Are you really a dog?"

But she is not speaking the dog's language, the dog whines, scratches at the door. It barks once, twice, probing her face with an urgency as familiar as her own.

"Lighten up," Joyel says, adopting a bantering tone. "What's crucial one minute is lost memory the next. My mother knew a Wisconsin woman who trained her dog to sit on chicken eggs. That dog knew the hatched biddies were not of her species. She liked eggs but was offended by what came out of them."

The dog scratches wildly at Jane Dearborne's muddy, rusting door. This car for three weeks was trapped under Orick mud up to its roof, everything was, rain and more rain, the Weichepec Range tumbling into the sea—but not that son of a bitch, apparently.

"The Wisconsin woman sold her pullet farm and moved to the city. My mother claims the Wisconsin woman took the dog to her own psychiatrist for treatment. He was a wonderful psychiatrist, blind, deaf, and dumb. In the end, during a thunderstorm, the dog jumped off the woman's sixteenth-floor-condo balcony. You could say I did the same. I hate self-pity, don't you?"

The dog quivers all along its flanks.

"The Estonian koerakoonlased," Joyel informs the dog, "possessed a mixture of human and dog sense, and their bodies were likewise both. These Dogheads murdered and ate anything and anyone they saw and could catch."

The dog lifts one ear, interested. Then it sneezes, despairingly, pawing the door.

Let me out, the dog says.

"*What?*" asks Joyel. "*What, what, what!* You're abandoning ship? You must go and lick the sores of Lazarus?"

The dog shakes itself, it whines a trope of misery.

"Some say the formidable American psychic Jeanne Dixon got her best visions through her husband James's pet pooch. Mrs. Dixon foresaw the death of Carole Lombard in an airplane crash; she foresaw the assassinations of the Kennedy brothers and of Martin Luther King. She had utmost privy to the futures of all our world leaders but none at all for the little folk."

The dog whips about in a circle, snapping at this and that.

"My grandfather, the one in the photograph I told you about, says he used to see Jeanne and James walking that dog every morning outside their real estate firm in Washington, D.C. Did you know that dog? I know how dogs get around."

The dog is at high squeal, in a panic for release.

"In England during the Inquisition, women were hanged for fondling their dogs. A black dog was the devil lover in disguise."

The dog growls, the lips curl back, saliva drips from its teeth.

Joyel pulls over on the shoulder.

"Traitor."

Not a word in response. The dog bounds off into darkness, galloping across dark grazing land, possibly bound for the dead-end road leading to the misguided, possibly lost, community known as Colony.

It's time I admitted it, Joyel thinks. Dogs don't like me.

Joyel crouches by the side of the dark road, her feet set wide apart. The wind is icy to her bare behind. To prevent her shoes from getting soaked she has squatted down on an incline; she is afraid that any second she will tumble over into the void or that something unseen will crack her across the head and drag her into the black high weeds. She hears scratching sounds all around her and is certain that something is crawling along her fanny, but, there, now she's finished.

Nothing is on this road, nothing is coming. The night is dark, empty of stars, and Raoul and Juliette, wherever they are, are snug in their motel beds. Isn't it funny that they've been to Anne's Ardor, and funnier yet that they will be barreling towards Cut Bank, maybe she will pass them on the road.

Joyel waits by the side of the road a long time, it's cold, but out here she can at least keep herself awake. Her shoulders ache, she's hungry, her stomach is grumbling again. To divert herself, she decides she will use this moment to count her money. She has the habit of doing this three and four times a day but today she hasn't done so since daybreak. She has built up a fine nest egg odd-jobbing in a dozen states. Raoul would laugh but she's pretty proud of her self-reliance, nearly twelve hundred dollars in the kitty. Twelve hundred is a good deal more than she had when she left home. It is wealth of a modest sort which does not take into account Jane Dearborne's credit card, a card to be used, by agreement, sparingly, only, that is, in direst emergency.

The son of a bitch had not found her in British Columbia, Oregon, Idaho. In Orick, California, he found her and her impression at the time was that she had left him dead under a sea of mud. She concedes now that this was not the case. It had taken him some little while to find her in Montana. But then he only found Jane Dearborne's car. He isn't God, therefore. He doesn't have all the answers.

To find Jane Dearborne's car, however, likely he first had to find Jane Dearborne, and that is a scary thought.

She has seen him close up only once. He's bespectacled, wears a three-piece Harry Rosen brown suit, and has big hands. The one time she saw him close up, in Zavala, Texas, this was, she waked to a cold rented room, middle of the night, and there he was in the open doorway. Then the door closed and—

Good. There's . . .

South Dakota

Joyel breezes along. Fifty, this crate's top limit, before shudders, clangs, oily clouds in the tail pipe, take over. The window is still down, stuck there, she has pushed and pulled, oophed and umphed, to no avail. The wind flings her hair, it is achingly cold, "Oh, poor Joyel," she says, and in the instant bursts into tears, "I'm a mess," she says, "not even dogs like me, I deserve gating, I'm a fuck-up."

Somewhere in this southwestern corner of the Coyote State, Joyel has heard, is the geographical center of the nation. There is something puzzling in this, although Joyel can't think what it is. Possibly political influence manifested itself on this issue. They must have chopped off most of Pennsylvania, New York, all of the New England states, in figuring this out. Being the nation's geographical center is a heavy burden to carry, and now it has begun to rain.

Joyel recalls that in whatever place she and Raoul visited, once they were able to afford jaunts to foreign soil, he derived immense pleasure in asking anyone he saw whether one could drink the local water. He asked it in restaurants and around swimming pools, swinging on hammocks under palm trees, and sometimes asked it of her while she was immersed in a hotel tub. But this was a long time ago. Maybe he has changed. He would pour grape juice into the toilet and drag Juliette in to look at it. "This is what happens when you drink the water," he told the child. "So from now on it is only tequila for little girls." Joyel remembers her daughter as a happy child. Joyel remembers being unhappy, for the most part, during her own childhood, shuttled one way and another: "You were awful as a baby," her mother likes telling her, "and awful all the time you were growing up. Fortunately we were not the kind of parents who believed in sparing the rod. And now that you've grown up you're an awful woman, you're consistent, I'll say that for you. Loving you has been the hardest thing I've ever done, I can't tell you the number of times I wanted to drop you on your head or drown you in your little blue tub, your father feels the same way, don't bother looking to him for sympathy."

But there's this: she has been happy nearly the whole of this day, possibly a record, it isn't easy being a woman and carrying the burden for all of humanity.

She wonders whether Raoul has been faithful to her during her year of recovery, it would be just like him to have remained true if only so he could point an accusatory finger every chance he got. She can almost claim the same fidelity, discounting that time in, well, those several times in, well, those innumerable times in Carter and Esther's bed, plus that one time on the mud raft, wasn't that funny, but this was all a part of the recuperative process, they were not days that should live in infamy, best though that she seal her lips on this issue.

An Idaho woman had said to her that she was born the year the Edsel came out. "Yeah," said the woman's husband, "everything was ugly that year." St. Thomas Aquinas, among many, believed the soul resided in a man's testicles, an idea which persists through to this day. But Brother St. Thomas, inventor of chewing gum and studded whips, was certifiable on many accounts and has much to answer for. The Idaho woman had said to her husband, "Yeah, well what if I kick you in the nuts?"

Another thing the woman in the Idaho bar had said was, "If I'm so bad, why did you marry me?" Sooner or later, Joyel thinks, every married woman she's ever met has had occasion to ask that.

"I married you," the man said, "because I believed I was as boring as you are. Then I got my teeth straightened."

Behind the bar counter in a rotting frame next to row upon row of liquor bottles was a photograph of, reputedly, the largest potato ever grown in Idaho. The potato had the girth of a largish stump, it wore human hair, sunglasses, smoked an El Bonito cigar. The bar was called the El Bonito World's Biggest Idaho Potato Bar, the guy had straight teeth all right, though he still looked like a weasel.

Joyel had supposed she would see a lot of men fighting each other in these northwestern states, terrain of rugged individuality, but the men preferred to fight with their women, who were not such sore losers. They were tender, however, with their dogs, their pickups, their fishing lures, they caressed gun stocks fondly.

She would pass a man fly-fishing in a river and say, "There's another one."

If Montana or Idaho had a slice of life devoted to sophisticated repartee, which it must, these smart people had eluded her.

"Talk to me," Joyel says aloud to herself.

She whips by a highway sign reading PRISON AREA, DO NOT PICK UP HITCHHIKERS. All over America she's seen these signs, you'd think half the citizenry had been thrown in jail. In her gated community back home there are seven Johns, five Dans, nine Junes, one Vern. They long ago formed the John Dan June and One Vern Club; in recent years they've had dinner together each Friday evening, nothing special, better in the summer when John, Dan, and Vern can play bigshot at the grill. They play cards, drink, talk politics and business, and reflect on the wording of the Official Constitution of Daggle Shores. It enrages them that despite a bylaw prohibiting such, opossums have infiltrated the grounds. Squirrels may be shot on sight, but no prescribed cure exists for the opossums, a surly breed. For the full year that Joyel has been on the road, according to Raoul, the John Dan June and One Vern Club has been drafting new legislation for the elimination of these creatures. Otherwise, life behind the walls is bliss.

Three of the seven Johns have been haberdashers, two were dentists, the two remaining were of independent means, which they and the five Dans, the nine Junes, and one Vern find extraordinary.

One of the Johns had a patient die in his chair. It was an old Negro woman with perfect white teeth, in for a routine cleaning. "It's eating dat cold food," John says, oh, you can see how fond he is of blacks, "day eats cold food, dat's why day have dem white teefs."

He can't be pinned down on why the woman died. "I turned my back," he says, "and she was gone."

The image John likes to leave with you is of that woman unfolded on the long chair with her mouth wide open, her legs splayed wide, "gripping those chair arms so tight we thought they would have to saw her arms off at the wrists.

"'I feel I'm going on a long journey,' were her last words, 'and me without my coat.'"

In the compound back home sixty-seven percent of the men and forty-three percent of the women are in their second marriages. A party with more than two marriages may not purchase property within the estate, a bylaw pushed through by Vern who holds family values dear, as do the others, despite their bylaw denying the visitation of their children's children even at Christmastime, children deflate property values, they make noise, who needs it, Vern said, you spend your whole life raising the little shits and then do they thank you?

"Then there's Doodoo, poor Doodoo," Joyel says, "I wonder if she got those roses I sent."

Jane Dearborne's heater is erratic, the windows have iced up, the defroster is kaput, she is motoring eastward to God knows where in a frozen box. The left ear, the entire left side of her face, is frozen, her belly is grumbling, her eyes itchy, her brow knotted, she's snatching brief patches of sleep as she drives, twenty-three hours now and the gas gauge touching empty.

Near a town called Faith, Dupree twenty-three miles ahead, she sees a blur and asks herself, "Was that an antelope, a deer?" The animal is loping alongside, looking at her with jewel-like eyes, gravel pings against the car's underside, she's off the road and steering straight towards the ditch, "Oh, goddammit," she says, "wake up."

Past Dupree, she sees the antelope a second time, swats her brow, shakes her head, she's traveling in a mysterious time that is neither night nor day nor strictly human time, "I've got to find a motel," she says, "I'm flagging, I'm near death, if I die out here, all the tears will be for Jane Dearborne. Our sojourner was a good girl, she gave her all for the common cause, she was punctual and thrifty, polite to old geezers and contemptuous of no one, she radiated charm and possessed the best of dispositions; poor Joyel Daggle, she stumbles, she staggers, would someone please throw her a warm greeting before she expires and ascends into heaven, glory is thy name.

"Where is that little girl going in her pretty party dress?" Joyel asks.

6

oop-edee-doo

RAOUL AND HIS DAUGHTER sit on homemade twig chairs at a homemade twig table in their rustic North Woods Best Western suite. Juliette, plugged in, watches his lips move, what's he saying now? Raoul is drinking a breakfast martini from his collapsible martini glass made especially for mountain climbers and other active sportsmen enthusiasts of the great outdoors. Three vastly magnified olives are speared on a toothpick inside the martini. The gin bottle, the vermouth, the ice, the martini shaker, marinating olives, line a nearby counter, together with oodles of spilled drink, overfilled ashtrays, someone's socks, broken glass, trashy junk to make you puke. Behind the counter is a kitchen, or kitchenette. Look at those pots and pans, look at the cute sawed-off icebox, the clever dwarf stove, look at all the neat gouges in the countertop, all that nice blond paneling, this terrific yellow shag carpet, the fine wear in the linoleum by the rustic door. Look at those beautiful fake plants from the tropics, the keg side tables, the lovely settee propped up on bricks, look at all those great real oil paintings devoted to a man's unfettered life ahuntin' and afishin' in these northern woods. "Oh, I love it here," Raoul is saying, "we can put down roots here, forget that shitty hellhole, the Daggle, forget Cut Bank and your mother, let's forget all the dead men she's left strung from here to Tippecanoe, call up Solly, tell him to drop the chase, I've got a new idea, I've decided to get off the chopping block, enter the meat market, name myself an eligible bachelor, just rove your eyes over that beautiful, sexy woman asleep there on the heritage settee, Lavender Blue. I've decided I love Lavender Blue, let's all marry Lavender Blue, she can teach us how to dance on table-tops, awaken us to moral imperatives gone slack from famine and drought, from misuse, go get that old ex-priest out of my bed, he can marry us this minute, she's got a Ph.D., you know, life hasn't been easy for Ms. Blue, plus she wouldn't set sail away from us in the dark of night without major provocation, she'd make a powerful mother, I knew it last night the minute I heard her say, 'Would either of you gentlemen like to kiss me?'"

Oh, Papa, pipe down, Juliette thinks, I'm wired, I can barely hear a word you're saying, but let your guests sleep, why not? You worry me, Papa, this falling in love with each woman you meet is ruinous to your health, you've fallen off the pier, Daddy, look at your beady, shriveled-up eyes, your pinched mouth, your hair gone white all in one year, look at your shaking hands, you're skin and bones, I love you, Papa, do you hate me?

Juliette has been a bad sport. "*A very bad sport, Juliette, I am disappointed in you.*" She has her head wired to one of Raoul's old tapes, Mel Tormé, and she must listen to that, in punishment for having been a bad sport. She has been a bad sport because . . . because he forgot to buy toothpaste, because . . . because he showed up in their Great North Twig Suite at three a.m. in the company of two drunks, one the detestable old alky priest with the purple nose, the other a shockingly beautiful Lady of the

Night, so he said, exotic dancer supreme at the Great North Woods Nite Spotte, Lavender Blue, by name, well, my goodness! Their trio was the loud and messy drunks, arguing and singing until dawn, but she was the bad sport, Raoul said, "You are just like your mother, you don't know how to have a good time." So here she is having to listen to one of her father's favorites, that top banana Mel Tormé. Poor dead Mel Tormé, so said the grieving Raoul, *You listen to Mel, get an education, young lady!* Fact is, Mr. Late Departed is, like, okay, he's cool, but it's all lovey-dovey stuff, where's the bump bump bump? This *oop-edee-doo* business is neat, it's groovy, but is she in the mood, who is being the bad sport around here?

Oh, goody, the zombies are waking, there goes the ex-priest in his stocking feet, thank you for not slamming the door, there squirreling up from the settee is the beautiful exotic dancer supreme of the Great North Woods Nite Spotte. "Oh, my head! Who are you? Why am I here? I've got it, you must be the brave Juliette I've heard so much about. Well thank you, Juliette, for a lovely time."

Go ahead, drag all yourselves off, I'm only a little girl, I shouldn't have to live like this.

What did she mean, "brave," maybe she likes me?

On the table in front of Juliette are folders, brochures, handbills, postcards informing guests what's going on in this neck of the woods. She has drawn circles around the most exciting opportunities.

On the table also is a black comb with all its teeth removed. She has broken these teeth one by one and now they are ugly black spears of no use to anyone. It is a comb she has found on the floor in the kitchenette, and she is prolonging that moment when she will sweep a hand across the table and knock the whole comb family back to the floor.

This motel with its fine kitchenette is run by a pair named Jack and Pearl Buck. There is Pearl and there is Jack and there is Pearl and Jack's fierce black dog.

Juliette in the bathroom says to the mirror, "Is that Juliette Daggle's exotic supreme face?"

She sits down on the toilet lid, looking down between her legs. "Hello down there," she says. "Are those Juliette Daggle's beautiful feet, are those her exotic supreme toes?"

These lines seem to fit in with the lyrics Mel Tormé is letting fly.

Jack and Pearl Buck have been doing repairs in this room. Shoved under the sink is a can of tile adhesive, tools, boxes of grout, stacks of broken and unbroken tiles which conform to no single pattern. The shower stall is only about three-quarters done. Occupants Use Cabin 12 for Wash, reads the taped note.

Juliette smears adhesive onto the wall. She presses in the tiles. Any idiot can do this work.

"Hello, exotic supreme wall," she says.

"What say we trash Pearl and Jack's whole place? What say we go at it with sledgehammers?"

Ice covers the windowpanes. Ice is in the toilet bowl, the towels on the racks are frozen, wind shakes the rustic doors, it's a winter wonderland out there.

The fingers of her left hand are stuck together, the hand is wrapped in a white towel, damned old cement. A moment ago she and her daddy looked through a window and saw Pearl and Jack seated on a sofa reading a story to a baby in a high chair. "Isn't that the most disgusting sight you ever saw," she had said, and it was clear her daddy agreed, they both wanted to pitch rocks through the window.

“Are you recovered, Daddy? Do you have your mettle back?”

“Don’t talk.”

Noon, the sky smudged, snow turning into rain, they are on the road.

Ironwood, Hutley, Saxon.

“Where are we going, Daddy?”

“Cut Bank.”

“Joyel Daggle doesn’t want to see us.”

“Yes, she does.”

“Joyel won’t be in Cut Bank. I want to go home.”

“Don’t snivel. We have no home without your mother.”

Odanah, Ashland, Ino.

“Do you know what one raspberry says to another raspberry, Daddy?”

“No.”

“If you did know, would you tell me?”

“No.”

“Then I won’t tell you.”

Iron River, Brule, Maple.

“I fell asleep, Daddy. Where are we now?”

Way up there in northern Wisconsin, on Route 2 through Little Runt National Forest, the Copper Range, Lovers’ Leap Falls, Jailbird Zone, No Hitchhiking—past scruffy hunting lodges, lakes, duck blinds, ski resorts, pasty houses, whitefish eateries, “Look at that, Daddy,” yes, it is worth a look, please slow down because here stretching all along the road are countless deer, deer or antelope, the odd elk, perhaps a moose, these legion in number, all munching leaves, moss, tree bark, and each one looking up as you pass, each one saying, Where are they going so fast, was that anyone I know, was that by chance the crazy Daggle pair?

"Turn up the heat, okay?"

"Okay, squirt."

"Do you miss Lavender Blue? Does she ache away at you?"

"I've given her a job at the Daggle."

"Doing what?"

"Looking after the moat. Head of family planning, security, landscaping, Indian affairs, things like that."

"How far is it to Cut Bank?"

"Two thousand miles."

"I guess you can tell me a story, then."

This is the story Raoul Daggle tells his daughter:

> A Delshi man, residing in Pintou, Guelph province, heard a heartbeat though his pillow during one recent night, and he slung away the *jiva* which covered him, and picked up the stick by his bedside, kept there in defense against burglars who were lately scouring the region, and with this stick he began beating the pillow.
>
> "What's a *jiva*, Daddy?"
>
> Then he lay his head again down and the heartbeat was silenced and he slept soundly through until morning. Upon awakening, the Delshi man residing in Pintou, Guelph province, said, first, "I will take my tea without sugar this morning." And second, "Why, beloved one, are you not stirring?"
>
> Whereupon he saw the soulmate beside him was a stiff corpse, and saw, moreover, that his stick on the floor was bloody.

"Stop right there."

"Happy people tell the unhappiest stories."

"Are we unhappy, Papa?"

"No, we're miserable."

"Why are we stopping, Daddy. Do we need gas?"

"We need you a *jiva*. We can't drive another mile without my little girl has her *jiva*.

"This is just an old woodsman's shirt, Daddy."

"No, it's a red-checkered *jiva* made in Pakistan for HuntsClub, one-hundred-percent cotton."

"All stories have their terrible sides," Raoul says to Juliette. "You have only to consider the late, lamented Daggle family."

> Later in the day the Delshi man arranged for a new soulmate, with old Eguchi of his same street, who had three sisters. Then he walked manfully to the police station to report his crime. Old Eguchi went with him, as did his new bride, and his bride's two sisters, all five of them gesticulating wildly, saying, "Justice must be done," until the two sisters parted from their group in order to visit Yuyu, the body man, who for a certain price, would journey to the house where the dead lay, and anoint the old soulmate's corpse with oils and incant over her the three days until she could pass on into the fires.

"Stop right there. This is not a story for a child."

"I can't stop, darling. Every story must be told, the bad and the good, without regard for a daughter's tender years, the innocent, or people who only want their tranquility, or Christian zealots who insist our violence be restricted to biblical atrocities, birth control centers, the coming Armageddon."

"Then get back to the police station. I want to know what is happening there in the realm of justice."

The police chief for the whole of Pintou, Guelph province, was a big man named Walpole Doe, who had a chest like a gorilla and a headful of hair parted four ways on his scalp, for the four paths in life available to a man of his station in life. He was a man steady as a rock, who could stare down crocodiles in the Hoo Loo River, which was why he was the police chief. He was also the twin brother of the Pintou man who had killed his wife with the cudgel, as alike to that man as you are to me and your mother.

"Why, brother, did you commit this dastardly act?" asked the police chief.

"I heard a heartbeat through my pillow and in my sleep-deprived state I believed my bed had been taken over by desperate burglars."

"Ho-hum, Daddy."

So word was given out that the dead woman had been sleeping with the gang of burglars, and they it were who had slain the wanton woman, in the land of Pintou, Guelph province.

"I hate this story, Papa."

"Not as much as I do."

"It's far-fetched."

"This is a true tale. Every story has its true side. If you had ever lived in Pintou, Guelph province, or if you were a Delshi man living in Pintou, nearby, you could go up and knock on the very door where the murder took place."

"So what happened?"

"I don't know."

"I bet that heartbeat business was merely a ruse. I bet that Delshi man already had his heart set on a new bride, one of those sisters of old Eguchi."

"That's right. He had his heart set on your mother."

"Joyel Daggle?"

"Absolutely. I've yet to get a confession from her, but I'd bet every penny I have that your mother had a secret marriage to that terrible Delshi man in Guelph province."

"Joyel was a hot ticket, known all over Pintou, Guelph province. It was her heartbeat that man was hearing through his pillow."

"Oh, come on. Now you're stretching matters."

"I bet she has a whole batch of other kids over there in Pintou, Guelph province. Will she ever confess? Do you suppose she ever feels repentant?"

At this point Juliette Daggle burst into tears. "I'm only a little girl," she cried. "People expect too much of me! I only weigh seventy-five pounds! I'm not brave! I can't go on living like this!"

There, there.

In Antigonish, Nova Scotia, way back when, they'd gassed up and the pump man had said, "Now isn't that a coincidence. Not ten minutes ago was another Daggle in here, used the potty, bought a Twinkie, and off she flew. Funny thing was, not one minute behind her, was a bespectacled gent in a brown suit asking which way she went, and there he flew."

"Look, Papa, there's Minnesota."

Upon entering Minnesota they saw countless roadside bill-boards announcing the world's eighth wonder. VISIT EBAN, the signs proclaimed, CITY OF INVISIBLE WOMEN.

"Let's go," said Juliette. "Maybe Joyel will be in Eban."

At a truckstop outside the city in question a man with long sideburns, a black stocking wrapped tightly over his head, told them not to bother. "You won't see any women and it will cost you ten dollars just to enter the city." Apparently a crew of refugees arriving by way of Afghanistan had secured a bank loan some years ago, bought up all the land they could get their hands on, and founded Eban.

There were women in Eban, upwards of a thousand, but they were not allowed to leave their homes unless they wore long robes that covered them head to foot.

"It's called a *burqa*," the driver said, "or something like that. They've got net eyes, wear veils, I mean. Anywhere these *burqa* women go they've got to have an Eban man accompanying them. They can't work except at home and even there they've got to wear that *burqa*."

Tourists, men especially, were flocking into Eban from far and wide, paying their admission to enter the city, and driving away with scads of these garments for their own wives and daughters.

"These invisible women work day and night," the driver said, "making more and more of these *burqas*, which the men of Eban sell in stalls all along Main Street, or Eban Street, they call it. They come in white or gray and cost $39.95."

"May one buy gin in Eban?"

Eban was on a winding road and Joyel liked winding roads, so Raoul and Juliette motored to Eban. The Infiniti was dragging; it did not seem to think an Infiniti 130 for the year 2000 should be seen in Eban, own one and you'll understand. They drove down Eban Street and did not see a single soul. All the Ebans were in prayer at the mosque. All the stall fronts were secured by heavy chains.

"This is such a disappointment," Juliette said. "This is worse than Hell, Michigan."

"Look," said Raoul, "there's your drinking buddy."

The old fat alky priest Juliette despised was sitting on a bench, looking totally forlorn, as if now convinced God did not exist in this place either.

"Don't stop, he'll talk our ears off."

As they were leaving town a small white figure was seen flapping in the grass by the side of the road. They backed up the Infiniti and saw the figure was that of a chicken with its head cut off. The feathers were matted with dirt and blood. The chicken looked as though it had been flapping there a long time, perhaps weeks, perhaps since the founding of Eban.

Juliette's face had a frightened look over the next miles. A dark mist spilled down from the hills, making their flesh damp.

Later on, a fire truck nearly ran them off the road. Then came a procession of other trucks in pursuit of the red fire engine and for the whole of this road ambush their hold on life was touch and go.

They passed a sign which said, REPORT LITTERBUGS, CALL 1-800-44-TRASH.

They passed a sign which said, SEE MAN-EATING CLAMS! SEE WORLD'S LARGEST CRAWFISH! SEE WORLD'S TALLEST CROSS!

They passed a sign which said, PRISON AREA, REPORT ALL HITCHHIKERS, CALL 1-800-44-TRASH.

They passed a sign which said, MINNESOTA, FIRST OUTPOST OF THE CIVILIZED WORLD, which announcement was not one they believed could be relied on.

"Strange things are done under the midnight sun, Gunga Din," said Raoul. "Did I ever tell you about the time Joyel was institutionalized?"

"She *wasn't!*"

"Oh, yes she was. Watch your tone with me, young lady. Joyel was institutionalized for one entire week. She wore this blue cotton wraparound, her feet always naked. Few things are more aphrodisiacal than a woman's naked foot. I've never in my life seen such beautiful feet on a crazy woman than were those beautiful feet on your crazy mother. She was like a young Elizabeth Taylor without all that front work to get in a man's way."

"Okay, why was Joyel institutionalized?"

"Time's hand, fate, found her out."

"Be serious."

"It was a case of mistaken identity. A real crazy person knocked on our door one day. Had I been home the whole ugly mess could have been avoided. But I wasn't and the two of them had this big shouting match, all about me, if you can imagine. When the police came they took one look at the situation and decided Joyel was the crazy one. So I guess you could say her institutionalization was a case of mistaken identity. It could have happened to anyone."

"I hate being a Daggle."

"By the time we got all the red tape straightened out, able to set your mother free, she didn't want to leave. She said she liked the asylum, it made her feel at home. She had free run of the kitchen and had put on seven pounds. She looked spectacular."

An old man was walking the side of the road and Juliette said, "Look, there's old Eguchi."

"I bet you don't know this," Raoul said. "Joyel has a rock that she claims was in Virginia Woolf's pocket when she drowned herself. Joyel claims she bought it at a Sotheby's auction in London, England. But I saw her pick that rock up off the sand in Gulfport, Mississippi."

"Good grief, would you quit?"

"You learned to swim in the Gulf of Mexico. The beached whale, we called you."

"Get stuffed, Daddy."

They were passing through the uninviting slums of some unpronounceable place in the lake country of northern Minnesota:

"The sun doesn't shine on those poor people's housing," said her father. "When the Bad Man comes to town, slums like this are the first place he visits. He's the one puts the cars up on chopping blocks, scatters all those broken tricycles and tin cans about the yards, and leaves all those rotting sofas on the porches."

"Will you ever be any fun?" said the girl. "Will you ever say anything interesting? In the early days after Mama left us you were a heroic tragic figure. Now you're just an old tired rag waiting for someone like Polly White to pick up."

"No gin for you tonight."

"Your mother also owns a chunk of rock from a Frank Lloyd Wright house, the one in Buffalo. She went to Buffalo with a chisel and hammer and in the dead of night stole herself that Frank Lloyd Wright piece."

"Describe your ideal woman, Daddy."

"Those space women. With the snake hair and the lizard skin. The ones that can read your every salacious thought and don't even think about hitting the sack until they have downed a minimum fifteen martinis."

"Those are my favorites, too. I like how they sleep all curled up together in a pile."

Juliette says this, although her mind is far away. Her mind is so far away it is like a little spinning ball spinning far, far away, in a minute it will be lost to sight, so to save herself before it is too late she shakes her dress, she smacks the faces of each of the little purple pansies, she screeches at them, "Put down those ice creams and get your fannies out there and *work*, *work*, *work* or there will be no dinner for you fat little pansies tonight."

Nearing Duluth, they halt for a red light. A black Honda stops in the lane beside them.

"It's the same car, Daddy."

Both Raoul and Juliette have the idea a black Honda has been following them through twenty-seven states and nine provinces. Raoul thinks it is the FBI, on his wife's tail for tax evasion, although Joyel has never in her life made a cent. Today they have seen the same car behind them out of Eban, in Castle Danger, in Two Harbors, and at Knife River.

But it is Mr. and Mrs. Minnesota in the black Honda, along with three Minnesota small-fry, each licking ice-cream cones, doing their bit for a renewed America.

At the next block up another light halts them. An old man dressed in the black robe of a judge stumbles by, then returns to pound a fist on their rooftop. "Same with a piano!" he shouts. "Call in the tuner or move your butt on!" The light changes and he staggers away.

A few blocks further on, Juliette Daggle lets go with a shriek.

"What what what!"

"There she is! There's Joyel!"

Raoul slams the Infiniti brakes so sharply their heads almost pitch into glass.

The woman Juliette is frantically waving towards wears a yellow tank top, yellow skirt, yellow shoes and stockings, on her head a yellow hat with a floppy brim.

She looks pretty stylish, the woman, seen from the rear. She has great legs. Joyel has lost a bit of weight about the hips, although the skirt remains a snug fit.

"Is that her, Daddy?"

It is *her*, for no other reason than it has to be. Raoul and Juliette sit immobile, as though stricken by the final ravages of a disease that has left them limp. Drops of sweat form on Raoul's forehead. Juliette's fists are white-knuckled.

"Mother!" she yells.

The vision in yellow turns. The eyes that meet theirs are blue in one instant, yellow in the other. One yellow gloved hand is up covering the face. The light in this Minnesota town has a peculiar sheen. It is all yellow.

Juliette's first thought is, *Mother has changed.*

Benevolent forces are at work here. The woman steps their way.

She says, "Why are you calling me, children?"

The woman bearing down on them has a face so latticed by the years that her flashing eyes are like glittering jewels in a cage. "Children?" She has a beautiful voice.

"My dear children, you are trying to get home, aren't you?" the woman says.

The skin at her throat is perfect and smooth. The shoulders possess a bodybuilder's girth. This old woman lifts weights.

She stands smiling by Juliette's open window, an infusion of sudden warmth.

"It is not within my province to be the person you would wish me to be," she says.

Raoul and the child are hypnotized.

"The person you seek perhaps was here. She *might* have been here. She still *may* be. She could have been here. She *could have been* me."

She touches Juliette's hair, her cheeks. "Life is like that," the woman says. "It was under strange compunction that I just now bought this yellow ensemble. It seemed to me, passing the shop window back there, that ages ago I saw a woman wearing a suit reminiscent of this one. That suit had remained locked in my mind all those years. It came over me that I had to have it. Is it my clothes, dear, that you recognize?"

She withdraws a tissue from the yellow purse. She wets the tissue with the tip of her tongue, wipes the ancient hand under Juliette's eyes.

"Hope is no more an enigma than is despair," she says. "Go on as you are going. The beloved may not remain lost forever. I am myself on my way to the fair. Such wonderful things happen at our fairs."

They have in the backseat boxes of fliers. The fliers say, HAVE YOU SEEN THIS WOMAN? Two million of these have been dispatched across the continent.

There are thirteen sainted towns in Minnesota. Juliette Daggle believes this is an unlucky number. She believes this because her father has landed her for the night in one of them. The sainted town they are in slants away from a lake, what a beautiful day, the sky so blue, yet seconds later there is turmoil on high, lightning flashes, thunder roars, and where has Papa disappeared to this time? Out on the lake a small boy in a metal rowboat is paddling furiously, he can make no headway, waves pound as on an ocean, the wind shrieks, you can see the waves breaking, the shooting foam, frequently boy and boat vanish, then there he is again, paddling furiously, he is being swept away, he will never make it ashore but oh how furiously he paddles, come on, little boy, but, no, he's lost from sight again, he's gone.

In a space of seconds wind abates, the sky is again an unblemished blue, sun is shining, the lake waters becalmed, but where is the boy? She makes a prolonged study of the lake's smooth surface but the boy is nowhere to be seen. Nor is there any boat of any kind anywhere on the lake or tied off at the pier or midst the bullrushes or anywhere anchored along the shore. She does not know what has become of the heroic boy.

She's locked herself in the bathroom, wracked with guilt, crying out her eyes, *What happened to that heroic boy, why did I not race into the water to save him? Please God, protect him, let me die in his place, Mutteyalamma, save him, Aramadoma, save him, Kalikalkali, save him from the House of Dust, I implore thee. May my platform shoes rot on my feet and my body be covered in bird feathers, may my tattoos bleed, save him, save him!*

That night in the cabin Raoul watches on TV the Pope speaking from his Vatican throne. The Pope is apologizing for the genocide practiced by the Church during the five-hundred-year reign of terror known as the Inquisition.

Better late than never, Raoul thinks.

The Church has so much to apologize for; in an hour of TV time, the Pope can barely scratch the surface.

Without the usual drink in his hand, the ice clinking, the glass sweating, matters to ponder, Raoul Daggle can confess that he feels incomplete. He casts his eyes downward, taking in his empty shoes as if he has suspicions they intend walking away without him.

The Pope speaks slowly. He's tired and ill, flagged out, every word is his last breath, he's recently back from East Timor, Rwanda, Kosovo, he's worn out yet his conscience continues to nag him, *My friends, we have unfinished business.*

Yes, Raoul thinks. We each have so much to tell each other.

"We burned them alive," Raoul hears the Pope saying. "Witches, fools, common folk, noblemen if we wanted their property, even our own bishops if they raised objections. We tore off limbs and ripped out tongues, we dipped them in vats of boiling water, a cry of innocence was the surest sign of guilt, no accused person was ever to be found innocent."

It amazes Raoul that the Pope is not lacing with sugar the Church's dastardly role through five centuries. There is sugar enough in his apology but it is not all sugar.

"We hamstrung every heretical bitch and bastard throughout the continent," the Pope is saying. "We set them aflame, one thousand at Como, seven thousand at Treves, four hundred burned on a single day in Toulouse, one hundred and thirty-three in Quedlinburg, in Silesia four hundred years before the Nazis we built ovens in which our victims were roasted alive, children, babies, we . . ."

Juliette enters, stepping from a cloud of luminescent steam, drying her hair with a thin white towel. Her head aslant, rubbing briskly, just the way Joyel would. Her feet, flushed a hot pink, leave footprints on the pile carpet of mystical precision.

"Make your papa a drink, sweetpea," Raoul says.

The Pope business drags on.

"Hell originally was conceived as a place of rebirth and regeneration," Juliette says. "It took a Christian to turn hell into a place where bodies writhed in everlasting torture."

"Now, now," Raoul says. "You've been listening to me."

The Pope says, "To the hundreds of thousands in our dungeons the Church applied hot irons, pincers, pliers to genitals, for five hundred years we . . ."

Juliette is already a tall girl. She does not yet have bosoms or even buds. Today she wears a ring on her right big toe.

"Why are you looking at me like that, Papa?"

"Babes-in-arms, infants two years old, they were all put on the rack, garrotted, dismembered, burned alive by papal bull, ad extirpanda, 1252, of Pope Innocent IV, among others, we—

"Turn him off, Papa," the child says. "As for drink, you said you've quit."

"I need to call Polly," Raoul says. "You go take another bath."

"Is it big?" asks Polly. "I'm going to come between you and Joyel, you know. I'm going to drive both of you crazy. How big is it?"

Life is short, what a ludicrous thought, the child thinks. How can this be, when the night is one long agony. Daddy is down at the Jumping Deer Bar, what's she supposed to do with herself? The bridal suite this time, no other rooms available. What, no one got hitched in this burg today, how wise of them. She's got a phone bug on tonight, she'd like to call everybody she knows and give them what for. Old Vern, she thinks, I'll call that prick, disguise my voice, the mean shit won't know what's hit him. So she does just that and a second later there the prick is barking, "Hello, hello," and she yells out, *"The opossums have landed. Get a life, you old fucker!"* Then slams down the phone, overcome by giggles, oh me, wasn't that a hoot.

But now she's really got the bug, she'll run up a million-dollar bill, why not, since her mama doesn't love her and her daddy is down in the bar heaping charm at any exotic supreme who will look his way. Flip those yellow pages, oh here's a good one, how groovy. An 800 number, yes, she's caught her father's disease, she too is now obsessed with these priests who have fallen from heaven.

We have all fallen, Juliette thinks, what makes that gang believe they are so unique? Dial a Fallen Priest, says the yellow pages ad, half a page, right there below Be Born Again's Dial-a-Prayer. She grips the hot phone, feels sweat puddling in her armpits, plopping into her eyes, dripping like folds of porkfat between her thighs. These rooms, they are either so cold you see your icy breath, or so hot you'll die of prostration, no matter, she's got a faithless old jerk-off on the line now.

The fallen priest speaking into her ear has a nasty tone, on certain words, *God* for one, his voice drips with sarcasm. "God so loved the world," he is snarling, "that He gave His only begotten son, which ought to convince you that our Father's thoughts on the sanctity of family life are highly suspect. Nothing lofty there, I assure you, and why 'only begotten,' how stingy of Him, how selfish. Just think if He'd had twelve sons, not to mention daughters, then one or two surrendered in our behalf wouldn't have been totally damaging to the family unit. But I suppose even God couldn't compel the holy mother to immaculately conceive over and over again, no, that would have been—"

Maddening, Juliette thinks. These fallen priests take everything so personally, as if God's crimes, should they exist, are directed solely at them, this requiring no deft aim on the part of God, since in a crowd, who are you first to spot? Yes, those scowling priests in their Reebok shoes, their white collars and shiny black habits, they've fallen but never so far they'll relinquish the churchly attire.

Juliette is disgusted, anyone over the age of six disgusts her, she wants to slam down the phone, to tear out the line, too bad her arm has gone numb. Well, rats, who next to phone, what about my good friend Teomi Feeolong, what about that old lady in the yellow neon suit over near Duluth we mistook for my mother?

A minute later she gets this same party on the line, Juliette says, "Let me see do I have this right, you saw that yellow suit years ago. Was it up in Niagara something or other that you saw it? Yes, okay, did you go out on a *Misty Maiden* boat to see the rapids, yes? Okay, did you see either of these two parties holding a dog over the rails? That was my dog Trash, you know, that dog was like a sister." "Oh dear," replied the woman, "I see now why Joyel left, the stress in your household must be beyond belief. You are all so high-strung, so *wrought*, however do you stand it?"

"We get along," shouted Juliette, overcome with a blinding fury. "You keep your nose out of our business."

Then to call Teomi: Hi, Teomi, let's jump off the roof the minute I get back, headfirst, okay?

"Why so glassy-eyed?" her father asks. "Who are you talking to? Why aren't you asleep?"

"None of your business," she snaps. "Just because you're my daddy doesn't give you the right to pry into every corner of my private life."

"We've come to a parting of the ways, young lady. What, you learned your manners from your mother?"

"You leave my mother out of this. What do you know about my mother? She left you, didn't she?"

"What, what, what!" yells Raoul. *"What did I do?"*

Raoul sulks. It is his aim to sulk all night and never speak again to his retarded daughter.

Raoul Daggle paces Best Western's much-paced carpet, sloshing gin, no way at a time like this he can keep his mouth shut. "It is not good," he's saying, "that a child should know all that an adult presumes to know, or that one adult should possess all the knowledge belonging to another adult. Knowledge shared is knowledge eroded, a set of facts, for instance, in my brain sent over to your brain, Juliette, is another set of facts altogether—witness your mother—which is why I am opposed to education for the masses, more especially education of the young, the young don't need learning so much as they need a cane against their britches, with the exception of the following, they should be taught rudimentary accounting, inasmuch as it's useful to have them run to the store for us now and again."

"Oh, Daddy, are you drunk again?"

"The rich man and the poor man do not speak the same language," he's saying, "and the poor woman who could speak it refuses to out of exhaustion or sheer stubbornness. If poor people spoke in concert, democracy would fly out of the window." His is a good lecture, he's thinking, solid as gold, and the fact that it is off the subject, the one subject being *The Case of the Runaway Wife*, the one subject to be avoided, makes it all the better.

"Stop gawking," he at last says. "Let me summarize, in summary, I want to drink my drink in peace, so you, young lady, you can just go over there and listen to the Pope's apology for two thousand years of crimes against humanity, or so it says here in the *TV Guide*."

And then he sat on the edge of the Best Western bed with every intention of drinking his drink in peace, although seconds later he is rising in a temper, bellowing and tossing away his glass, shutting himself away in the Best Western bathroom, because what he has seen when he sits on the bed is Joyel seated on the second bed, dressed in a white half-slip and otherwise naked, taking pins from her hair as she crosses her legs but then uncrossing them, Raoul temporarily remiss in noticing the dark triangle of her exposed sex, inasmuch as sight of her unbound breasts is sufficiently riveting to him. So it must have been a subsequent crossing of her legs which drew his attention away from her breasts, first to her slim ankles, next to her kneecaps, her thighs, a brief upwards glance to assure himself the naked breasts have not vanished, only then to drop his eyes to that beautiful triangle where so much lusciousness is stored, how incredible that year after year and under wear of ten thousand acts of love that entry and its hallowed chamber go on renewing, even advancing, the one irrefutable glory. A mistake, though, to follow this line, despite its being the line of least resistance, at least for Raoul Daggle, given the deprived state he's in. His wife's bare breasts have mesmerized him, but those uncrossed legs, that inviting artistry known as the parted thighs, the lovely hirsute mound in camouflage of the beautiful cunt, these are more than Raoul Daggle can contemplate, certainly not while under the watchful scrutiny of his daughter. So then, we are never to know whether it is his wife's appearance on a Best Western bed or the sudden memory of his daughter's presence that compels him to let out a wounded cry. To cry out in great anguish, a shriek of unbridled pain, to hurl down a nearly full glass of deluxe drink onto Best Western's much-paced carpet, and flee with a second, even more heartrending cry into the Best Western's marbleized bathroom. At which juncture we might remind ourselves that we are booked tonight into the Best Western bridal suite, nothing else available, and to ask ourselves to what extent these somewhat luxurious quarters are contributing to the improbable occurrences related, both as regards Joyel's visitation in naked form, her husband's breakdown, and now Juliette Daggle's pounding on the Best Western door, shouting,

"You're a fruitcake, do you know that? You're fruitcakes, both of you, and I want to die."

Nor can we know for certain that Joyel Daggle in apparition and through whatever spectral means has followed Raoul inside the bathroom, now to stand on the white-tiled floor on legs every bit as real as yours or mine, her face and shoulders, those bare breasts, repeated in squeaky-clean mirrors along three high walls, those long legs now parting, real feet separating on the cold tiles, as she strides directly up to him, angrier than any spirit creature has any right to be, saying, "So, you slimy weasel, you would sleep with that siren, Polly White, would you? You lust after that exotic supreme, Lavender Blue, do you?"

Unsaid, perhaps, are the fated words, Is this all our marriage means to you?

If only this, then that; if only that, then this. Juliette, pounding on the door, is versed in the "if onlys," if only because her parents' blood pumps, pools, simmers, boils, is ever seeking undiscovered routes inside her flesh. For all of that, she's a rational soul, content as lake water which ever reflects on its surface the sky's hue whether bright or muddy. "Come out, Papa," she calls. "Let's hold a prayer meeting and form a circle of hands, let's bring in all your exotic supreme girlfriends, Polly White and Lavender Blue, let's get that old purple-nosed priest to lead us, let's all of us fallen people sit at a Ouija board and see if we can't summon Mother."

7

CAUTION: Deer-Crossing Road Next One Hundred Miles

JOYEL HITS HARD RAIN SOON. God is weeping because not even He could create a perfect world. He is weeping because He has made a thousand mistakes, because not everyone loves Him, because a billion people in nearly as many languages bombard Him minute by minute with requests for favors, because billions insist on giving Him news of this and that disaster, miracle, triviality and most asinine thought, as though He had turned stone-blind, couldn't read minds, had a need for such contemptible clutter. He's weeping because these billions feel obliged to thank Him for every little bite enters their mouths, Cheez Whiz, chips, Twinkies, Kraft macaroni. God help them, He must count the very hair of their heads, must never sleep, must lead them not into temptation, must intercede at every sporting match, every public unveiling whether sewer or citadel, even little schoolchildren's piping voices assail Him, people on their knees beseech Him morning, noon, and night, as if He had nothing better to do with His time than a common retiree or pensioner, as if His kingdom is little more than an elevated Daggle Estates. Jesus Christ, isn't that enough to bring on hard rain, His gale of tears, buckets and buckets. Let the earth slide off into the seas, let the oceans percolate, let Joyel Daggle, who hasn't addressed Me once, not once, this vile woman who has forsaken husband and child, the explanations existing in abundance, as many as My blades of grass: he beat her, which he did not, he ridiculed her, which he did not, he was unfaithful, which he was not, he refused to help around the house, which he did not, he was tightfisted with money or threw it away at every opportunity, which he did not, he did not love her or she him, which is an utter untruth, they had a lover's spat, no not that either, she has lost her mind, there's a good possibility, she needs this year of recovery, needs to find herself, get her act together, there's another feasible explanation if you're accepting of such psychobabble, she's running from something or someone, not from husband and child, did I hear something about a bespectacled son of a bitch in a Harry Rosen brown suit? Fine, show Me a taggle of proof. She hates motherhood, forget that, Joyel Daggle has developed amnesia, don't be silly, she abominates the gated community, well, pardon Me, Ms. Daggle, your Lord happens to share the values of that crowd, they personify My views totally, dear Vern will be seated by My right hand. Let's not bore ourselves with endless speculation. How could even God on high be expected to know why the creature abandoned the family hearth, I have long since thrown up my hands, I forgive you if you do likewise, not for nothing were you made in My image. What headway can your likes make anyway? Let Me remind you that after five hundred years you still do not know the answer to such a simple question as why Mona or Monna or Madonna Lisa is smiling, certain affairs are meant to remain mysterious, divine intervention cannot be practiced seven days a week *ad nauseam*. As some of you will have noticed from the thousands of fliers posted on My trees, walls, My bulletin boards in public hallways throughout the land, this fugitive from the family nest bears an incredible likeness to the smiling Mona, much to our surprise, even to My consternation, her face displays a wholly developed benign and integrated humanity, the face of a woman in tranquil harmony with her universe, traits highly at odds with any extrapolations you will have made from the oppressively larded narrative in your hands. Had your Savior time—meaning Me—He might remind you that the smile of Leonardo's Mona, approximate date of creation 1503–1506, if memory serves, is a smile precisely identical to that of Georges de la Tour's all but equally famous and much more significant *St. Mary Magdalene with a Candle*, dated 1630–1652, the one difference being that Mary of Magdala's face is turned away from us, we see on the canvas only a fraction of one eye, it apparently riveted upon a flickering candle, the barest hint of lips, this obscured by an uplifted hand, a lazy, somewhat slothful body, a despairing woman, I say, one beaten down by the world, whipped into obedience by My son's maniacal physical love of her, if you must know, a woman who bedded with ten thousand men, men and women, as I recall, before My son saw her walking a brambled trail with a jug on her head and fell instantly in love, a woman now exactly as Georges de la Tour paints her, one smote with repentance, melancholy, defeatism, guilt, characteristics undeniably the influence of My son, a woman so disheartened she dare not show you her face in the painting of which I speak, yet I assure you doubting Thomases that Mary showed her face to Me, it was in fact not the candle but My Own Self she was regarding as Georges de la Tour brought her to his canvas, and I am telling you Mary of Magdala's face and Mona Lisa's face are the perfect duplicate of each other, and furthermore that Joyel Daggle, should she ever smile again, is the third of these triplets, as alike in their features as My blades of grass, and if now after five hundred years of studying the one smile known to you, you cannot interpret what's behind that expression, nor even now do so under fresh impetus of all hints contained in this harangue, then I forsake you, I give up on you, Eli, Eli . . . as My son exclaimed, because frankly you will have proved yourself unworthy of Me yet again, so if I am weeping now that is why. Should My weeping flood your rivers and bury your homes and turn your every highway into a sea of mud and you drown in the downpour, annoy Me with screeches from your rooftops, forgive Me if I only send more rain, snow, ice, hurricane, tornado, and other such weaponry chocked to overflowing here in My armory in the sky, amen.

Joyel Daggle, alone on the black highway, sees rain turning into ice, *Salaam, peace be with you, God.*

God has a bad cold, Joyel thinks, He has influenza, His nose is dripping, He needs Contac C and (that cold remedy, what's it called?) lemon might be the preferred flavor.

Or it could be that this icy curtain is South Dakota's personal weather, nothing freakish or untoward about it. You're in the Dakotas, you take what's given or move your tail on. The ice to Joyel's mind swishes by like bullets and more than once she finds herself ducking. She accelerates and the ice sweeps off into darkness. In the high beams the ice pellets are a curtain fully horizontal. If she drives fast enough, the ice will not hit the car at all, just as when she was a child learning to ride a bike she never hit anything so long as she whirled along with closed eyes, air dynamics, luck, works that way.

Frigid winds, not to mention ice, blow in through the broken window. "I'm freezing my butt off," Joyel groans. Ice drums against the car roof like an Irish dancing troupe, Joyel's eyes are cherry-red, the lids hanging like funeral wreaths on doorknobs. Being on the run, she thinks, is pure livin' hell.

She wallops a fist against the radio, good, there's static, better, here a voice fading in, a deejay saying, "Fellows and gals, groovy nighthawks, take the needle from your arms, the snow from your nose, here's Sippy Wallace singing 'Zootcase Blues.'" *I'm afraid to travel down that long bad road by my lonesome*, sings Sippy, way to go, girl. Next, whiny Saffire is going strong with *"Ain't Nobody's Business,"* Joyel humming along, this is so damned good, now Koko Taylor doing "Sixty-three-Year-Old Mama," whoops, more static, wheezes and crackles, fade out, no more radio.

Ice falls harder, such a macho temper God has.

Nancy the babysitter had said, "Why would I want to go inside your stupid cave?"

Joyel's mother had said, "Wouldn't you like a picture of Mummy and Daddy inside your cave?"

They had said, "What do you do all day in there?"

Parents couldn't crawl through the cave's entrance because of how big they were. They could lift the cave up and look inside at how their little girl had dressed up the cave, but lifting and looking were not nearly the same thing as crawling on your knees inside your very own little house, the one you yourself had decorated without outside influence.

She had play magazines on a play coffee table in there and a grand piano by a curtained window and a kitchen with a real self-cleaning oven, a microwave, Triscuits on a wide shelf.

"I think you should put this little 'Prayer for a Happy Home' inside your cave," her mother said. "You need a wall plaque saying 'Home Sweet Home.'"

"No I don't."

"Young lady, don't argue with me. You need pretty play towels and shell-shaped soaps in nice colors in your play bathroom."

"No I don't."

"You need—"

"I don't, I don't, I don't!"

"What, what, what! What did we say?"

The best thing about that cave was that it could be moved anywhere you wanted it. Joyel could drag the cave from her own room into Mommy and Daddy's bedroom and watch Nancy sleep. Santa Claus, not her rich circus-owner uncle, was supposed to have given that cave to her. She had written a note to Santa at the North Pole to thank him and Santa had answered, Don't mention it, kid. He had said, I'm glad you appreciate its features, thank goodness there's at least one other in this family has brains.

Before her parents returned from their outings Nancy waked and said, "I'm a big lizard and I'm going to eat you up, whether you cry or not."

Such a whiz, Nancy was.

Nancy was Joyel's absolute favorite-most babysitter of all time and if she couldn't have Nancy she would erupt into tears and stomp the floor. She could remember well the stomping, the tantrums. Her parents ran a silent household but to the babysitter's mind that house was so noisy it was all but unbearable. Too much hum in the fridge, too much rumble in the furnace, too many things holding their breath inside the walls. Nancy preferred a residence so silent you could hear deer jumping invisible fences in an invisible world populated solely by yourself and the jumping deer.

"Close your eyes. Listen to the jumping deer," Nancy would say.

"I see them."

"You're a big liar. You're too young to see them, you gotta be older."

Nancy said her own brain was such a special place she could go inside that very brain and sit down the same way ordinary people sat at their kitchen table drinking coffee or whiskey. She could sit inside her brain and paint her nails, do her hair—things like that—anytime she wanted to. Often she held parties in there, Nancy said, serving only lemonade or tea because she didn't want a lot of drunk people who did not know how to behave in there.

But it was exhausting work. It was "rueful labor," Nancy said, keeping your brain neat and tidy.

"I hire housekeepers but they never work out, the fair, imploring face is the least trustworthy of all. They steal things, especially my thoughts, while they are in there. It's best, really, if you have to deal only with imaginary people or with immigrant laborers who cannot speak the language."

Nancy's brain had a secret door she entered by. Her brain had a white picket fence on a nice secret street which you reached through a canopied pathway of secret elms. It had a nice English garden and yellow lattice windows with panes of glass like diamonds all in different colors, climbing ivy-covered every secret wall and the key to the secret door was kept in a secret locket on a necklace around her neck.

"Where did you get the key?"

My mother the renowned trapeze artist gave me this key on her deathbed, after flying through the air without swings, ropes, or nets. My father, the equally renowned aerialist, put this locket in my hand. They were the great daredevil duo Ceyx and Halcyone, than whom none were greater. When I was no older than you are now they were already training me, they said I was a prodigy with excellent potential. Ceyx and Halcyone performed before the great royal houses of Europe and Asia, honors of every distinction were bestowed upon them, gifts of precious rubies and pearls, musical instruments from the Paleolithic Age, golden diadem from the tomb of Pharaoh Sethos the First. From a pole one hundred feet high, nightly they leapt into a space lit by powerful spotlights and for fifteen minutes to waves of thunderous applause they flew unencumbered through naked space, with a freedom of expression normal only to birds of the air. People gasped, many of faint heart swooned and had to be fanned back to consciousness, only to swoon a second and third time, for nothing like it had ever been seen, they were like soaring swans, though better than swans since Ceyx and Halcyone flew without wings and all in a manner that was perfectly natural. At times they would fly off into a darkness far beyond the reach of the powerful spotlights and the great crowned heads of Europe no less than the humble ordinary folk such as you and me would hold their heartbeats, scanning the sky for sight of them, and just when everyone had given up hope, when they had begun to believe all this was some sorcery done with mirrors or flight existing only in their overwrought imaginations, here would descend Ceyx and Halcyone like radiant parachutists from the dark heavens, more graceful and beautiful than ever, then to swoop, dive, and glide in ever-widening circles over the hushed crowd, my mother often with strange white objects pressed to her bosom—What is she holding? the people would ask—a great murmur of awed reverence gradually swelling up from the throng, many with their heartbeats locked in that strange chemical conspiracy of the senses that confounds us when reason and logic depart, then my mother to fling out her arms and, as though expelled from her very bosom, suddenly flew scores of birds white and luminescent within the powerful lights, birds which Ceyx and Halycone had plucked in flight from the dark clouds, and a deafening volley would sound, like a clap of thunder, the people rising as one, all in a fever of unparalleled excitement, as ever so slowly Ceyx and Halcyone leisurely pirouetted back to earth, there to take their bows before the tumultuous applause.

How did Ceyx die?

One night my father reached out his hand for my mother's, he saw a blank look in her eyes, her hand wasn't there to take hold of his, the next second she was in the grip of gravity's terrible law, plunging to the rings below.

Poor Ceyx.

My father never flew again, nor would he allow me.

What happened to him?

Heartbreak and melancholy, within a month he had withered away.

Poor Halycone.

"Stop blubbering. Do you want to see my locket and key?"

"Yes."

"Then go inside your cave and if you're nice and quiet there for a long time, I'll show you."

The key in Nancy's locket was so small you could hardly hold it between your fingers. But it was a real key, of purest gold, which Nancy said people would give a fortune for, since it was this key which had unlocked her parents' hearts and enabled them to fly.

"They'd give a million dollars just to see behind my secret door. How much will you give?"

Joyel Daggle has not seen another vehicle in hours. She does not know what has happened to the rain, the ice, the loping antelope, her life.

She's got herself a stone wedged over the gas pedal, her driving foot nowhere near the floor. Her shoulders are killing her, her eyes are gritty, she's hungry, cold, sleepy, every bone aches, a bespectacled son of a bitch in a brown suit wants to kill her, why then is this woman smiling, why is she nodding her head, saying aloud to the dark, "What a good question"?

Another thing Joyel remembers Nancy the babysitter saying was that her boyfriend licked her tears. He licked them right off her face, as a genuine sign of unfettered love. He could come inside her brain, too, though she couldn't go inside his because men's brains were not as accommodating as a woman's, they had a sign up there like those seen along this Dakota highway, No Trespassing, Violators Will Be Prosecuted.

The ice is back.

Drivers finding themselves in fog speed up. Joyel has often noted this. In Florida one time, on I-95 below Jacksonville late at night, she and her parents were in a pile-up involving 367 vehicles. The fog that time was so thick you could not see beyond your nose. No one slowed up. In fact, the thicker the fog, the faster drivers go; it is some strangeness of the brain that causes this, some whimsicality that discerns infinity in the mist, an infinity you can't deliver yourself into fast enough. You can say "Not me," but fog fogs the brain, motion deludes the steadiest mind, the dreamworld enchants, it lures you into its heart, the fog's heart must be such a lovely place, if only I can reach the heart.

Her father swore he was only creeping along. If he slowed down, someone would ram his rear end.

The same thing happens when a person falls in love, Joyel believes.

Her parents' car was number 314 in the 367-vehicle smash-up. Their front end went right through the boot of a 1972 Cadillac Eldorado, an Oldsmobile 88 got them, God lets men and women invent such things so that they may kill themselves and save Him the trouble—Trouble, my good woman, is all they are.

For decades Joyel's mother retained the neckbrace a doctor decreed she wear; she would pull the brace out while entertaining friends and say to them, "This is what my husband did to me."

In Florida on that trip with her parents she'd seen a fat woman on the beach draining something from her left ear into a silver cup.

The woman said to her, "Go away, you stupid girl."

Then the woman buried the cup in the sand.

It was a beautiful silver cup with initials engraved in Old English script.

Joyel had rooted the cup free with the yellow shovel that went with her yellow bucket. The waves carried away the cup and her shovel, and when her parents said, "Honey, why don't you come in the water?" she ran away screaming. The juices in that woman's ear had tainted the ocean and anyone went into it would drown and many did, as will many more, for how long does it take the earth's waters to renew themselves unless they come blessed with dramatic falls like exist up there at that Niagara something or other place where Joyel and Raoul Daggle and Trash and beautiful Juliette, at that time just a baby, vacationed one time, the four of them on that tourist boat, Misty something or other, Raoul saying to Trash, "Trash, either you get your act together, dog, or I'm pitching you over the side."

The woman with the silver cup, the pile-up of cars, are Joyel's sole memory of the Florida trip, except that they stayed in a place belonging to a rich man, possibly related, for whom her mother had sung "Tell Me Where the Violets Are."

This was out on cool sand under a deluge of palm trees. Her father was eating coconut with a knife. He carried cotton-wadding in a pocket for those moments when his wife was moved to sing and he would tear off tufts for his and Joyel's ears, *Let's let it be our little secret, okay, hun?* They missed the hurricane by two hours. She grew up hearing her mother say to stony-faced guests, "We missed the hurricane by two hours." Then the brace: "This is what my husband did to me."

Joyel says, "I hope my poor Colony dog did not get caught in this ice storm. A dog should not have to experience such misfortune."

Tests have demonstrated that fully ninety percent of drivers succumb to what is known as the fog phenomenon.

Ice, however, is another story.

Joyel stops on the road and scoops up a few cubes. She'll have a highball once she finds a place to flop, lucky Lake Oahe is set as her next designation. Twenty-one hours on the road in one spell at the wheel isn't so bad, may that son of a bitch back there on her tail drop dead.

On the outskirts of one of the towns she has passed through, after Cut Bank, near Rock Springs, was a string of billboards patterned after the old Burma Shave signs. The billboards said:

AROUND HERE
THERE IS THE NOTION
THAT HEAVEN IS FULL
THINK
AGAIN

The last one said, SLUMBER-A-WHILE CEMETERY.

Joyel, lightheaded from so many miles, has found this amusing. Then she thought how often it is that things that are funny are really so sad you have to cry.

She wondered if the people who had done the actual paintings of the billboards had thought about how sad humor often is, and whether, thinking about that, they had sat down on the road and cried the way she is crying now.

Joyel's friend Carter in Orick had used something on his hair that he called Utt's Grease. This was an actual product made from a secret formula manufactured only in Paraguay and shipped to Carter by mail order from an importer in New York, New Jersey. Carter liked that his grease was shipped to him from a city in a state the city wasn't supposed to be in. Carter liked the toothmarks his comb left in the Utt's Grease. He admitted that occasionally he rubbed this grease over his testicles. The import company, with each order, sent him a folder in which it was said that groin anointment was a Paraguayan custom widely practiced by both men and women.

Elvis Presley was said to have endorsed Utt's Grease. Ronald Reagan used it.

Carter would have been a handsome man, Joyel thought, except for his Utt's Grease. Salvador Dali used Utt's Grease on his mustache.

Ronald Reagan used it to color his hair.

It surprised her that Esther hadn't minded Carter, a tasteful man, anointing himself with the stuff.

"He's building me a tree house," Esther said. "Carter says everything in my tree house is going to be remote-controlled, including what time we get up in the morning. He's so romantic. What do you think?"

Joyel told Esther her English was coming along really well.

"You don't even speak with an accent. Hardly anyone else in this country can say that."

For herself, Joyel was not keen on much from Paraguay or Argentina. She blamed this bias on the Nazi shelters these nations provided. She wonders how numerous skinhead neo-Nazis are in Paraguay and Argentina and whether these skinheads are devotees of Utt's Grease.

Paraguay is the world's largest supplier of petitgrain. Petitgrain is a flavoring; it is an ingredient in many famous perfumes, though not of any, so far as is known, worn by Joyel Daggle.

Free of the storm, Joyel sees car lights behind her so feebly distant, so bouncy in the reflection, they are like a chain of winking jewels.

"Son of a bitch!" she says.

It's *him*, somehow she knows this, the stalking Camel-smoking Othello-quoting son of a bitch is back there.

That has been her policy through the whole of this period of recovery, her year on the lam, *Always think the worst.* Jesus Lord, will I ever get through this night? The globe's circumference is 24,902 miles, must she soldier through all of them?

Arriving at a crossroads, she sees a Dakota Highway Department mobile trailer spelling out in flashing yellow lights DETOUR, ROAD CLOSED AHEAD, "Oh Christ, just my luck," Joyel shrieks, "what next?" A long time passes, no further signs loom up to assist her, she's somehow missed the proper turn, got on the wrong road, she's traveling on bumpy gravel now, fog teems about, such a soup, now the gravel is giving way to a weedy lane, she should turn the car around, but how, where? Eyes gleam in the darkness, limbs scrape and stab, she goes on slowly through the black night, the path arriving at elbow turns one after another, clearly she's climbing a high grade, the car pinging, sluggish, the steering wheel so stiff in her hands it might be mounted in concrete, "Go," she cries, "show a little oomph, you!" The engine putters, coughs, spits, she pumps the gas, yanks the choke, but the engine is silent, the car lurches, jounces, coasts to weary standstill. A good thing, too, she now notes, because the path has quit as well, she's in a surround of frosted bushes, tall trees, deadfall, an icy wilderness. Heavens to Betsy, why me? She douses the lights, sits in utter darkness, within a silence so profound her very ears must enlarge to appreciate the breathtaking hold this silence has on earth, really it's rather marvelous, if you can bring yourself to look upon it that way.

She does not hear the hooves of an animal crunching over snow alongside the stalled car, nor see the animal touching its lips to the icy window by which she sits, the animal sniffing at the crack in the window, licking moisture from the glass as it appraises her twisting form. Joyel switches on the lights, involuntarily emits a gasp: there in the swirling mist is a horned beast of some kind, she squints, is it her antelope, is it a deer, an elk, surely it isn't big enough to be a moose, nor can it be a true antelope. Joyel is well aware these creatures are confined to Africa and Asia where their seventy-two secret names rival those of God—*I conjure thee in the name of Ele, Elo, and Aho. I invoke thee in the name of Abra, Amo, and Infinitas, in the midst of mountains and snow and mists. In thy names may all infirmity be struck down, may our many legs run as one*—why don't we make it easy on ourselves and simply call it a deer?

The animal stands perfectly still in the high beams staring back at Joyel with unblinking eyes, its expression one of tranquil inquiry, not the least bit menacing, perhaps even sympathetic. Joyel releases her held breath, her eyes widen, What's this? she asks, for now the deer is thumping a front hoof into the leaves, its bleats, such a language these creatures speak, and now here it is to be seen approaching in a measured gait. It submits her to a lingering gaze, sniffs, gives a sudden snort, a shake of the head, a single antler rakes the glass, then the deer turns and pads delicately away through the forest, in the distance turning to bestow one last lingering gaze: Are you going to continue sitting there, stupid woman, or will you follow me? Where the deer has halted, a footpath, and there, nailed to a tree, a crudely painted sign, This Way to the Powwow at Crazy Horse Falls.

The pathway climbs the mountain, eventually emptying onto a lit clearing where any number of people are gathered. Drums, chanting voices, hoop dancers. Couples walk abreast in the snowy mist, some holding hands, embracing, lovers they must be, others dart this way and that in adherence to unknown duties, servants to whim or circumstance, many another is seen in assemblage around picnic tables by open pits where foods of diverse description simmer under thick smoky drifts. Up the way, a crowd congregates by what appears to be a long rope bridge spanning a deep gorge, rocky cliffs to each side, all beclouded in mist which the dawn's rays just now are penetrating. The roar of rushing water, vibration that Joyel's legs detect in the breathing earth, and there the falls are, magnificent, a great gushing curtain topped in sheets of ice, in spray and foam.

This is what Joyel feels: a shudder of delicious ecstasy, you are about to be kissed and you do not know where the kiss will fall or where the lips next will go or whose lips they are, and how it is that they may in one breath encompass your body head to toe.

Men and women are in flight from the rope bridge, beautiful exotic birds, nocturnal Furies attired in the strange garb of sorcerers from another world, one leaps, there goes another, another, and here comes the first springing back, arms aflutter, somersaulting on invisible wings, how can we account for the fact that people now can fly, there goes another, another, some forty or so in flight from the rope bridge, spray churning up from the falls, these bodies gliding above the turbulent depths, such a besiegement of water—But what is going on? you ask. Well, I am glad you raised that question, you have come to the right party and happy am I to oblige. Look at that fellow over there, that's Tom or Thomas, known in these parts as the New Indian, surely you have met the New Indian who takes our Chief Crazy Horse to the winter fairs that our great chief may render verdicts in the livestock competition, and the others, well, they are your usual ragtail First Nations bunch, together with interloping priests weak in the knees from having fallen from heaven, if God did not make us then we must make ourselves, worse the luck, we are all, let us say, poets of the cloth at this powwow, no less than is the innocent deer whose tracks you followed to this place.

Ages back, Joyel was holding something in her hand, her hand in a tight fist, and Raoul asked, "What do you have in there?" "It's a secret," she said. "But why would you have a secret, what can it be?" She ran, he gave chase, both were laughing at that point, it was no more than a game. Then Joyel trips, her wrist snaps, Raoul rushes her to the hospital. “Doesn’t look too bad,” the doctor says. “Mild discoloration, hardly any swelling, most likely a sprain. But what’s that you’re holding in your hand, young lady? Let me see what you’ve got in there.” And the doctor, a kindly man, makes the mistake of wanting to open that hand. Her arm pinned, he’s peeling back the fingers. She screams. For Joyel, it is quite the scream, obscene, if you want to know the truth.

“Get this cocksucker away from me!”—that was the scream. And in the instant, she shoots that hand up to her mouth, they catch a glimpse of tightly wadded paper, in the next second she’s swallowed that paper, she’s eaten the secret whole.

“Oh, well,” says the doctor, “I’m certain nothing is broken, still, we’d better X-ray.”

Joyel is in a rage, it is perfectly clear to her that this doctor, abetted by the man she loves, means to X-ray the whole of her body solely in order to discover what this secret is. She’s off the table and running, “*You sons of bitches, you fucking woman-haters, leave me alone!*”

Peel back my fingers. When we die, we die inside each other. Now open yours.

8

master, master,

Lend Me Your Horse that I May Ride to Samara

"Look at that sunset," Raoul says. "It's the damnedest thing."

"Look yourself," says Juliette, in a mood.

"I bet Joyel is watching this sunset. She's a big softie when it comes to sunsets."

"Can't you shut up one minute about that woman?"

"That woman?"

"You heard me."

"Cripes, what a mope."

"Shut up, shut up, shut up!"

"My shoulders are killing me, my eyes are gritty, I'm hungry, cold, sleepy, every bone aches, Daddy, let's pull in."

In the Best Western motel room, Ah-Gwah-Ching, Chippewa National Forest, Minnesota, Juliette says to her father:

"I have been to beautician's school, today I received my diploma. I have my combs and brushes, my shampoos made from secret recipes. May I cut your hair, madame?"

Raoul did not want his hair cut. He has picked up Juliette's churlish mood, it is at his backside like an Inquisitor's torch.

"You can't cut hair," he said. "You're a bogus beautician. Let me see that diploma."

Juliette drew her diploma on a paper sack, using the hotel pen. She stuck the sack diploma on a wall. She rearranged the chairs. "We have special perm rates today, madame," she said. "Sit right down. Will that be plain wash and rinse or would you like nice silver streaking to highlight your wonderful cheekbones and those chiseled lips?"

"Leave my hair alone," Raoul said. He trotted off into the bathroom, disappearing behind a slammed door.

Juliette trotted after him. At the door she said, "I am happy to announce, madame, that today we feature manicures and pedicures on the house. Will madame partake?"

"Quit bothering me."

"At the conclusion of your sitting our man Upton will take you home in our limousine. There will be a small charge."

"I'm warning you."

Juliette rattled the doorknob. "Madame?" she said. "Madame's behavior is unacceptable. If madame does not improve her manners, I am entering madame's name in the black book."

Silence.

Their room was an oldish one. Over the bath door was an open transom. Juliette pulled up a chair, stood on the chair, and looked through the transom at her father. He was standing in the tub in his jogging clothes. He seemed to be crying. Some kind of strange animal noise seemed to be issuing from him.

"If madame will consent to appear," she said, "madame may join the staff for delicious tea and cake." Her father put his hands over his face; he sagged back against the wall and slowly began sinking. "There will be a modest charge," she said. "Will madame be joining us?"

Her father slumped down onto the tiles. His shoulders were shaking and the strange animal noises more pronounced.

"Has madame considered therapy?" she asked.

He shook more. He seemed in gyration from the huge sobs overtaking him. Juliette had never seen him like this but she didn't have her mother any longer and someone was to blame.

"Did madame miss her glorious sunset? Is that why madame is so bereaved?"

Her father's reply was awful. The voice cracked, his pain rode a dozen aching syllables, despite the single word produced. "*Please!*" he said.

After watching him for a few minutes, Juliette hopped off the chair. She sat another several minutes on the foot of one of the two single beds, staring first at the closed door behind which her father sobbed and then she stared at the wall. She stared at the wall in such a state of absorption that her mother no longer existed nor did her crying father. She thought, My heart is cold, as indeed it was. It was dripping ice with such ferocity that only ice existed. My lost mother, my crying father, what are they to me? As for that, what am I to myself? I exist, certainly I do, I'm here in this stupid room, but I don't care. The more her father cried, the longer her mother stayed away, the less she cared. Fuck it, she said, who are they, who am I, what does it matter? But these were fleeting thoughts, here and gone, and all that mattered was the spot on the wall that had caught her attention. She had to keep reminding herself, focus on that wall, because there were terrible sounds now coming from behind the closed door. It was the sound in there of a strangling man, maybe even a hanging one, someone dangling from gallows, but what had these sounds to do with her?

She got up and examined the spot on the wall which had been absorbing her. Well, my goodness, she said to herself. Good gracious. Just look at that. On the wall, the spot that so enraptured her, turned out to be a beautiful ladybug. Such a lovely little bug, yellow with black spots. What brings you to our domain? she asked of the ladybug. Why aren't you in hibernation? You certainly are a beauty, though, and I wish I could get to know you better. The ladybug of course, didn't care about her thoughts. The ladybug was in the room to eat the aphids off the plants, but it was hornswoggled because the room had no plants. "There are three hundred and fifty different species of you guys on this continent alone," she said. She blew on the ladybug and watched the ladybug fluff out its wings.

Juliette climbed back up in the chair. Her father had pulled shut the shower curtain. She couldn't see him and didn't know whether he still was crying. Was he there? She sat back down on the bed. She examined her hands and the dirt beneath her nails. She did not have hair growing on the back of her hands the way her father did or the big knuckles he said he had from his days in the boxing ring when he was known as Raoul the Bull and had sparred with the great Canadian champ, George Chuvalo.

The shower was running. She jumped up to the transom again and looked a long time at the top of her father's head under the spray.

"Madame is such a silly woman," she said loudly. "I wouldn't care if madame croaked in there."

All at once she had a wonderful thought. She shot away from the door, ran to the table, snatched up the scissors, and began snipping off her hair down to the very roots.

Everywhere she looks Juliette Daggle sees young couples kissing on the street. They are going to the Vikings game, Raoul and Juliette have seen the signs. About are untold restaurants and pubs and wing Kwikstops, Viking this and Viking that. "*Stop the car, stop the car, there's wings!*" Juliette screams. Juliette has never eaten *wings*. But all over North America, where her father has stopped for his quick pick-me-ups, she has seen people gnawing on these wings.

Juliette thinks these Viking women ought to be careful who they kiss. You kiss a man and the next thing you know he's holding your head underwater. He's got his hands around your neck. She's seen this happen so many times on so many motel TVs it is now a thing to be expected.

She's glad she's eleven and only her daddy has kissing rights. Her daddy has seen those floaters in the water, too. He watches out for her. He'll let no one do her in.

Juliette Daggle is engrossed in waves of flickering neon. This is how she learned to read in the beginning, in secret. Studying a word's lettering was like looking into unfriendly faces. She remembers *cat* and beside it the picture of a black creature hissing, its fur raised. She remembers the letters tumbling and when the letters righted themselves there was the cat hissing.

"What's that?"

Raoul Daggle has pulled a slip of paper from his pocket. He's reading it up on the steering wheel.

"None of your bizwax."

That words represented actual things had unnerved Juliette at the time. "Oh, that's all they're for!" Until then she believed it was gibberish, gibberish alone, erupting from all those mouths. Fish. And then the cat again hissing, the *fish* swimming, bumping into each other, the hissing cat and the swimming fish madly swirling, and when swirling ceased there was another word, *catfish*.

Amazing.

"The Fall from Heaven priests are having a meeting tonight," Raoul says. "Minnesota chapter."

"Spare me."

"At a place called the Bottom Dollar Inn. No charge."

A small child, not much more than a baby, has his face plastered against the window of the blue Plymouth ahead of them. Raoul has been trying to pass the blue Plymouth and the almost-baby, but they are climbing a long No Passing hill. Raoul wants to pass anyway but they've come in for a long stream of logging trucks, engines grinding at the hard grade. Juliette has been making faces at nearly-a-baby, wanting to see if she can make the infant cry, so far without luck. The near-baby is too thick to realize she hates him, hates their ugly Plymouth, hates the trucks, the road, the woods, hates her father. I do, Daddy, I do. The ugly blue Plymouth has a sign beside the near-baby's face, Handicapped, it says. "The damned truth," she mutters. The boy has showed her his muscles, gone cross-eyed, poked out his fat tongue; he has stood on his head, flapping his teensy wee-wee. He and all she hates has come close to making her cry.

Raoul is riding the Plymouth's tail, patting and repatting the brake because the Plymouth is strictly cruising the legal limit, fifty-five per.

"Beep, Daddy," Juliette says. "Run them off the road."

Raoul beeps. He is on the Plymouth's bumper. They can see the driver looking back, see the alarm plastered over his face.

Then the Plymouth's wheels are rumbling onto the road's shoulder, throwing up gravel, casting the ugly Plymouth within a cloud of yellow dust.

Whish, there they go. "Way cool!" Juliette cries.

Moments later Raoul says, "You get too trapped by meaningless detail. What did that baby have to do with us?"

"I want artichokes for dinner," Juliette says. "I want mussels. Let's say grace now. Let's go prepared."

On the outskirts of a burg called Migraine they see three men hopping by the side of the road. The three men are dressed up as chickens, in suits with actual feathers, wings, tails. The biggest of these three is not actually a chicken, he is a rooster sporting a high red crown; the three are on the road in a brave attempt to halt every car. A fiddler somewhere is playing. A man beside a washtub fitted with strings plunks away. He is another chicken. The chickens wear yellow socks that climb to the knees, immense padding in their behinds, yellow running shoes with painted claws. The chickens are passing out coupons good for one free soft drink for any purchase exceeding five dollars. The town of Migraine, Raoul and Juliette learn, is under siege of a powerful Minnesota Chicken War. The chicken men, and several hundred people of routine appearance, are celebrating the grand opening of Migraine's new Minnesota Chicken Diner. A sign flapping above a cinder-block building conveys that idea: *We Will Eat All the Chickens and When There Are No More Chickens We Will Eat the Eggs*. A Migraine radio station is broadcasting live from a platform erected by the diner's entrance. The radio host is another chicken. He is eating chicken wings as he speaks, telling those people out in radioland how good those wings are. The radio man tells his audience in radioland to hustle butt down. "Shake a leg, Meg. Tiny toddler to grandpa and grandma, hustle butt down. This is a day that will go down in Migraine history," the radio chicken says. He's so excited that Juliette has caught the bug. "It is one for the history books, this latest development in the Minnesota Chicken War, and all you stay-at-homes will have nothing to pass onto your children about your life on planet Earth if you do not . . . hustle butt down. Hidy there, young lady!"

The radio personality is issuing an invitation to Juliette Daggle to step up onto the platform, shoot the breeze with him. Have you ever tongued better chicken? Don't it go down good with that free soda pop? Hustle butt, all you folks, hustle on down. Later today Minnesota Chicken Diner will be giving away to some lucky bird a free console TV courtesy of Migraine TV and Appliances. And that's not all, folks. There's a grand prize, hustle butt down. Take a chance on Minnesota Chicken Diner's lucky draw. Hot dog! An all expense-paid trip to beautiful Hawaii, can you believe that? So drop what you're doing and hustle on down.

"Having fun?"

"Yes sir, this is my first chicken war."

"And what's your name, pretty one?"

"Juliette Daggle."

"Well, folks, here's another live one with shorn hair, practically bald-headed, has hustled butt down."

Juliette likes it up on stage. She likes the bouncy plywood, the frenzy of wires, the host's zealous spiel, likes all the faces smiling up at her, the fiddling chickens and the big rooster's cartwheels on the road. A car out there has hit one of the chickens, a chicken is wounded in action, but no one pays any attention. Feathers swirl in the air above their heads. A greasy lard scum covers every leaf, the air is laden with the smell of frying chicken.

There is Raoul. He is over under a tree talking with considerable animation to a woman who looks exactly like Polly White.

The Polly White woman has a hand on her father's shoulder. She has locked eyes with him and must touch, touch, touch him. Her father is so handsome women cannot resist. The Polly White woman's arms are tight around her father's neck, there, goddam Raoul Daggle, now she's kissing him.

"Now you, little girl," the radio chicken says. He thrusts a mike under her chin. "You look to me like a girl who has come a long way to eat chicken and make your personal contribution to our world-famous Minnesota Chicken War."

"Yes, I have," Juliette says. She's not the least bit on edge, she's in full sync with all these strutting chickens and has a full smile for all those below offering their grinning encouragement. But her father and Polly White are suddenly no longer under the tree, where have they gone?

"My daddy and I," Juliette says into the mike, "are on the road in search of my mother Joyel Daggle. She's run away."

Now isn't that cute! Aren't you the sweetest thing! Let's give this bald-headed youngster a big hand, and you out there in radioland, shuck those traces and hustle on down.

Seconds later someone is lifting her up, pitching her into the air. "You were good," her papa says. "Why didn't you give a description?"

"He snatched the mike away. Where's Polly?"

"Who? What good is a name without a description? Let's go to the car and get those fliers."

"I saw you kissing."

"Now don't go haywire on me."

"Allow me to introduce you to Olga Doss," Raoul Daggle says. "Olga Doss is an enchanting woman of Finnish origin. She instructs in holistic medicines in these parts and is or was—"

"Is," the woman says.

"A professional kickboxer."

Olga Doss, the Polly White lookalike, says, "I am a woman fallen by the wayside. That deejay is such a sexy-looking chicken I could eat him up."

"This Chicken War has been an inspiration to us all," Raoul shouts. He is in the Finnish woman's kitchen mixing martinis. Olga Doss scurries about, scooping up untidy objects from sofas and chairs. Now Olga Doss's eyes are all for the speared olive in her glass. "Where I was?" she asks.

"You were telling Juliette of your childhood in Finland."

"Oh, yah. Was a big grand tree, century's old, one day cut down. Mother claim Father have the treecutter that tree take down to—how you say it?—spite her. Father claim he have nothing to do with the tree's coming down. I say, 'What tree?' I am four years old. They not to speak to each other the next umpteen years."

"Family life can be a terror," Raoul declares.

Juliette oversees this pair with her mouth hanging open. Olga Doss has drained her glass and now she is shoving sofas and chairs to the walls. "Now for me to show you my kickboxer lethal moves," she says.

They are in the living room kicking out at each other, stomping the floor, spinning on toe and heel, yelling the wild cries. All three are dripping with sweat. Olga Doss, Juliette has decided, is a beautiful woman. She has blinding moves. She has wide shoulders, all muscle; she has powerful, wonderful feet. "Balance resides in the tailbone," Olga says. "You must ever know where your tailbone is." It turns out that Olga Doss is able to kickbox and sip a martini simultaneously.

Juliette, kicking, shouting killer threats, cannot recall a time when she's had so much fun.

"I am known as Olga, the Blue Lightning Bolt. Because of my eyes."

Juliette Daggle loves Blue Lightning Bolt, her blue eyes, her great feet. Blue Lightning Bolt is now her mentor.

"Father in Finland was a seaman. We lived in Oulu, it was very cold. In winter, a child, I skied all across the Gulf of Bothnia to Sweden."

"My goodness."

"And back again. My father and little Olga, like you and your father on the road."

"She's been gone nearly a year."

"Only nine percent Finnish land is arable. We make excellent glassware and porcelain."

Juliette Daggle loves Olga Doss. She wishes Olga Doss was her mother.

At Migraine's last traffic light they see, crossing the road, a man Raoul says looks exactly like Albert Einstein. Then he's at their Infiniti with a battered squeegee slapped angrily across the glass.

"I void thee," Albert Einstein says. "Please surrender one dollar."

On the road, Juliette says, "Olga Doss could have been my mother."

"If I had surrendered to temptation," Raoul says, "you might be soon having a sister."

"I saw you kissing."

"Something in her eye."

On the Infiniti backseat, under thick coats, under scarves and socks, maps, shoes, boots, a sorrowful litter of traveling debris, crates of fliers depicting the fugitive, is a slew of postcards sent by Joyel Daggle.

"Read them aloud," Raoul tells his daughter. "I'm in the mood for a good cry."

Juliette reads: "'Ereh erew uoy hsiw.' What does that mean?"

"Wish you were here."

"They all wish we were there. Joyel's a lousy correspondent."

"You set your heights too high. You've got to bend a little, be grateful for each swab of happiness sent your way. Why should mothers be on such a high pedestal? Who says there's room for all of us up there? It's hard being a mother. Imagine going around nine months with that lump. You've got to turn sideways just to get through a door. Your ankles hurt. You suffer hemorrhoids, diarrhea, cramps, dizzy spells. You have hankerings for strange foods. You're carrying something vital in there, alive. It's a considerable responsibility. It can warp a person. So lighten up. Give the woman the benefit of doubt."

"Doubt is no benefit."

"Give it anyway. Suppose you were a child cooped up in that little cave the way she was. Wouldn't you be nuts?"

"She's nuts?"

"Not as much as us, but close."

"Speed up, Daddy. There's a car trying to pass. Suck that crowbait up your exhaust."

"When you and Joyel married," the child asks, "did she wear a white dress?"

"I don't know."

"You don't know?"

"She was wearing something. I got it off her as fast as I could. I think it was white, maybe yellow. I seem to remember yellow panties, stockings. A yellow hat and veil."

"Your own bride and you can't remember?"

"I was blinded by her beauty. By lust. I think I really was blind there for a while. It was like I was moving in yellow circles, in pools of yellow light. I said, 'I do, I do, I do,' and likely still would be saying it had she not pinched my behind. I got my sight back when she pinched me. Then I saw her face behind the yellow veil and sexual appetite whirled up like a blizzard. I was blind again. But I heard her saying, 'I do, I do, I do,' and knew I had to pinch her."

"I know why most brides wear white."

"Keep it to yourself. Then about a year ago Joyel started saying things like, 'You pay no attention to the me that is me.' I took to saying, 'There is no me. *Me* is all of us.'"

"That's some shit you're laying on me, Daddy."

"Let's list the things about Joyel we don't like."

"You first."

"She ran away."

"That's all?"

"All I can come up with."

"She was always giving my toys away to other kids. She gave my favorite doll to Trash. She said, 'Mangle this, please.' I hate her for leaving us."

"Look upon it as her small vacation."

"You can take off, too. I'd be better off."

"Your hair is coming back beautifully, don't you think? It seems more curly somehow. How to explain that?"

The Infiniti hums along, how this Infiniti adores the open road, here comes a little Honda roadster, s2000 for the year that is the same. Now my day is complete, the Infiniti says, those s2000 chicks are mad for sex, look at her swing that tail, what a vixen, here I come, honey.

Juliette sprawls in the soft-leather seat, her eyes closed. It is a beautiful white day. She and Olga are skiing the Gulf of Bothnia from Oulu to Sweden. Joyel and Raoul are two yellow dots far behind them, parents ought not be allowed in this beautiful place.

Juliette has decided she's going to be a good girl. She will be Joyel and Raoul Daggle's good girl. She wasn't a good girl, which is why Mummy left.

"Why are you so morbid?" asks Raoul. "Is it because God's love is a sometime thing?"

Juliette feels her face go hot. She clamps her eyes and mouth tight; she will give this goodness thing one more minute.

She has a friend at school, Teomi Feeolong. Teomi Feeolong likes her hair in long braids, uses lipstick, wears the unfamiliar clothing of those living in a far, far place. Teomi is considered unapproachable by others in the school. She and Teomi often sit hidden in the school bushes discussing their latest suicide attempts. Teomi is an orphan. She had parents once, but they went down into Davy Jones's locker when the boat bringing themselves and Teomi to the New World capsized on the high seas. Teomi rode a plank in the water for days before being rescued by a trawler out where it should not have been, catching illegal fish. The fishermen had to hide her in a hole, Teomi said, or be hit with horrendous fines and possibly shut up in jail for the rest of their lives. They spoke a strange language and laughed riotously as they ran their fingers over her ribs and peered inside her mouth. They fed her rice twice a day. After a while, they began to think of her as a good omen, in that way that fishermen have of turning a thing. They put her in a small rowboat and lowered the boat into the sea. It was night. She could see lights. She was to paddle for those lights, Miami. Miami had been the very destination of her parents when their boat broke apart on the high seas. Teomi thought that was hilarious.

Hilarious? *Hilarious* was not a word Juliette thought appropriate to the situation. But Teomi often came out with the surprising word.

In Miami, her saviors had given her doughnuts and coffee. They'd let her relieve her bladder. All the time in the sea Teomi had not peed once. Teomi had pretended not to understand English. "In general," Teomi said, "it was always best to pretend ignorance when dealing with adults in a strained situation."

In her homeland, Teomi had lived in a palace whose toilets were fitted with gold. She'd bathed in golden pools. But that of course was before the coup. As Teomi understood the matter, locked away in a Swiss bank was the sum of thirty-eight billion dollars which belonged to her alone now that her parents were dead.

"My parents raided the nation's treasury. They salted away hundreds of millions in Swiss banks. That is why I want to die. Why do you? I would not lose a minute's sleep over a triviality such as a mother's desertion. Your energy should go towards helping me. Did you steal the sleeping pills? Did you secure the razor blades? We could jump from a tall building or lay down on railroad tracks. When I am dead you may have all I own. Please arrange to have my body burnt when I am dead. At home the corpse is taken by cart to a special place. The poor people save up for this. It is a very beautiful tradition, I believe. At home now this would not happen to me. At home I am reviled. The people spit when they hear my family's name."

"What?"

What, what, what!

Further on, Raoul stopped the Infiniti by the side of the road in order to snap a few pictures and pour himself a drink. "Stand by that bush," he said, and Juliette stood by the bush. "Eat this apple. Pretend eat." From the bush she watched him stride away, looking for other pictures he wanted to snap. He had in the Infiniti thousands of photographs he'd snapped. His idea was that if he took enough he'd find his wife in the background. The Fall from Heaven priests were in his photo portfolio in abundance. He had snapped a whole roll of Polly White giving her four-corners lecture and of beautiful Olga Doss kickboxing.

"Did you get the chickens?"

"You bet I got the chickens. Joyel will love those."

He had a good shot of Trash lying on the pavement in Hell, Michigan, before she said "Trash?" and Trash got up and followed them inside. He had lots of snaps of scandalized faces in that café in Hell. These photographs documented their year on the road. They were for Joyel's enjoyment once her travels were over.

"I wonder what it's like to be blind and dumb and deaf," her father said. He had come up out of nowhere. He was always doing that, just when Juliette thought she had lost him. "I wonder what it's like to get all your news from vibrations within the earth, like a smedgehog."

She went quickly back to the car. He stayed on. The smedgehog reference has angered her. She doubts such a thing as the smedgehog exists.

He's out there now alone, kickboxing. He can be such an irritation. She wants to cry. She's alone in the world without a mother and one of these days Raoul will be gone also and where will she be then?

When Raoul returns his trouser knee is ripped, blood streams down each cheek. For a second she thinks he has shot himself.

"I tripped."

She snuggles against his shoulder. He pulls her close. They hold each other.

In Juliette'e life at five, before drowning in a cake, a deer had come up and eaten apples from her hand. Doves had hopped upon windowsills. She'd had five-dollar binoculars you could look through and when you were done looking you could eat the binoculars, which were made of licorice. You could even eat the lenses, although it felt funny to do so and fragments wedged between your teeth. When she was five, her birthday, Raoul had presented her with an exploding cigar. Joyel was enraged. Joyel hated practical jokes. Juliette hadn't minded. She liked her black nose. Joyel had given her a music box. When you lifted the top the box sung her name.

A moment ago she had been thinking of her friend, Teomi Feeolong, when her father abruptly said, "How's your friend, Teomi Dingaling?"

"You should learn Latin," her father says. "It is all that is missing in your life."

They are entering Minneapolis. Two dozen roads enter Minneapolis and St. Paul, the twin cities, from every possible direction. It is easy to get lost when there are so many roads to choose from. They have hit the 694 beltway, which betrays them, and are now on Highway 47, apparently heading away from the city whose heart they have not yet penetrated. They are heading north, the direction from which they just came. They don't care. Minneapolis can wait. They are in Anoka

County, shooting into Coon Rapids. "Is it a Sunday?" asks Juliette Daggle.

She asks this for good reason. It must indeed be a Sunday because here they are in Coon Rapids, stopping in the middle of a teeming street. Hordes of people are taking the crosswalk, in no hurry. The First Baptist Church of Coon Rapids sits on one corner of the busy intersection where they find themselves, the First Presbyterian Church of Coon Rapids sits opposite. Every man, woman, and child resident in Coon Rapids, it would seem, has been in attendance at one or the other of these churches. It is noon. The Presbyterians, on the whole, appear the dressier bunch. The competing preachers are bidding worshippers adieu. The church structures are about even on the stained-glass front. The Presbys have more trees. Churchgoers fill the yards and streets, among them a handful of fallen priests, ever under summons of steeple bells, forever lost between heaven and hell. "Look," exclaims Juliette, "there's that old alky with the purple nose, he's waving at us." "Out of primal chaos he came," replies Raoul, "into primal chaos he goes."

Ahead, a pregnant girl in an ill-fitting smock has her thumb hoisted, she wants a ride.

"Thanks," she says. "I guess you can see I'm a single mother-to-be."

A pimply, scrubbed-face boy chases after the Infiniti. He is shouting something dramatic but unintelligible.

"Don't stop," the girl says. "I've seen enough of that son of a bitch."

Dawn comes. Later it goes. The day wanes.

9

DAY, NIGHT, WANING MOONS

WE HAVE ARRIVED at a time where goodness prevails and evil is the carpet we wipe our shoes on before entering that Parnassus where goodness resides. Even so:

Joyel Daggle can walk into almost any room and the energy she finds there astounds her. She crumples to her knees at times, and, your thoughts to the contrary, she isn't faking. Energy pours from the paint on the walls. It pours from the window glass, the casings, the heating unit, the bed and tables, chairs, TV, the carpet on the floor. Oh, that carpet! All those footsteps, the heavy bodies, the flow of feet back and forth, the lives that carpet has absorbed. Enough! Enough! The carpet, the walls, the glass want their revenge. The lights sit moody there, hissing their rancor: Oh, just wait. Any minute now some busybody will be flicking our switch.

A fire poker in 1824 got so fed up it jumped up and cracked a man's noggin. It flew through the house and whapped the husband on the behind, then broke his neck in two swings. Then it hastened up the stairs to the nursery where children were crying.

The poker did this its own self. The deeds are fully recorded in *The Omaha Annals of Nature's Bizarre and Outrageous Crimes*, a book Carter stuck into Joyel's rucksack when she departed Orick, California.

Oh, there's mention of a becrazed governess who indeed was beheaded for the crime, but don't you believe it.

The poker did it. Or the light switch does it. Or the carpet. The glass can shatter and pierce your neck. The paint from the walls can slide down and smother you.

The plants can.

The bird in the cage would, only it is so small. It can get you only in the long run, by infliction of disease. Its little stools, the mites within its feathers, the sediment between its claws, only your cat is immune and not the cat always.

You know about gas in a room, asbestos in the walls, what they can do. But do you know about vinegar? Do you know about salt and sugar and tins on the shelf, about meats in the meat tray or the vegetables in theirs?

Every room is a killer, that's what Joyel Daggle is saying to herself.

That's the one practical advantage of mating. With two people, the room shuts up. The goods hang in there, waiting to catch you alone.

That morning in the Best Western, tribute to Raoul that she's hanging her hat in one, Jane Dearborne's car parked in another place, she hears a rattling at the door, in the instant is zipping for the preexamined exit, a bathroom window, when she hears a female voice saying, "Room service, I not got all day."

She sleeps through the balance of morning, wakes, scrubs her teeth, showers, grabs a bite, and by noon is on the road again.

The First Nations people, the New Indian, the priests fallen from heaven were very beautiful flying on their bungee cords at Chief Crazy Horse Falls. There the New Indian is now, his rig pulled over by a traffic cop, well I'll be damned, what a small world.

The rain in Orick, California, was unlike anything Joyel had ever seen. Night and day it poured and by the third day the strip-logged ridges and valleys of the Weitchpec Mountains of the Coast Range were pouring onto Orick and environs a sea of mud. The mud streamed over Orick's windswept spruce, the dwarf evergreens and scrub, inundated and covered the massive tangle of vines through which for years wild goats had cut a low maze of intricate, seemingly endless trails. The mud took with it cabins and homes alike, it dislodged and took away into the angry ocean the hamlet's gas bar and video, a restaurant by the lagoon, the Trailer Stop, the sawmill, Bud's Fix-it Shop, it swept away untold automobiles, bicycles, wheelbarrows, thousands of pounds of debris, logging machinery from operations high in the Wiechapec, it took away logs and stumps, the animals in its path, nesting fields, a three-mile span of the famous old Highway 101, the odd man and woman, too, and all of these it dumped into the angry sea.

And still the rains came, twelve days, fifteen, twenty, no end in sight, high-grounders waked on beds adrift in mud, look from your window and all to be seen were miles and miles of flowing mud, the Wiechapec denuded, lifestock and people and birds alike all on their way into the angry sea. One came and went by poled plank float, by rowboat, instinct, foolishness, daring, as National Guard helicopters dropped parcel after parcel of rations, these too by and large destined for the angry sea.

"What is Esther recuperating from?" Joyel asked her friend Carter.

"Life," said Carter.

With few except Joyel's high cabin surviving the flood, come evening Carter and Esther lay on a damp mattress on the other side of the room's dividing blanket, there whispering to each other until sleep claimed them.

"What progress is she making?"

"None yet."

For a time Joyel feigned a jealousy, then came to realize the jealousy had taken root. No one had the remotest interest in her own recuperation. But did this matter, because they were all going to be claimed by the rain, the mud, the angry sea.

The rain still poured and more and more of the Wiechapec drifted out to the angry sea. One cold wet evening Joyel yanked down the blanket partition, she said to the shivering lovers, "Get in my bed." Their arms wrapped around one another, they coiled together like snakes, they slept a warm sleep side by side and when one turned over, so did the other two.

On the twenty-seventh day the heavens relented.

Half-drowned gulls passed in silent rage over the mud sea, eagle, cormorant, and hawk kept vigil from bleak outpost among barren trees.

One wet day they saw an unidentifiable creature out across the mud's horizon. It was a large bespectacled man in a brown suit laboring over a pole, a cigarette in his mouth, the raft, the man, the pole, and the cigarette slowly drawing near.

"Who is it?"

"Unidentifiable."

Joyel's heart took flight. It was the son of bitch coming for her.

"Carter, where's your rifle?"

"Won't do you any good, it's rusted. Are you going to shoot him?"

"Yes, I am."

The figure was sometimes there and sometimes not. He was poling close to shore, not a son of a bitch accustomed to the Wiechapec's wild ways. Up the Wiechapec incline were swooshing streams, rivulets, mud slides large and small, rock and boulder unloosened by torrential rains.

Carter and Esther shouted warnings, but who could hear?

Here it came and there the son of a bitch went.

"We are all recuperating," Carter said. "We are not reliable witnesses. Was that man there or was he not there?"

Driving through Mud Butte Joyel decides to find a phone booth. She roots out quarters from the bottom of her purse, she must call Jane Dearborne, must do so now.

She picks up the phone, her quarter poised to drop, and discovers a conversation already in progress. Two women with hard singsongy voices chatting about someone's hair.

"I wouldn't let Arnold touch my hair for all the money in the world," one is saying. "Dorothy only goes to him because she thinks he has a crush on her. He tells her she has the prettiest boobs in all creation. Dorothy adores talk like that. She's pretty sure he wears an instrument of some kind, you know, down in that area."

"To make him big?"

"I suppose so. Men are so worried about that."

"What? The size of their apparatus?"

Joyel hangs up. She wants to make this call. An urgent need to do so has whisked in from the blue, overtaken her. She has alternating visions of Jane Dearborne. In one Jane is by her phone, sipping the Bristol Cream she loves, waiting for this call; in the other she sees Jane in a hospital bed, face puffy, eyes black and blue, her every limb in plaster.

She snatches the phone up. The women are still talking. "I have an emergency here," she says. "Please get off the line." The voices pause only a second, then chat on. "They have their own agenda," one is saying. "They refuse to cooperate with anyone. They are terribly antisocial, which I believe must go back to something their parents did to them."

"They are everywhere, aren't they?" the other says. "They are underfoot, like acorns. Well. Not this time of the year."

"Forgive me, dear, I believe a very rude person is on the line."

The receiver emits a crackling noise. Joyel jiggles the mounting, the cracking subsides. She shoves a quarter through the slot. It rattles about for an uncommonly long time. She shakes the receiver. There is no dial tone.

Poor Jane Dearborne. Human beings should be fitted with black boxes like those airplanes carry in the event of disaster. *This is what happened to me.*

In Mud Butte a man wearing a deerstalker hat read a book the entire time he was filling her car with gas. He didn't look at her, the tank, the gas nozzle. He was unaware of the severity of her gaze as she cleaned insects from the windshield. When she asked where the rest room might be found he shrugged a shoulder in the presumed direction. He did not look at the dollars she offered in payment. She, the car, the gas hose, all in his realm except the world within his book, were invisible.

Approaching Lebanon, she sees a burning house. A man and a woman stand embracing near the fire truck rushed in to fight the blaze, around the woman's shoulder a shawl made of the most exquisite fabric Joyel has ever seen, a jiva that mirrors exactly the many hues of the burning house.

Entering Seneca, she has her third antelope sighting, antelope or deer. A deer, let's say, as earlier we agreed we would and also because this is obviously the same animal that revealed itself when her car stalled near Crazy Horse Falls. The deer lopes alongside, then ahead of her, paying no heed to Seneca's many traffic lights, pausing now and then to nibble moss from the occasional tree or rip away a mouthful of leaves.

The deer stays with her through Faulkton, Rockham, Zell, and Flying Horse Pass. Uplifting though this is, it is with difficulty that Joyel keeps her eyes open, bad weather looms, her shoulders creak like old flooring, the car is an icebox, she has cramps, a headache, her hair feels like steel wool, a child is only granted a short childhood and one year of Juliette's has been missed entirely, on the phone Juliette sounds like an adult, no blessing is that, she never giggles as a girl is supposed to, they should have been kinder to Trash, God knows what madness Raoul is teaching the poor child, Joyel is a year older herself but has she truly recuperated, is she still in recovery, if she has recovered, what magical wand has engineered this amazing feat, and as for that, other than ennui, apathy, asthma, anemia, chapped lips, pill-popping, insomnia, flaky nails, earwax, flat feet, an occasional discomfort in the urinary tract, stupidity, pronounced deficiencies in the kitchen, an obsession with tidiness, a neurotic temperament, the son of a bitch behind her, a marriage that wasn't one hundred percent the rosy ideal, a baggy fanny, falling breasts, fat thighs, cracks and fissures in the sternum, other than believing life was the pits, Daggle Estates a sanctimonious version of hell, other than this and the malaise generally afflicting nearly everyone, aside from these trifles, what was it a year ago that had spiked her tea, set her footloose and fancy free upon the grueling road?

A man fishing from the bridge spanning the Mud River in Redfield shouts at Joyel, "Your muffler is dragging." Tears immediately flow, a year on the road taking hard knocks and the smallest remark still can make her bones go limp as a dishrag.

In Caviar near Sidewinder Gulch the man in the diner drawing Joyel's mug of coffee tells her he is doing so with a heavy heart.

"Hip-hip," she says. She isn't in the mood, she must toughen up, which means resisting the allure of another's life tragedies, because you will then be reduced to a wet spot on the floor.

Over the grill is a hand-lettered sign, BROTHERS AND SISTERS, WHAT HAVE YOU DONE TODAY IN AID OF HUMANITY?

"May I use your phone?"

"Long or local?"

She's gobbling down one of the man's hamburgers, wondering at the apple pie under glass.

Jane Dearborne isn't home.

She dials Carter, no reply.

"You want to talk to someone," the counterman says, "I'm available."

The next second Joyel's mind has gone blank. She sees a swirling phone, the counterman's cloudy face; she's inside spinning, then she's tumbling.

"How long was I out?"

"Two minutes."

She's on the floor, her head cushioned. The hum of coolers, the tick of a clock, vibrating walls.

"Who is that drumming above us?"

"My wife. She's been sick a long time. Now she's recuperating."

"What is her illness?"

"Undiagnosed as yet," replies the counterman, on his face a pained expression as the fates have booked him for a long cruise not to his liking.

"I'm sorry."

"While in the hospital she fell in love with those green smocks they make you wear. She'd strip naked, have me bring home the smocks under my coat. The nursing staff thought it was wild, how she kept being found naked. It was a mystery to them how those smocks kept disappearing. 'Has the nudie been given her codeine?' they'd say. That's kind of cute, don't you think?"

Joyel laughs, she is feeling better now. It was starving herself, then belting back all those greasy burgers, sometimes eating is a luxury best avoided.

"Do you know how many of those green gowns she's got now?"

"How many?"

"Eighty-nine. Fifty years we've been married. By each other's side every minute."

"Has she always been a drummer?"

Joyel can hear the drumming quite clearly, a full set, snares, bass, cymbals, this caviar wife could be the Caviar Marching Band.

"I had the drums waiting as a surprise when she came home. I figured it might be good recuperative practice. She accompanies the big bands, she really gets hopping."

"She's hopping now."

"Yeah. They give her one month." He bangs on the wall, "Rock, Mama, down and dirty!" he calls.

Mama, upstairs, is rocking.

"Go on up. My wife loves a friendly face."

"If you want to sing along," the dying woman in her green smock shouts as Joyel comes through the door, "just push that karaoke button."

Onida and Doesmore beckoned. Blunt, Harrold, Holabird, Highmore. Suddenly it was morning. It had been morning for some time but for Joyel its awareness arrived as slow revelation. Wafts of smoke billowed up occasionally from the car hood. The muffler clanked and roared. Drivers were honking, more than one party shouted, "Get that trap off the road!"

Highmore, hours along, Joyel sipping a coffee that inflamed her lips. Three teenage girls in red silk pajamas occupied a corner booth. They were laughing uproariously at everything. They were having a sleepover. One of the girls' mother owned the restaurant. The girls were showing off for a trio of boys seated in an opposite booth. Their fingers were often at work on the pajamas' buttons. Now and then one of the girls flipped the cloth free of a breast. Then the second girl would, and the third. Then they'd hoot.

The boys were gigglers, too young for them.

Each girl had before her a dish of soft ice cream. They were dipping their fingers into the ice cream, sucking those fingers slowly, laughing and heaving themselves about, then when the boys could stand it no more, the three simultaneously exposing a breast.

The boys died. They were not boys deserving of such fine girls.

Joyel was on the phone.

She had been on the phone nearly fifteen minutes and the woman whose phone it was, was beginning to twitch. The restaurant keeper had the sagging shoulders, the wearied face, of a single mother.

Carter's dossier was rich with news. Esther, he reported, was fully recovered, her period of dementia, her long year of recuperation, had reached its end, and now she was going to become a forest ranger and live in one of those towers.

"That's wonderful, Carter."

"She's over the moon. It turns out that being a ranger has always been her secret quest. She loves those green uniforms they wear, and I love her, did I tell you? You were the first to spot it, I can't wait for us to have our babies. How are you, did you hear about their finding the dead man?"

Joyel had made the call a collect one, she could see the nickels flying. I'm innocent, she thought, what dead man? The three girls were in a sedate mood now, combing and arranging each other's hair, impervious to the stricken boys.

"The girls at Eureka Escorts are devastated, they baked Esther a goodbye cake, it was extraordinarily moving. Do you know there was a detective guy out here asking all kinds of questions about you? He'd heard, you know, that we'd had one of those three-party things going, what you call it, something à trois."

"Oh, that would be Solly. I know about him, he's in my husband's hire."

"You're married? Jeez, such tight lips."

"I've been a woman in exile. What else, Carter?"

"Jane is in Eureka General, all beat up. You couldn't have saved her, Joy, it was her ex. There was another fella here, too, guy in a brown suit, spectacles, hell, you got the whole world looking you up."

It is so hard getting out of South Dakota, as so many have discovered. South Dakota has Harney Peak, over seven thousand feet high, that's pretty high. There are many high buttes and peaks in South Dakota, more than you can shake a stick at, Bear Mountain Lookout (7,166), Signal Hill (6,483), for instance. But Harney gets the nod. Harney is over Rapid City way, in the Black Hills; too bad Joyel Daggle won't be going that direction. Fine coffee beans undoubtedly can be grown on Harney Peak, you'd think at least one of South Dakota's 700,000 people would have tried it. Joyel's crate can't manage the climb; on level land it huffs and puffs; it strains, it overheats, it shudders, it emits a funnel of black oil on the mildest grade. This is Crazy Horse Country. This is Badlands Country, Custer Country. The Standing Rock reservation, Cheyenne, Pine Ridge reservation, they cover nearly a fourth of the state. A town called Little Town on the Prairie is somewhere in South Dakota, too bad her overheating chariot can't take her to these places, perhaps another time.

Here she is coming into Box Elder, S.D., just imagine.

At a gas bar in Box Elder she asks of the woman working the cubicle, "Do you sell pillows? South Dakota pillows?" She and the woman fall into conversation, marriage the topic. "The something borrowed at my wedding was my husband. Honey, the directions are printed right on the tank." Joyel is having trouble with Jane Dearborne's bank card. The machine time and time again spits the card out; it flashes an urgent message, with three exclamation points: *Take your card!!!* It puts Joyel in a panic to think what might happen if the card is not yanked out quickly enough. Her hair might catch fire. Someone might shoot her, rip off her clothes. The gas nozzle is in her tank, her hand pressing the handle; yet the numbers refuse to budge. Life has got so complicated. You have to be a child to know how anything works.

Start over!!! the machine says, what a laugh, that's my life, she tells the spitting machine.

Joyel gets no more than two blocks and the car shudders, shimmies, halts. She grinds, grinds away, but the car won't go.

Joyel cries, she whimpers, she pleads, and when she tries again the motor still won't kick over. Whistling sounds, fizzing, muted gunshots, the car is dead.

She kicks a tire the way she's seen so many other people do, she peers under the hood, her shoulders sag, God does so love the world.

An old man, his head and hands enormous, with great bushy brows that remind Joyel of waving palm fronds, sugarcane fields aswirl in wind, says to her, "I was not put on this earth to do good deeds. I was put on this earth to make money and my wife was put here to spend it."

Eubanks of Eubanks Fix-it is the man saying this. He's a kidder. He's not taking her dire straits seriously. Eubanks Fix-it, he explains, deals only with lawn mowers, with "implements of strategic importance to the home gardener." He does not fix cars. He has never come near another person's car, has never sat in any automobile unless out of extreme provocation. He has ridden in a streetcar once, in San Francisco, California, in the old days, and that was quite an experience, though not one to be repeated.

"So you will just have to go elsewhere for your repairs," he says. "I'd suggest Thruway for the muffler, since that's the one muffler outfit we got here in town. But Thruway is not open on a Sunday, which day this is, and they will be no more impressed by that five dollars you're waving about than I am. What's wrong with that vehicle anyway? you ask. Old age, disease, a failure in the kidneys, I'd say, just like me. I'd say that car is fit for the graveyard. One of my lawn mowers would offer a gal more driving comfort."

"I'm a woman in distress," Joyel tells him.

"You're dying, that's distress. No sir, car trouble is only a little blip along life's road. Don't blip your eyes at me, young lady, I'm immune to the womanly influence. I'll look at it, that's all I'm promising."

Joyel could see the second it was that Eubanks got interested. He crawled under the car, she dropped to her heels to watch. He touched a pipe and the pipe disintegrated. It fell onto his face as dust. He touched other spots and more rust, rot, and mud fell. The entire suspension of her car was about to go, he said. All that was holding up her seats, her transmission and gearbox, her engine, seemed to be a layer of foot-deep mud.

"It's caked hard, that mud. It's turning to stone. But even stone mud is not Super Glue."

"Yes," she said. "But can you fix it?"

Old Eubanks laughed. He looked about at the earth and sky. He scratched his bald head and hooked both thumbs under his belt.

"My wife will tell you Eugene Eubanks can fix anything put on this earth except her rheumatism and the national debt. Now she'll have to add your car. No, I can't fix that heap, nor could Jesus Christ Almighty fire up this job, it's a waste of time trying. But this is California mud, you say? I've never seen a car held together by mud. I guess I could weld in a few rods. I might find an old muffler. Ain't never an engine defeated me yet."

"How long would it take?"

"Three weeks. Yes, yes, I know, you're in a hurry."

Joyel had lunch with Opus Eubanks while her husband worked on the vehicle. They lived in a house to the side of the shop.

The house seemed to be made almost entirely of grasses, leaves, twigs, one and another of nature's friendly fibres. The floor was mossy, spongy to the foot. The ceiling was composed of blue-green bottles held aloft by a clever crisscrossing of beams out of which strange plant forms grew, many in bloom. The place smelled of vanilla extract. Opus explained that she had been baking.

"We had moles visit us in June," Opus said, announcing this with considerable pride.

The walls were of earth. Out of this stacked earth grew vigorous grasses, these grasses perfectly trimmed, Joyel saw.

"Irrigated and fertilized from within," Opus said. "It attracts snakes, sometimes, but they are mostly harmless. Sit right down."

Joyel sat.

Opus served iced tea. The tea was of a kind Joyel had not previously tasted.

"Will you have more?"

Joyel did.

"Where are you going in your wounded vehicle?" Opus asked.

"Home," she said. She blushed. It was Opus's joy at her own strange home that forced this lie to her lips.

Joyel was suddenly crying.

"Tell me your story, darling," the old woman said. "You'll feel much relief getting it off your chest."

When Joyel finished relating her story she was wrung out. She had wrapped into the tale a good part of Jane Dearborne's tragic life, Doodoo's harrowing marriage with Vern at Daggle Estates, her old babysitter Nancy's story of the fabulous aerialists Ceyx and Halcyone, the dying smock woman's tale, her deer or antelope, the daredevil flying of the New Indian, the First Nations people, and the fallen priests at Crazy Horse Falls, an incident on Mars beheld in a dream, the woman with a silver cup on a beach in Florida, the terrible flu virus suffered by purple pansies on the pretty dress sent to her daughter on her birthday, various grave (alleged) episodes not mentioned in this document *The Fall of Gravity* but having to do with a bespectacled son of a bitch in a brown suit on her trail, not to mention other exploits and terrors, real and imagined, experienced by her during this year on the road away from her beloved husband and child.

"You stretch out on this cot, dear," Opus said. "Let me take your shoes off, let me put this warm compress over your brow. There, that's the ticket, have yourself a good cry and soon we will be as good as new. All my life," Opus said, "I have demanded the extraordinary of love, I have demanded a great love, and I see no reason why you should not. Thank goodness my Eugene has been up to the task. I am sure your Raoul and the lovely Juliette will do no less."

Then Opus told Joyel of their own great misfortune. "We have a daughter, too. Our Katarina is out in the dark world. Her absence has broken our hearts. It would give us great peace of mind if she came home, if only for a visit. We worry sometimes that it was our strange ways that drove her off."

"How long ago did your daughter leave?"

"Close by one full year. Yes, one full year it will be next week. There's not been a day we've not longed for her return nor smote ourselves black and blue."

After the exchange of tales they sat drinking tea in yellowing china, eating strange sandwiches of some vegetarian variety, their knees touching, the two women often laughing and, more frequently, wiping away unbidden tears.

Eugene Eubanks repaired Jane Dearborne's car with such exactitude that the engine and its exhausts emitted barely a murmur.

Sitting under the wheel, Joyel sensed enormous power. He had fixed the heater, the radio, the door, he had installed, he said, a pleasant voice which would address her intimately at the first indication of impending wrong.

"I feel so grateful," she told the happy pair.

He had painted the car a grassy green.

"The paint isn't yet dry," he said. "But that's no great matter."

Over the paint he had sprinkled a thick turf of yeast, earth, precious seedlings, a nectar of his own devising that would keep the new roots moist and juicy. Already, a mossy yellow growth was taking root and the car from front to rear exuded a scent remindful of spring. Joyel loved it.

"If you run into anything that's ours," Eugene said, meaning their lost daughter, "kindly point it homewards."

Joyel felt wonderful. She had napped in the runaway Katarina's bed. She had washed. She had freshened her face, draped herself in new clothes, put on lipstick, scented herself with unknown oils. She had eaten well and constantly. She had Opus's cake in a box, tied in a yellow bow. Dangling from her left wrist was a hammered silver bracelet Opus said had come down in the family from Teutonic times and a pair of soft white leather shoes such as a baby might wear had been hooked over the rearview mirror above a carpet of living grass.

The pair trotted alongside at the open window as she departed.

"Here I go in my beautiful machine!" Joyel cried.

"Watch that buggy, for she will fly!"

She blew kisses, they blew theirs, there she went.

Commonplace language is a language usually reserved for realistic novels, for the life under siege, who knows why, nor does Joyel Daggle know why at this moment she feels like singing, feels like breaking loose in a brand-new manner, realistically speaking, yes, that is how she feels, the song comes and her musical notes soar over the fields, there is the deer once again loping alongside, I was dead now I am alive, I was entombed and now I am not, I sang false notes and then they were not, I loved but I did not, I would but I could not, I will because I am, I must because I should, I will because of them, because which of us will, let us kneel to our Buddha, let us sing for there is air, let us break bread where there is none, let us bathe in the pool and shout at each other our foreign names, let us slay the demons, let us . . .

10

advanced biogenetics

"GIVE ME A SIP OF YOUR DRINK, Papa. You said I could sip, but now you're not letting me. Watch that car, Papa. You don't want to put a scratch on this Infiniti."

"You're absolutely right, daughter. You have said a wise thing. Here, have your sip. You've earned it."

"Thank you. Watch out, Papa!"

"I'm watching."

"I'm your little navigator. I'm your right-hand girl."

"Yes, you are. You're my both-handed girl."

"Stop swerving, stay in your lane. Watch that light. You don't want me taking away your license, do you? Well, you'd better begin acting with some responsibility. Where are we going, Papa, why are we leaving the highway?"

"To the tennis courts. We've got to work on that serve of yours."

"It's wimpy, isn't it? I've got the wimpiest serve of any person alive."

"Throw the ball higher. Stop crying when you throw up the ball. You can't see the ball for all of those tears."

"You're right. This time I won't cry. This time I'm going to kill you. I'm going to leave you flat-footed every time."

"That's the spirit."

"I get all my spirit from you, Papa. You're my spirit."

"You were born in a roomful of screaming babies. Did I tell you that?"

"Maybe you told me."

"I'd say a minimum fifty women were in that room. Babies were being born right and left. An open room, no curtains, screaming babies. It was how the hospital was doing things that year. I think you were the forty-ninth to be born. All girls. It was fifty to zip on the gender front, that night of the screaming babies."

"The number on my tennis jersey!"

Her father slammed on the brakes. He spun the wheel, bumped up over the curb. Cars honked their horns, whizzing past. He snatched open the recessed box between their seats. He tied a cloth over his mouth. Tied another over his eyes.

"Who am I?" he asked.

"Pope Pious XII!"

"Why am I Pope Pious XII?"

"You're turning a blind eye to the Nazis' murder of Jews. You've shut your mouth."

He unfolded across the seats to give her a big embrace. "You're my big and bright girl," he said. "You're the apple of your father's eye! Open your hand. I'm going to read the future in your palm before we go another mile."

The child loved it when her daddy read her palm.

He envisioned such extraordinary occurrences. Everything he had ever read there had come true. They had come true even more fantastically than he predicted.

"Yours, too, Papa! Let me read yours."

"No way, José! I died."

"You didn't die. I won't let you."

"I passed away when Joyel left me. I wasn't looking where I was going and suddenly I wasn't going anywhere anymore."

"You're making that up. Only a part of you died. You're a fraud."

"Before I was married and had you, strange companions helped me make it through the night. The strangest one of all was a twenty-three-year-old Scientologist from Omaha, Nebraska. Do you know her name?"

"Jane Doe."

"Look, there's a boy hitchhiking. Let's give that boy a ride. Maybe the two of you will fall in love."

"I am already *in* love. I have all the *in* love I need."

"Oh, there's always room for more. Take myself. There's always room for more so long as I have you beside me singing."

They pick up the boy. He is nineteen. His name is Otis James McKinley. He is on his way home to visit his sweetheart in Winnipeg, Canada. Winnipeg, the boy claims, is Canada's second-best city "after, after . . . after whatever another person would say is the continent's utopia." The boy is in training to be a long-distance trucker. He will be driving one of those sixteen-wheelers whose rubber you always see littering the highways. Once he has his diploma, he and his sweetheart are getting married. They will live in Winnipeg, Canada. He can't wait. He wants children and so does his sweetheart. They are going to name the first one Otis James McKinley, Jr.

Take my word for it, there will be much to pay for this "second-best" business. An author is accountable for every word issuing from any mouth, such is spelled out in their contracts, thank goodness, too, for otherwise who knows what rubbish might appear.

"Otis," said Raoul. "Now here's a conundrum for you."

"Huh?"

"Papa doesn't really mean 'conundrum,'" the child said. "He's only going to ask you a question."

The boy said, "In that case, okay. I thought he said 'condom.'"

"No, he said 'conundrum.'"

"Okay. I'm in."

"Otis," said her father, "here you are going home to your sweetheart. Suppose we had an accident. Suppose we all were taken to a hospital. Suppose two of us died. And suppose you got to choose which two it was that died. Which would you choose?"

"I don't know you two," the boy sensibly said. "I'm only along for the ride. I'd choose me as the one to escape."

"Good. Now suppose God was to choose. Which one of us would he choose to live?"

"That's hard."

"Yes, it is."

"Is God in a good mood or a bad mood?"

"We don't know."

"Am I supposed to say which I *think* God ought to choose? If so, I'd have to say me again."

"Good. Suppose we were all carted off to the hospital and two of us died and the hospital wouldn't release the third until he or she paid the bill for all three."

"They couldn't do that. The little girl here, your daughter, she's what? Nine, ten? So they couldn't expect her to pay. And I'm nineteen, not even in my first job, so they can't hit me for it, they can't expect me to pay a stranger's bill. That's what I'd tell them."

"How about this? How about they tell you Blue Cross has got everything covered?"

"Great! Yeah, that's groovy. Wow!"

"But how about they tell you our bodies must be released to your keeping? They'll ship our bodies, wherever you say, but you can't be released yourself without signing for our bodies."

"I'd say they are crazy. I don't even know your names, so I'm not signing for any bodies."

"Why not? You like us, don't you? We're giving you a free ride, aren't we?"

"Yeah. But bodies, that's something else. My parents would kill me, I signed for the bodies of perfect strangers. Jesus, I might even have to postpone my wedding."

"How about there was a plus in this for you? How about you didn't know this until now, but it turns out I'm an extremely wealthy man. A millionaire. So now you've got our bodies and you won't release these bodies to our kith and kin until they fork over a fistful of money from the estate."

"'*Kith*' is stupid," the girl said. "Associated with *couth*, also stupid."

"That's like a payoff, right? They pay me, your family can have the bodies? I wouldn't do that. I'd give the bodies to them for free. I've got a 'how about' for you. How about I'm nineteen. I got my whole future in front of me. I'm going to drive those big trucks, marry, raise a beautiful family. When I'm old, then I'll deal in dead bodies. Now here's another 'how about' for you. How about we close this subject? Your daughter here is what, nine or ten? Frankly—frankly—I wouldn't submit any child of mine to your 'how abouts.' Fact is, I hate your goddam 'how abouts.' I think I want to get out. I don't want to ride with you anymore."

"Good," said Raoul. "That's really good. You're a fine young man. Isn't he, Juliette?"

"I've never seen better."

Later on, the boy dropped off, her papa said, "What grade would you give that boy?"

"I give him a C."

"Not a B-plus?"

"He was just ordinary, Papa."

"You won't even consider a B-plus?"

"No."

"You grade hard. You're a tough cookie. You've missed your big chance. You could have sat up beside him in the cab on those long hauls, shifting the gears for him. You could eat at truck stops, I know you like truck stops. You could be a beautiful mother, have a potful of McKinley babies. I could come visit you, bounce them on my knees, what other reason do I have to live."

"Drop it, Papa. You're flogging a dead horse."

Grow up, she thought.

"Cut Bank is just around the corner," he said. "A few thousand miles, that's nothing."

Oh, Papa, Papa, Papa! . . . We are lost and abandoned, wayfarers cast adrift, afloat in uttermost sorrow.

Raoul Daggle, forty, in a motel room somewhere in Minnesota this present moment, startled Juliette in the middle of the night with a scream. He lay sprawled within a sea of rumpled sheets, in heavy sweat, his eyes disbelieving.

"What, what, what!"

"Dammit to hell!"

"What?"

"She's sleeping with someone. I could feel it, I wasn't dreaming. Here I was in bed, she's there beside me, a surprise in itself, then I hear this strange hick voice saying, 'Move over.' I hear myself saying, 'I'm not moving, you move.' Your mother says,

'Would you two please hash this out another time. Would one of you please get down to business?' Suddenly there's this guy in a yellow nightshirt crawling over me. He's rooting out a spot beside her. The next thing I know they are—well, how can I say this to a child?—they are tumbling about together."

God in heaven, what a child must put up with.

"Who is that dead man found in the mud? That's what I'm wondering. Who has your mother murdered this time?"

"You take that back," the child screams. "Take it back this minute or I'm jumping from the car. My mother is not a killer."

She opens the car door. Wind whirls, spray shoots up from the highway. A red alarm on the Infiniti dash beeps insistently, Door open, Door open, a voice warns. Raoul, fist clenching the girl's collar, has swerved off the road. In another second they will be jumping the ditch, plowing through a stand of diseased elm, mowing down a soybean field.

This having been said, the gruesome wreckage imminent and ever the dreadful possibility of a loss of lives, broken bones, crippling accident that might ever after demote our subject's quality of life, we should be aware that Raoul Daggle has not for a moment taken seriously this report by his investigator Solly of a man washed up in the mud in Orick, California. Such a corpse may indeed exist in Orick's mud, likely does, but his husband's brain finds it inconceivable that anyone so wily, so slippery of foot, so blessed with the power of invisibility as Joyel Daggle, would ever have to resort to killing a man. As a matter of fact, this husband's irateness at Joyel is altogether disconnected from dead men, is instead directed solely by a thought which pinged across his brow minutes ago and which is this moment still pinging there as the Infiniti jounces over furrows in the aforementioned soybean field. Dead men, no, it's the living male, all raunchy as the dickens, who makes his stomach churn. In the year since Joyel deserted the family compound Raoul Daggle has invented an army of these macho devils, each more vibrant and sexy than People magazine's Sexiest Man on Earth. What dishonor, therefore, if he submits to the clutch of desire for that enchantress Olga, that exotic flower, Lavender, or basks in the radiance of, the unparalleled wizardry of, that seductress Polly White. Marry all of them, why not, like that old shit in *The House of the Hanging Lanterns*. What harm there, put the issue to old Vern, see what he thinks.

I'm at the end of my rope, I'm done with Joyel Daggle, let her go climb flagpoles.

It is all a ruse to assuage his guilt. Raoul now nightly is telephoning either Polly White or Olga the kickboxer, usually both. He wonders whether he isn't a tad smitten with now one, now the other, perhaps both simultaneously, plus hooked on dynamic Lavender, because sometimes a whole hour will pass during which he hasn't thought of Joyel once. At other times, when he believes he is thinking of Joyel, Polly White or Olga, and now Lavender, will prance into his mind wearing a white Armani suit, frequently the trio arrives together, they say, *Take us, fool*, or they say nothing, they disrobe, they wait for him in bed, each with a big grin, they say, *Come and get us, you big beautiful stallion*. Often at such times Juliette intercepts this vision, she will say, "Why are you smiling, what on earth can you be happy about?" And when next he looks the bed is empty, no woman in an Armani suit or otherwise is within a thousand miles, and never will be, because he's become an old irritable bastard, with gray in his beard and what looks suspiciously like the inroads of a potbelly, plus he has rings under his eyes and is beginning to reach for another gin even as he has an unfinished one in the reaching hand.

Beyond this, he is also wondering whether Olga the kick-boxer might not be talked into taking on the job of recreational director at Daggle Estates. After all, they have there the sports complex with its weights room, bowling alleys, swimming pools, tennis courts, badminton courts, spa courts, the new eighteen-hole golfing facilty, all of which until now he has been managing, or forgetting to manage, himself. He figures a cool one hundred thou, an automobile only slightly less grand than a Lamborghini, may win her over. Three beautiful women on his team, Polly, Olga, and Lavender Blue, how can he lose? He has to look after himself, dammit, and the presence at Daggle of these exotic supremes, each apparently available, will help salvage his damaged ego, even save him, should, as more and more seems likely, his runaway wife never return. Period of recovery, my ass. Recovery from what?

It isn't just the women, however. He is getting more and more intrigued by this idea of establishing a center of some kind at the Daggle for all those wayward, dejected sojourners from the faith, the priests who have fallen from heaven. The main holdback to this plan is that they are such an utterly useless bunch. He can't figure what they would do with themselves, short of spending their remaining time on earth concocting a foolproof scheme for doing away with Vern. But if they rub out Vern, then police are apt to be swarming all over the place, disturbing Juliette here in her formative years. So this idea is not one he wants to go into without the deepest scrutiny.

"How you doing, Papa?" the child asks. "Are you hanging loose?"

"Listen," Raoul says. "The simple greeting, 'How are you?' is the bravest of questions. 'Fine,' the most courageous of answers. Lives alter, often totally, on the basis of such flimsy exchanges. Without these civilities our entire culture would flounder. So, no, to answer your question, I am not 'hanging loose.' I am 'fine.' I am 'fine and dandy,' so please don't ask me a second time."

"Jeez, such a grouch you are this morning."

Here we have it, catastrophe, the Case of the Chapter Which Ends and Ends Again, yet has no end, for how can it end so long as that unthinking woman, that coldest of hearts, Joyel Daggle, is spending her time with bungee-jumping New Indians, in poisonous rooms, in treacherous memory of a long-ago babysitter named Nancy, someone call the police, why will no one help us, our friends are suffering, they wait by the phone for your call, they weep in anticipation of your arrival, how adept we are with the social graces, Hello, darling, how nice of you to call, am I desperate, quite the contrary, I am free of all physical sensations, God rules, my heart is light and buoyant.

"We've followed a thousand false leads. We'll never find Joyel."

"She isn't in that gin bottle between your legs. That's one place she isn't."

"You want me to throw it out, I'll throw it out."

"Don't litter. We're coming into a town. Maybe this will be the one."

"Dream on."

"*Shut up, shut up, shut up!*"

> Now listen, Juliette. There was a certain Delshi man, residing in Pintou, Guelph province, who heard a heartbeat through his pillow, and he slung away the *jiva* which covered him, and picked up the stick by his bedside, and with this stick he began beating.

"Not again, Papa."

Then came old Eguchi, the three sisters, the one wife chosen from these sisters, Yuyu the body man to cleanse the corpse, the brother police chief in Pintou, Guelph province, who would cloak the crime.

"We've been down that road, Papa."

Now we come to the spirit of the murdered wife who would not depart that room where the new bride and the Delshi man slept. In the night she crawled in between them, and when they were aroused to lovemaking it was her limbs entwined within theirs, her spirit flesh that received their caresses, their lips parted upon her own, their tongues met her tongue, all this in a manner that was unseemly for a house of their high status in Pintou, Guelph province, becoming to none in their party, I am saying, and imparting not the smallest satisfaction to any of them.

So the man from Pintou, Guelph province, went to old Eguchi with his complaints, saying, "Old man, what shall we do? Our kisses are without rudder, our cries of ecstasy not our own. And that's not all, far from it. Our tea is bitter, our food unsucculent, our fruit trees wither, we walk on nails."

And old Eguchi, no fool in these matters, said, "There is nothing for it but you must burn your house down."

"Burn my house down?"

"Yes, first making assurance that every possession in rightful ownership of your late wife is heaped in a pile onto that bed, including the dishes you supped from, your spoons and wall adornments, the mats on your floor, your teapot, and most importantly, every garment her hands ever touched, each cloth that might ever have touched her body, your mosquito netting over that bed, her footwear and yours, your money hidden beneath the floor, any sprig of hair between the pages of a book, her jewelry, her combs, any slither of soap her hands might have touched, your birds in the cage, each doorknob touched by her hands, in fact, everything."

"But I will be left a poor man," said the husband. "I will have nothing."

"You will have your soul," said old Eguchi. "Go forthwith and do it."

Which the husband did.

He did so and the conflagration persisted through seven days and seven nights, always with some new object discovered, which object must of course be added to the flames. The smoke of that fire, the evil fumes, lay like a yellow pall over the whole of the region, through seven days and nights, so that even as far away as a thousand miles people knew well enough what was transpiring in Pintou, Guelph province.

But in the end there existed only cinders where once had stood the proud house, and the yellow cloud dispersed and the cinders swept away, and with money borrowed from lenders within a fortnight a new house stood where the former one had, with fine windows and a carved door, a golden roof, paths beset with precious stones, a garden through which flowed perpetual water. Radiant!

And all seemed resolved for a time and the murdered wife's spirit was seen no more.

But the new wife had in secret laid-by one *jiva* belonging to the old wife, this of exquisite silk, a fabric so fine, of such lightness of being it could hover about in air never to settle, and a dear favorite of the new wife who could not bear to part with cloth of such unparalleled virtue. It was a cloth of highest yellow, iridescent in the sun, each thread a line of winking diamonds yet when there was no sun the *jiva* had the transparency of glass, lacked any color whatsoever. In the heat of day the glorious cloth cooled the skin and when the day was cool it warmed the flesh to the utmost satisfaction.

"How did you come by this most exquisite *jiva*?" inquired the husband. To which the wife replied, "I have brought it with me into my new life from my former home."

And thus was the saving of this cloth, the wife's lie, the undoing of all concerned, and indeed the undoing of the whole of Pintou, Guelph province. End of chapter.

"Thank goodness. Slow down, Papa, we're coming into a town. Did you see those street signs? No maniacs welcome."

Kindred is a small town a coyote's breath out of Fargo, a hare's breath from the Minnesota border. Entering Kindred one sees strung over the main street between utility poles a hanging man. SPEEDERS DON'T LAST LONG IN KINDRED, a flashing sign reads.

"Would you like your own room tonight?" Raoul asked Juliette. "You are too old now to be sharing a room with your father, perhaps you desire your privacy. You're the only child I've ever had and I'll never have another. What do I know about what children want or what I want myself, but if you want your own room, I have no objection, you can come and go as you please without having to offer explanations, we can even have dinner at separate tables like that time in Puerto Escondito, Mexico, when you refused to sit with me because your little dress pansies had a bad cold." What on earth was he saying, he sounded dejected, this was manic depressiveness talking, she'd go crazy in a room by herself, maybe both of them needed what Joyel was having, a long period of recuperation, of recovery, or possibly Daddy had caught Joyel's disease and this separate-rooms business was a ruse for him to go on the lam, she'd be an eleven-year-old helpless child abandoned to the vicissitudes. To forestall this, perhaps she should be a good little girl, a good and loving daughter over the next few hours.

There she now sits, gnawing her nails down to the quick as the Infiniti plows through slushing snow, past the hanging man, how gross, she wonders what her mother would think if she could see them now, Joyel would say, Stop biting your nails, I'm going to paint poison over those nails, and what if someone else could see her mother's vigil over them, what would that party think, that party would say, I disown you, I am coming like a thief in the night to drop you Daggles into hell, what if the quiescent hanging man suddenly blurted out, Fuck all of you, including Him, what if the Infiniti suddenly found wings and carried them away from this sordid earth, what if . . .

"There's a quaint place," her father says, "the Best Western Cold Toe Motel and Bar. What if we pull right in here?"

From their room in the Cold Toe Motel, Raoul and Juliette Daggle can see both the hanging man and the flashing sign warning one and all of the fate awaiting those who indulge in anticonforming acts. The lifelike figure's neck is in a noose, his eyes bulge, his arms droop past his sockless shoes so as to suggest to passersby that hanging alone in Kindred is insufficent punishment, the lawbreaker's bones must be pulled from the sockets also.

"That man looks like you," Juliette observes. "Jesus Christ, I think he's wearing your suit!"

"Well, by God. By God, I think you're right. What's going on here?"

Snow is coming down. More is expected. Whiteout conditions are predicted.

A long rig is pulling into the Cold Toe Motel and Bar. A high cab, a dark, hooded driver behind the wheel, maneuvering slowly, some would say blindly, through the gusting snow. On the trailer rides a giant carved and lavishly painted figure, arguably of wood, arguably carved from a gigantic tree and thus still a tree. But a man. Injun.

"I've got to see this," Juliette says, flying from the room.

"Wait for me."

"Oh, yeah, you got that right," the bartender tells them. "That's the New Indian and Crazy Horse, the great warrior, on their winter tour. Probably on the way to the Fargo Fair."

The rig driver enters, stomping his feet, shaking off snow. He's a tall man filling the doorway, half of his thick frame in shadows, the other half under wash of a yellow globed light above the door, a man in two halves come in from the world's whiteness to pause there while his eyes adjust to the darkness. His face is ringed in fur, eyes black as buckets, head hooded, feet in white mukluks, the rest of him under a long coat perhaps made of down given how it seems so puffed up, so inflated. A youngish man, good-looking, they now see, as he steps from the doorway, pitching back the hood, unzipping the huge long coat, advancing upon them. Injun.

"Daddy, buy that man a drink," Juliette whispers, feeling a wave of something like history, the pulse of a gone time, ripple through her bones. A hand brushes the soft drink in front of her, a spectral hand or is it an Injun's, the glass clatters to the hardwood floor, rolls. Rolls and rolls. The glass rolls to the approaching man's mukluks, jumps from the floor, comes to rest in the New Indian's waiting hand.

"How did you do that?" asks Juliette, her face flushed, her knees knocking, this is such a beautiful guy.

It is cold in the Cold Toe Bar. All speech is dispelled within misty bags, "Nah," the barkeep says, "this isn't cold, let me refill that glass."

Juliette sits on tingling hands, knees spread wide, the pansy dress at fold between her legs, the pansies awed into silence, her feet hitched over the chair brace, Juliette speechless now, unable to unlock her eyes from this bewitching newcomer to the grossed-out world.

"I've seen you somewhere before," are the Indian's next words, this to Raoul as the Indian pulls out a chair, removes frozen gloves, slaps these against a palm, sits down at their table under leave of no as yet proffered invitation.

"Yes," he says to morose Raoul, "I've seen you." He's a hearty sort, clapping Raoul's shoulder with a big hand, "How you doing, Daggle? How goes it in the lovelorn's gloomy cellar?"

"Who are you?" Juliette asks, a tremor in her hushed voice, her hands shaking, why can she not sit still, why is her heart fluttering?

"I am the New Indian. You can call me Tom or Thomas, Thomas Kingdeer for short."

"What is a New Indian?"

"It's like this, Juliette."

How does he know their names, why are his eyes so deep, why has he now picked up her hand, why is his finger now tracking a path over her palm, why does his touch ignite leaping flames that shoot down to her very feet? "It's like this, Juliette. The Old Indian has gone like crows across a field, but each winter he returns to lodge in the New Indian's heart. So you could say the old Indian and the New Indian are one and the same."

Tom or Thomas the New Indian looks into the girl's eyes, his own eyes water just as tears well in hers, now they waver, his sight dropping to the table in mute study of the montage of old worlds, names, initials within hearts, hieroglyphics carved into the ancient wood, silent in the interim as though these engravings, other voices, former times, are in secret dialogue with him.

"I am making history," he finally says, his voice low, afloat in wonder. "I am the first Indian to sit at this table."

"We are looking for my mother," the girl feels suddenly compelled to say. Her eyes bore into the Indian's, her brow is sweaty, she feels feverish, she cannot make her knees stop knocking.

The New Indian nods, smiles a warm smile, he has a long knife out now, gleaming slender blade made for gutting fish, he's carving TOM, Tom the New Indian, into the wood.

"Joyel, that's her name. Joyel Daggle."

"Oh, you Daggles," Tom the New Indian replies. "In mine and the old Indian's lifetime we keep crossing trails with Daggles, always the same bunch, always trouble."

"My mother's been gone a year."

"The old Indian has mothers so numerous that if one is lost, the New Indian has only to pick up a stone from the earth and there will be the lost mother in his hand."

The Indian withdraws a stone from a pocket, folds the girl's fingers around it. "There is one hour in every year when each child's wish is fulfilled. Is your hour approaching, Miss Juliette? Your mother has gone on a long hunting trip. Perhaps she will return when her quiver is empty and the snows have come." The Indian's knife is still, he looks out, and soon they all are looking out, in bewitched wonderment of the swirling snow. The roof creaks under its load, windows rattle in the wind, wires and pipes everywhere sing. Snow pelts the glass, bush and tree out there are slung over, squatting down, the whole outside earth under white cover. In the distance can be seen Kindred's hanging man at sway under tether of his rope, under snowfall, the long arms flailing in wind, a man doomed ever to pace back and forth the few steps allowed him.

"There," the Indian says, sitting back, closing the knife blade. "Tom. Now I know I exist. I have sat at the table." He laughs a long laugh, casts off his long coat, unzips the mukluks around which a pool of water has formed, shakes ice from the fur collar. "I have sat at the table," he repeats, his sight floating wide, his mind seemingly adrift over a sea of memory, as if the table on which he has carved his name is an item of no precise dimension and perhaps not even a table, perhaps other Indians are arriving at the table, they are looking at the table in amazement, Look at that, they say, Tom has sat at the table, perhaps we all should sit at the table, they are bringing more chairs to the table, they are sitting down, with long knives made for gutting fish they are carving names, hieroglyphics, symbols significant only to other Indians, initials within hearts, a tree, a cougar, buffalo, all these they are carving into the table, Running Arrow loves the She of Immeasurable Light, Lotto the Magnificent Loves Cold Water, Little Crazy Mud Was Here, George Armstrong Custer Was a Gutless Shit, and the like, all of which takes a considerable time, such writing does not come easy, teeth clamp down over tongues, breath is harried, they are all sweating, they must remove their furs and skins, unzip their wet mukluks, the table in question is now afloat in a pool of water, someone must hold down this table or how otherwise may an Indian write, Yes, they say, we have sat at the table, they are all in agreement on this, We have sat at the table, someone must run and get Crazy Horse, that mean mother, he, too, must sit at the table, the New Indian only then to emerge from his journey to throw a hand over Juliette's shoulder, to laugh and say to Raoul the lovelorn, "Did I hear something about a drink?"

"You go ahead," Raoul says, lifting a hand in signal of the bartender: "Drinks for everyone. I'm dry this evening."

"Pardon me," says his shocked daughter, only this second emerging from her own mental journey, "while I faint."

"That was one weird New Indian," Juliette said to her papa in their room, splashing cold water over her face. "I didn't understand a thing went on."

Her father did not reply. He has pulled a chair up to the window, scraped frost away, and sat now with legs reposed on the sill, chin on cradled hands, staring absently into the world's whiteness.

"Could I fix you a drink, Papa?"

"No, darling. No, you couldn't."

"Would you like to hold my rock?"

"Thank you, yes."

Solly of Seattle, their hired detective, a retired police officer, finds people. He's good at this, though he hasn't been good at finding Joyel. He's found her, that is, but always too late. What he's found of her has been her tracks, her shadow only, for Joyel has shot on to another place.

"I'll take a whiskey," he's saying now. He's saying this in the Cold Toe Bar, Kindred, North Dakota. "You're not drinking?"

Solly is fattish, breathy, slow of foot but quick of mind. He follows his impulses. When Raoul Daggle called, he came. They've had these meetings off and on during the year. Today he flew into Fargo, rented a car, motored the few miles to Kindred and its famous hanging man.

"Another hour or two and I would have been stuck in snow up to my elbows. So let's get down to it. A man by the name of Jack Dearborne has been using Joyel's charge card. That's how I tracked her to Orick."

"How did this Jack get her card? Is he a boyfriend?"

"Long story. As for boyfriends, I gather they've not been at the forefront of her mind. This Jack is the ex of one Jane Dearborne, residing in Orick. Our Jack, a few days ago, beat the shit out of Jane, that's how he came to have your wife's card."

"Why would Jane have Joyel's card?"

"Joyel and Jane hatched this scheme whereby they switched cars, IDs, the cards got included for one reason or another. If you're hiding, the best way to hide is to become someone else."

"So how does Cut Bank come in?"

"Forget Cut Bank. Joyel speaks to you on the phone, tells you she's in Cut Bank, you start barreling-ass to Cut Bank? After all this, do you still believe every word she says? Okay, I can see you do."

"She's not in Cut Bank?"

"Her last known sighting was Alzada, Montana—"

"Alzada?"

"—about twenty-four hours ago. A guy, Yew, out there, a police officer, thinks she's the best ever came down the pike. Smitten. Anyway, she's headed this way, God knows with what intention."

Through the rank of frosted windows they can see the rig conveying the great Indian warrior and the hanging man between the telephone poles, whose head now is piled high with snow.

"What about the dead man in the mud?"

"Joyel was in Orick a good spell. Longest I've known her to remain in any one place. Working her butt off, apparently. Daily shift at the Maiden Mist. Evening shift, the Lumberjack. Rented a room up the Wiechepec, that's a mountain range, you probably read about the floods. She made friends out there, got along."

"Who's the dead guy?"

Solly shrugged, he seemed to be thinking about something else, perhaps of the hanging man, the snow, of this entire year in futile chase of, how might we put this without offending, an ordinary housewife.

"Mud," Solly said, "all you see in Orick are miles and miles of mud, really quite extraordinary. Humboldt Lagoons are filled in, the entire seashore pushed back so far you could move in a state the size of Rhode Island. The dead man? No one knows. A drifter, probably. Joyel comes into it only because the body turned up pretty near her place. She was trapped up there, you know, for about a week. Had two people with her, a couple named Esther and Carter."

"She was always good at making friends," said Juliette. "I knew she hadn't killed any dead man."

Solly nodded, then solemnly said, "Trouble is, there is a party on her tail. For a long time I thought it was nothing but coincidence. Everywhere I've gone there's been another man either ahead of me or arriving soon after I've gone. A guy in a brown suit, smokes Camels. Any idea who this might be?"

11

dakota secrets

As father and child are gassing up at a Git 'n' Go station in Kidder, South Dakota, the child says, "Here's a secret. One day when I was in second grade a heavy snow fell. School closed early because the teachers were worried we wouldn't be able to get home. They called all the mothers to come and get their children. There were about a hundred of us lined up in the hallways in our mittens and scarves and heavy coats. My mother came. She snatched a boy's hand. She said, 'I'm glad to see somebody else had to get you in that gear and not me. Come on.' She was wearing those yellow boots she liked, and a flimsy see-through kerchief on her head. She marched the boy out to the car, she pushed him in and slammed the door. Then she slipped and slid out of there. She bolted into the street without looking. Cars slipped and slid every which way to avoid hitting her."

"Motherhood is hard. She's a loopy driver."

"The whole time, I was standing in the open doorway calling as loud as I could. Then one of the teachers plucked me back.

'Stop letting in that cold,' she said. I said, 'My mother went off with the wrong child.' The teacher said, 'That's perfectly understandable. There isn't that much difference between you little shits.'"

"Wait," the child said. "I want to hear what this woman is saying."

She turned up the radio volume.

"The scud that hangs over our cities is not produced by toxic gasses, automobile emissions, and the like. There is a direct relationship between this cloud of smog and female sadness. If all the sad women left town tomorrow, the air would be clear as day."

"Next caller, please," another voice said. "Our lines are open."

"I have to pee," Juliette says.

Raoul pulls off the road.

"If you added up all the little girls who have said, 'I have to pee,' their lines would stretch to China."

Juliette can see them, all the squatting girls, their lines stretching to China.

"I don't believe this!" cried the child, marveling. "What is a deer doing in downtown Kidder, South Dakota?"

The deer is standing in front of the Infiniti. It has taken the pedestrian tiger-stripe walkway, walkway lights are flashing. The deer regards with disdain the screeching vehicles, it looks at Juliette Daggle, What are you doing here? the deer asks, and that is when a dumbfounded Juliette cries out, "What is a deer doing in downtown Kidder, South Dakota!"

The girl scrutinizes the night's walls. She will touch nothing in this room. Each object is contaminated, including the phone, which her father is speaking into.

"I observe your checkout time is eleven. For your information, that is about when we will be falling asleep."

Fluorescent tubes flicker and spit. Good. She knows precisely how they feel.

"That story about the people in Pintou, Guelph province," Raoul said, "isn't a nice story. It's a story like ours without your mother."

"I hate that story."

"So, remember, Eguchi gave his good advice, 'burn your house down,' the husband burnt down his house, but the new wife in secret kept back one exquisite *jiva* belonging to the dead party."

"You think I'm a dunce? Just get on with it, okay?"

"Temper, temper."

> One evening the man from Pintou, Guelph province, was lighting his carbon, his carboni, his charcoal, in preparation for their meal. A spark blew up. The spark fastened onto the woman's fine *jiva*. Although the *jiva* itself would not burn and would at the end be as exquisite as it was at the beginning of its journey, the *jiva* was carried by wind all over Pintou, Guelph province. It was, many afterwards said, like a great bird pouring fire from the mouth. The *jiva* set afire every rooftop in Pintou, it carried sparks to every tree and shrub, to every garden and stall, every shock of growth in a field, and in the end all that was left of Pintou, Guelph province, was scorched earth, death, and ruination. Everyone perished. Some in the lower provinces to this day claim they saw the dancing fiery *jiva* and within its flaming strands rode the precise form of the wife who had been murdered.

Heavy snow is predicted. "May I not fix my esteemed padre a martini?" asks Juliette.

"No, you may not. I've quit."

"Are we going to tonight's meeting of the priests who have fallen from heaven."

"I am not."

"Is Juliette?"

"Juliette may do as she pleases."

"Would the esteemed padre like to hold my magic rock?"

"Yes, he would."

"Daddy, have you ever told me any lies?"

"Not many."

"Is that one?"

"No."

"Tell me the truth, Daddy. Tell me the truth about everything."

"Okay."

"You won't do it, will you?"

"Yes, I'll tell you the truth about everything, although it's a tall order."

"Fire away."

"I do remember, about a month before Joyel took off, we'd had this party, I'd had too much to drink, and after everyone had gone, I'm in the kitchen cleaning up, I break a glass, she's in by the fire talking to this Vern, always the last guy to go home, Joyel hears that glass break and she shouts to me, 'Goddam you, Raoul, I told you from the start I wouldn't be content with a happy marriage, I told you what I demanded was a *great* one!' Just screamed that out, and not by any means was this the first time."

"It's her theme song, Daddy."

"Fucking A, she thinks she's Cole Porter. But that time it was like, in there by the fire with this eat-thunder fireball Vern who won't go home, she knows in my drunkenness I've broken a gold-rimmed five-hundred-dollar fifty-thousand-year-old irreplaceable glass, a circus hand-me-down presumably from the clouds of Osiris who conquered the nations of his time with, according to Bulfinch, music and eloquence. I think that's why she took off. Because in one way or another I kept breaking everything we had of value. And here I'm not talking about value, per se. I'm talking about the squandered moment, about how every minute you're not demonstrating your regard for everything precious is a moment lost in the annals of human endeavor. And all those lost moments add up until one day you discover that what has been lost adds up to more than was possessed in the first place. Do you get what I'm saying?"

"I think so. We're really talking now, aren't we, Papa?"

"Yes, we are. Your mother and I had the notion, picked up somehow, that ours was to be a great love, that we were the picked party. God had picked us, the Pope had picked us, Fidel Castro, hell, Christopher Columbus had picked us, someone somewhere had picked us, and we were to be the fucking example. Damn right, too, it was what we both wanted and expected, we didn't care who had picked us, we were a pair in step one with the other, paving the golden trail. Others could have 'okay,' they could have 'good enough,' but that was their bag, not ours. So that's why I think she took off. Because in that respect, the only one that mattered, I wasn't cutting the mustard."

"Not the mustard again, Daddy, please?"

"I apologize, I'm here mouthing off, but, honey, I believe every word. I let her down a thousand ways. I was not up to the high standards. I was a guy who let the daily grind usurp my honorable intentions. I was a guy who, without even realizing it, had come to accept 'okay' could cut the mustard."

"You're swerving, Daddy. Mind the road."

"Do you remember how your mother tears the covers off every book we bring in the house?"

"Oh God, yes."

"She tears off the covers, tears away the titles, because those books, wonderful though they are or may be, tell only a part of the story, no matter their excellence. With the covers off and the books stacked mile-high they tell almost the whole story, with the covers off they become the one book. But the whole story is a thing that is always expanding, which is why there are always more and more covers to tear off."

"You're ranting."

"I know, darling. And that's why we are both so sad this minute. We are both so sad because there is no way I or anyone can ever tell you the whole story, although tonight when we are in our room and you are drifting off to sleep I will make another doomed effort."

"Fine, Daddy. Don't forget, okay? Do you promise?"

"I promise."

"You know, when I was growing up, I'd see my grandmother polishing the silver, polishing one or another piece every day. By the end of the week every piece in the house would have been polished, and then Monday came and she started all over again. I used to think it was a silly thing to do. What's the big deal if a serving tray, the teapot, shows a little tarnish? But I would take a gander at the flowers in the shining vase, I'd pick up and study the fork in my hand, and slowly it dawned on me what my grandmother was up to. It dawned on me that her polishing had not a damn thing to do with the items themselves and wasn't being done because she was excessively house proud. Her idea was that in polishing the silver she was in fact putting the shine on love, she was creating an environment in which loftier gradations could flourish. She was doing it for my grandfather, for us, and for anyone who chanced to come into the house or looked through a window while passing on the road."

"Jesus Christ, my mother left because we didn't polish the silver?"

That night at the Bide-a-While Best Western, Dropped Ace, Minnesota, as Juliette was falling off to sleep her father told her the true and happy story of that man in Pintou, Guelph province, who heard two heartbeats through his pillow. One was his own, the other was that of his beloved, and he said to his beloved, "Dearly beloved, what do you hear?" And his beloved said, "I hear your heartbeat and mine through my pillow, my darling, and if you will but draw your body nearer, I will tell you a lovely story." So the man drew nearer and every evening thereafter was the same, and they had many sons and daughters whose own sons and daughters begat the same, these many populating the earth and everyone in every corner of the globe doing the same into perpetuity, and each and everyone of these many from the beginning through to this present day living happily ever after.

"Oh, Daddy," Juliette said after a time. "You are doing it again. Please tell me a true story about you and Joyel and when you met and got together and had me, and like that, because those are the only truly true love stories."

"Okay, hold on, this is the true story."

So this is the true story Raoul told his daughter:

> Joyel Moffit was an up-and-coming girl, bright and attractive as could be. No other girl had quite what Joyel had, whatever that was being a mystery it might take a guy a lifetime to unravel. Which was fine by Raoul Daggle, the guy

with the inside track. Of Raoul himself, there was less than a consensus.

"That's the whole story?"

"No, love, that is only the beginning. You can't have a love story without a beginning."

"I'm sleepy now, tell me more in the morning."

Even those who disliked the talkative hotshot agreed that he was smart and handsome enough for Joyel; you snapped a photograph of the two and you wouldn't be horrified to find Raoul standing beside that gorgeous woman. But if you thought of Joyel as up-and-coming, then your next thought would be of Raoul Daggle as the up-and-going kind, since that is what he was always doing. A traipsing guy, gone off and yonder, doing what no one knew, anymore than they knew who he might be doing it with or why. Why he was always shooting off like that when he had the divine Joyel Moffit here was a mystery deeper than most minds cared to ponder. You don't ponder the imponderable, is what they might have told you, assuming they thought Joyel and Raoul were any of your business.

Joyel was of course aware that she and Raoul came in for a good deal of speculation, envy, concern, things like that, but she was too much the with-it sort to lose sleep over this. She was as certain of Raoul as she was of anything else in her life, and there wasn't much in her life she wasn't assured of. She had momentary doubts of considerable variety, as was natural to everyone, but after a good night's sleep she customarily arose refreshed, sometimes with alarm at what the day might hold but always with a zest to get at whatever it was. She wasn't one for twiddling her thumbs, not Joyel.

She was as aware as anyone, probably more so, that Raoul Daggle had his darker side, was prey to wanderlust, and although she rarely had even the vaguest notion where it was he periodically disappeared to, she wasn't overly concerned. She had her own life to lead, after all, she wasn't wrapped around Raoul's thumb. And usually he was thoughtful enough to tell her he wouldn't be around for the next few days or weeks; in fact, he usually held her in a tight embrace, kissed her, and with troubled eyes told her he would miss her, miss her like the very devil, and think of her every minute he was away. Joyel didn't necessarily believe the whole of these passionate orations, though they made her smile, they sometimes made her melt in her very footsteps, but she knew a girl with her wits about her would be wise to accept such declarations with a grain of salt. In any case, invariably she told him to go, "Go on where you think you must be going, and when you come back I'll be here waiting."

It was a kind of discipline exercised between them on the eve of these departures, the scene sometimes being played out on the bed in his small apartment, sometimes at a motel on the highway, not a "cheap" motel exactly but whatever their purses could stand at whatever given time this wanderlust, if that's what it was, came upon him.

He left, she waited, and the minute he returned they were in each other's arms, and nothing, so far as either could see, had changed between them. She would catch him up on what had happened in the town during his absence and he might, or might not, usually didn't, tell her what he had been up to.

Raoul's absences varied, as I say, from a few days up to a month or so, and one fatal time, six months, but rarely did it cross Joyel's mind that one day he might go, never to return.

Oh, well, barring some terrible calamity, an accident, say he gets run over by an automobile or falls off a cliff or is unlucky enough to be inside a place when a madman comes in and shoots everyone. She had these thoughts sometimes, these small worries, but what she was assured of, aside from the unlikely prospects of the unseemly hand of fate touching their lives in a nasty way, was that both she and Raoul were the lucky sort, always had been, and why should that suddenly be reversed? It was always someone else who slid on a patch of wet grass to break an arm, or walked through a plate-glass window, or drowned, or was so plagued by mosquitoes they couldn't sit outside in the sun. So many things, really, that could befall a person, but she and Raoul, childhood sweethearts and still going great guns, seemed to have an invisible shield surrounding them, or maybe they were spared such misfortune as these because theirs was an optimistic nature, they were attuned to the universe in which they lived, and neither of them ever got so drunk they didn't know what they were doing. They got high, though, they got high quite often, and perhaps a point or two beyond that during those times when they were having reunions, since it was almost traditional now that Raoul would show up with two bottles of fine champagne, flowers and such as that, because he really was quite a romantic guy.

The longest time Raoul was away, those fatal six months I spoke about, he pulled into town, pulled into Joyel's parents' yard about ten in the evening. A bright moonlit night, people out sitting on their porches enjoying the perfect weather. He had left town in his old black beat-up Pinto, now here he was driving a sleek yellow convertible, spanking new and looking as though it had just that minute emerged from a car wash, which in fact was the case. He was running late, he was eager, but he took time to run the machine through the Kwikwash there in town, which may give you the idea he was rightly pleased with that car, which he was, because the truth of the matter was, as he saw it, this yellow convertible was his and Joyel's honeymoon car, the wheels that would deliver them into a new, fantastic life. He had on the front seat beside him the flowers, the candy, the gifts for everyone including a bone wrapped in nice paper for the puppy dog Joyel's parents had recently acquired, Trash's father, as it happened. Raoul was wearing a new suit, obviously expensive, new shoes, a watch that Joyel's father kept sliding over his own wrist until Raoul, laughing, finally told him he could keep it. Told him it was meant for him to begin with, this being either a lie or the truth, no one, not even Joyel, being able to ever figure that one out. Whatever the case, it was a gift, why can't we leave it at that?

A few minutes after arriving, the greetings having been made, Raoul took the car keys out of his pocket, he said to Joyel's father, "Why don't you take your lovely wife for a spin wearing your new watch?" They did, and the minute the pair was out of the house, Raoul and Joyel embraced, they kissed, they drove their bodies one into the other. He said, "I've missed you every minute, I've loved you every second of every day," or something like that, and she said, "Me, too, I've waited, I love you to the moon and back," or something very similar, the way lovers talk, and their clothes were likely about half off by this time, making love that way, standing up, in a hurry because they both knew her father would do no more than drive around the block a few times, let everyone out on their porches have a good long look at him there in the hotshot automobile, his hand up high on the wheel so they could see the new hotshot watch as well if they chose to, and his wife beside him, her neck for once not hidden by the old neck brace, no, she's there smiling a greeting to the neighbors, even dipping her head to people she hasn't spoken to in years.

So Joyel and Raoul were presentable enough when the parents returned, both sitting on the sofa with the dog between them chewing on its new bone. It was maybe understood by the four of them, five if you included the dog, that this was a special night. Raoul had been gone so long this time, with not so much as a postcard, a phone call from him, and Raoul was, what, now in his late twenties, somewhere in there, and Joyel was now twenty-three, twenty-three and getting on, and maybe she figured, perhaps they all did, that it was time for the two young people to settle down and get on with their lives. There was that feeling in the den that night in any event, if you can believe what the parents afterwards said. Raoul had uncorked the first of the two bottles, they were about at the bottom of that bottle, even Joyel's mother taking perhaps half a glass—much to everyone's surprise, which should indicate to you the celebratory mood evident that night, Joyel's mother being one who pretty firmly believed that drink doomed one to everlasting hell—when Raoul took from his pocket and placed on the coffee table a small wrapped package that all involved took to be an engagement ring.

Well, it had to be, what else could possibly be that size, and so luxuriously wrapped? So it was a ring, either a ring or a joke of the grossest kind, and Raoul was not the kind who went in for bad jokes. But Raoul was just letting the box sit there, everybody staring at it, and him not saying a word, just holding Joyel's hand when they were not stroking the puppy, and now and then the two of them exchanging soft smiles, the clock ticking, the parents beginning to feel a bit embarrassed for Joyel, that little unwrapped box just sitting there. It is perfectly possible, in fact, that the presence of that box, Raoul's silence, triggered in her father some old enmity, an intolerance or impatience, let's say, an animosity that he hadn't given voice to or allowed to surface in that house in a good many years, because suddenly he was standing, jabbing a finger at Raoul, his face set in a gruesome rage, saying to Raoul, "Goddam you, you're the same little fatso no-account Daggle you always were, aren't you, aren't you?" Repeating that "aren't you?" over and over, like it's a thing he really meant, some hatred that went so deep in him that he himself, if he ever did, could no longer understand how or when it had lodged there. Or maybe it was occasioned by his being pretty much the teetotaler, holding pretty much the same views as did his wife when it came to drink, or so he claimed, and the—what?—two teensy glasses he'd had—had gone to his head. "You son of a bitch, Raoul," he said. "You've been gone six months without one word, no explanations to Joyel or to us, and now you've put that goddam box on the table!"

Well, they'd all hopped up by this time, of course they had, a room explodes, you're going to hop up. All now speaking at once, the father shouting, "What, you robbed a bank, you come back here with your new car and new suit, those white shoes, a new watch that you expect me to wear. What are you, some kind of secret criminal? And now you've put that goddam box on the table!" The wife with her arms around her husband trying to hold him back, Raoul saying, "Why you sorry sack of—" but not finishing that particular thought, while Joyel is pulling at his clothes to keep him away from her father, because it is perfectly clear by now that what both these men want to do is kill each other, and the women screaming one at the other, because, really, this has sprung up so completely out of the blue that neither woman can yet believe what is happening. The father lunging forward, taking a swing that by chance clips his own wife's chin: "I wouldn't have your goddam fancy watch. What I'd like to know is where and how you got it, plus your car, what are you, a goddam bank robber?" Like he's some kind of record spinning around and around, you know, apparently unaware that his wife is down on the floor at his feet moaning from having been clipped and Joyel fighting to clear a path between the two men, clawing at their chests in a panic because, what, for all she knows they will be happy to kill her, too. Because, what, her teetotaler father is in truth a secret alcoholic and tonight has come out of the closet? Hasn't he been periodically quitting the room, trotting off for his secret shots? Can't you just look at his purple bulbous nose, the veins, and see what has been going on here? Doesn't anyone remember those years ago, Joyel a child, when these parents drove to Florida and had the smash-up, 357 cars in a sea of fog, and him on the old Highway 301 with a brown paper sack between his legs? Isn't that why, even these days twenty years after the event, his wife will pull out the ancient brace, fit it about her neck, and say to anyone present, "This is what that man did to me"? Isn't that why Joyel's father hates Raoul? Because Raoul knows too much about him? And doesn't respect him? And because Raoul doesn't like how the man browbeats his wife and daughter and ever affirms he's nearly the teetotaler, that veined jelly of a nose to the contrary?

"Have you both gone crazy?" Joyel is asking. "Would both of you shut up, what is the matter with you?" And saying other such stuff until finally Raoul is just standing there, hands by his side, nodding, now and then looking at Joyel as though to say, Can you believe this? Is it possible that this son of a bitch, your father, is saying to me—that both of you are saying to me—what I think you are saying to me? Joyel and her mother crying now, in a rage one second and on a crying jag the next, both at a complete loss to understand where this storm has come from. You're laughing, stroking the puppy, sipping the bubbly one minute, then boom! How to explain it?

Or how to explain what happens next, which was this: Joyel snatches up the little wrapped box from the coffee table, she screams out, "I hate both of you!" and the next second she's flung the box at the picture window. There it flies.

They all see it happen, see the box hit the glass, drop to the floor, they see the puppy streaking towards it, they see the dog going at the parcel with tooth and claw, they spot a patch of blue which later turns out to be the box lid, and then the goddam dog has swallowed in one big gulp the rest of the box and whatever it was in there.

There they are, all four, all in perfect silence watching this happen. Rage has gone, anger has gone, they are just four stunned people in what appears now to be a state of collapse, watching that dog gulp down what was in there, an engagement ring, if that's what you want to believe it was. The dog then looking at the assemblage, cocking his head, wondering aloud, if you can credit this, why it is that things have suddenly got so silent in there.

But only for a second, because next that dog is over licking up the juice around the overturned bottle, he's even putting a paw on the neck of the bottle to drain out the last wine in there.

So everything is on hold while the puppy goes about this dog business.

Then the wife is saying what everyone later will agree was a strange thing for her to have said. She is saying, "Maybe this is all for the best."

Maybe this is all for the best?

What? What did she say?

The trouble is no one is sure exactly who she is saying this to, whether she means it as a fairly accurate description of how both she and her husband feel about the general situation, or maybe in her own mind she is speaking for God who is otherwise choosing an unobtrusive position. Or maybe the statement is somehow intended to make them all feel better, who knows? In any case, Joyel, this loving daughter, seeing her world tumbling, her future in shreds, is suddenly slapping at her mother, slapping and shoving, saying things like, "You dumb underfoot goose, what do you know about any of this? Don't you dare, you mollycoddled bitch, you ides-of-fucking-March woman tell me all this is for the best! And you, Daddy, you, how much of your poison have you poured down your gullet?"

So now it is Raoul having to restrain Joyel, hold her back from raking her claws into both parents. As in the meanwhile, unknown to all of them, the dog is up on the sofa making gagging sounds as he tries to upchuck some lump that looked great for a minute but is now plugging up his throat. But finally they do look, the barfing puppy is making such a noise, they look and look and the dog goes on barfing and nothing comes up. They are looking at the dripping mouth, expecting that box to emerge, but will it? No it will not.

After a minute, father and mother are sitting down, they look a wreck and the house is definitely an earthquake zone, and, frankly, they are hiding their faces, hiding their eyes, they are both so much ashamed. And our lovers, the dog as well, are looking at them in this shame, sharing in it, I would expect, although still more than a little removed from its center. For a second or two, Joyel and Raoul, standing right beside each other, their hands touch, the fingers intertwine, then they, too, are looking at the floor in what certainly could be construed as a look of shame, of regret, of despair, although in another second they are parting from each other, turning their backs on each other, and after a few seconds of this Raoul simply strolls to the door. He strolls there in no hurry, you can see that door is the last thing he wants to go through. You see him there with his hand on the knob, you see the knob turning, and Raoul looking back as though he has in mind saying something, My apologies, thanks for a lovely evening, goodbye, something like that. But he falters, no words come. He opens the door and goes through it. He's slumped over a bit, tarrying, you could say, perhaps out of the expectation, the hope, that Joyel will follow. Yes, for a second he stands still on the porch, hands in his pockets, looking up at the moon. He's waiting, he won't look back, he won't say aloud, *Joyel, please come with me*, but you and I both know that's what is going through his mind.

Joyel isn't, though. She isn't coming. Another second or two and she might, probably she would have, but as Raoul likely was seeing the matter, he was not going to wait forever. There's such a thing as pride, you know. She isn't going to come and she isn't going to say, *Don't go*. She's only going to stand there like a pillar of stone. Stricken, Speech a thing she's never even heard of.

So Raoul with the look of a man trudging behind a hearse moves down the bricked path to his shining new car. He gets in, softly shuts the door, turns the ignition, the engine smartly purrs, he switches on the lights, adjusts the rearview mirror, and there he goes.

There he goes.

Goodbye love, goodbye to the rest of my life.

But the funny thing is, his wheels have turned around hardly once when he sees a jumping blur and in the next instant there's the dog sitting up high in the seat beside him, Trash the First, I guess you could call him, Trash thumping his tail, saying, Let's go, burn rubber, we are two dogs made for the open road.

Well, my God. Well, Jesus Christ, what kind of dog are you, to desert your own family?

But Raoul has had enough confrontation this evening, so what he does is pat the dog's head, thumps its hindquarters, "So you're to be my life's companion," he says to the dog.

And there they go, man and his dog, Joyel's father racing after them, shouting, "Thief, thief, come back here with my goddam dog!"

There they go, never to return.

Joyel, watching all this behind the screen door, knows this. She knows it as surely as she knows the alphabet or where Orion, the Pleiades, the Three Wives, the Seven Women of the Auroral Gown, are to be found in the night sky. Her happiness has gone. She has no hope, love is lost, her life is over, trees will never again bear fruit, the sun will not shine.

Why? Because the mind lives on the heart, Juliette, like any parasite, just as Emily Dickinson said.

"Is that the truth, Daddy? Did that really happen?"

"Hey, don't be so glum, we got past it. I thought I saw you drifting off. I thought you were asleep."

"Trash's father ate Joyel's engagement ring? That's really gross? Now tell me about the truly gripping part, the best part, the part where the two of you are back in soulful harmony and about your having me. Tell me about when I was made."

12

joyel's other *daughter*

JOYEL LOVED the nation's highways. She loved how the highway surfaces altered mile by mile. The builders insisted on inconsistency; black asphalt here, white concrete there, pebbled here, rippling there, potholed every mile. In diversity is the peculiarity, she thought. It was like new art, those highways. It was the call of eccentricity, surrender to serendipity, like it or leave it: the American way.

Thanks to that dear heart Eugene Eubanks, the radio works beautifully. The second Joyel touches the dial a warmly modulated voice, so near the speaker might be at her elbow, says, "Hello."

"Hello," says Joyel back.

"What do you have to tell me?" asks the radio woman. "If you're here to tell me he doesn't love you, I'm not listening. If another woman is in the picture, forget it. If you're here to tell me he doesn't know how to love, then we can talk."

"Right on!" Joyel says. "Woman, let's talk!"

Soon after crossing into Minnesota, Joyel stops to pick up a hitchhiker. Normally she would not do this. Picking up this hitchhiker is a test of character. Also, the party in question is female, a child thumbing in frigid weather, weary as Jesus, emaciated as a stick.

The girl says she is going to the city of Marshall, in the state's southwestern corner.

"What's in Marshall?"

"Me when I get there."

"Where have you come from?"

"Back there."

"How far?"

"Far enough."

Another runaway.

"Neat car," this one says. "Little shrubs everywhere. Is that a lemon tree?"

The girl reveals that where she came from the water had wormy creatures swimming in it, which you could see if you looked at that water under a microscope. But no one else back there troubled themselves to put a drop of water on a slide and look at the wormy water.

"They say it's my imagination. Believe you me, if I wanted to use my imagination, I would use it for something other than seeing worms."

"Jesus Christ," Joyel exclaims, "the highway is packed with runaways but you're the first to be here because of worms under a microscope!"

The hitchhiker picks at a scabbed lip. She's a glum, reserved thing with baleful eyes. "It isn't just that."

"What's your name?"

"Amber."

"How old are you?"

The girl bolts forward, tightens the strings of her big black boots. Yellow leotards cover her skinny legs, two silver loops pierce the right eyebrow.

"Fifteen yesterday."

"How long on the road?"

The girl's eyes swivel about. She thumps out a cigarette from a crumpled package within her ruck. Lights up.

"Jesus," she says, "you're not my mother. Can we stop this?"

The cake Opus Eubanks gave her has remained untouched in its box. Joyel slides away ribbon, plunks a fistful of cake into her mouth.

"Feel free," she says.

The girl watches Joyel eat three of four fistfuls.

"You eat just like the pigs at home," she remarks, "except that they use a fork."

Joyel laughs. The girl laughs also. "I don't usually make jokes," she says, blushing. "I don't know what's come over me."

"What will you do in Minnesota?" Joyel asks the girl.

"One, I intend to find romance. Then I'm going to tie-dye my hair. Hang out. I'm going to enroll in school, if they'll let me. I like science courses but the teacher in my school only knew what he'd boned up on the previous night. A dope. I love the sciences. All that stuff is so way cool. I want to get into cell structuring, genetic espilliration, genetic time or molecular chronometry, molecular phylogeny, I like that, too. Or I might get into quantum gravity, that's a dynamite field. Cloning, that's neat, too. I already did a mouse and a mole, which came out rather as expected. That's why I've run away. My parents pitched a big fit when they discovered my project, they hated that idea of a burrowing rat. Listen, if you wanted to give me twenty dollars, I'd accept it."

"What will you mate next?"

"No correcto, mating. Mating, ha! But something beautiful. I've decided that. I was thinking I'd work with butterflies, butterflies, maybe, and hummingbirds. That, I think, would be neato."

Joyel and the girl spend the night in Marshall's Best Western, by the sprawling university.

In the middle of the night, seeing Joyel with a stunned look high on the pillows, Amber says, "What are you doing?"

"I thought I heard someone rattling the doorknob."

"My mother is like that. She sleeps with a vial of poison by her bedside. If a rapist breaks in, she's going to take the poison before the man can rape her."

The girl is up now, strolling about. She pulls on the yellow tights, Levi's, ties the yellow strings on her heavy black boots.

"This vial thing was my father's idea. You can see now where I'm coming from. Weirdsville."

"Where are you off to?"

"The next century."

"I mean now."

"The university is across the road. They must have science labs. I'm going to see if I can sneak into one. A lot of scientists work late at night, like any day they might overturn Newton's Law."

"I'll go with you."

"Hey, way out!"

Joyel and Amber hold hands, walking along. The moon stalks them, big and beautiful, the sky clabbered, the air icy, the earth frozen, their breath like ghosts running on ahead of them. In Marshall the sky scoops low. You look out through your muffler and there the horizon is, down there on a level with your shoe-tops.

"People my age, we're on the pivot of big breakthroughs. There's a zillion things we know fuck-all about."

It has been ages since Joyel has held a child's hand. That it is not Juliette's hand matters, though not that much.

"Some scientists, though, have a closed mind. I might have to go to Bolivia. I'm fifteen. What are you, thirty, forty? I bet you've lost a child and that's why you're holding my hand."

"Be nice."

"Yes, you're right. I'm sorry. I took off, my parents were watching TV. They hardly even looked up."

The next morning they wake to whiteout. Snow, still falling, obscures every window, sweeps in enormous drifts past the very roofline of Best Western's one hundred rooms. The entire world is white, cottonwood trees are invisible, roads nonexistent, not a house is to be seen, no shadow lurks anyplace.

Out of the whiteout appears a truck-and-trailer rig driven by a young man whose extremely pleasant face is ringed in fur. On the trailer is another native man standing all but high as a telephone pole and way wider, secured by ropes and thingamajigs, this one wooden, though, and painted for war, his raised tomahawk so massive one swipe could disperse the many.

"I've got to see this," Amber says, already running.

Joyel is spellbound, of course she has seen this man before, of course it is the New Indian who flew on invisible wings at Crazy

Horse Falls along with a pastorate of fallen priests, though none to pluck birds from the clouds for release before the assembled multitude as had happened nightly with Ceyx and Halcyone. How small is the world and peculiar the workings of coincidence that three times now her path has crossed this New Indian's yet never once have they exchanged the smallest word. The wonder of it is that coincidence has such a low reputation, when without its arduous labor in our behalf so few of us would be partnered with our present mates, we would not recognize ourselves, our children would be other than who they are, our ancestors might carry names strange to our ears, the entire world's history would be as raked as the sands of the seas, why it sounds almost obscene.

"That's Crazy Horse," the rig driver says. A beautiful young Indian who gives his name as Tom. "Crazy Horse is seeing the country. Crazy Horse can't get over how much has changed, although not that much has for the Indian. Crazy Horse has just come from the Fargo Winter Fair. He had a fine time judging the livestock competition. Now he's here for the Lyon County Winter Fiesta. Then it is on to Polska Kielbasa Days in Ivanhoe. What's your name?"

"Dearborne. Jane Dearborne. She's Amber."

Is that so?

Minnesota inventors are holding their annual congress at the Best Western and many of those inventors are showcasing strange new wares. A helmet with a propeller blade, for instance, that allows its wearer to skim along inches off the lobby floor. Prima donnas, all. The priests who have fallen from heaven are also convening. A squabble is in progress as to which of the two groups has rights to the Best Western's Bison Room. "A skulk of fat friars out of the devil's ort-hole," one of the inventors says of God's fallen crew.

"Crazy Horse won't go for this," the New Indian says. "He had a hard night. Today he's recuperating."

Crazy Horse has two wooden eyes larger than Joyel's head. Snow stacks around and over him and over the vicious tomahawk raised to strike. His face is painted for war, a warbonnet in descent to his waist, out of which protrudes the great beak of a carnivorous bird, the bird eyes there as well among the carved feathers. On his chest is carved a vest of beads, bones, the teeth of a great many expired animals; the many skulls of old enemies hang by web belt around his middle, scalps at dangle from a thrusting spear.

"Show biz," the New Indian explains.

He leads them inside the old warrior's belly, entering by a waist-high aperture on the backside. The belly interior is lit by an eerie yellow light, the source of this light itself hidden but it's color illuminating a bevy of gears, pulleys, cables, wires, ropes, sprockets, cranking wheels. The arms move, the legs also, the enormous head is mounted on a swivel, so, too, the old Chief's eyes and mouth. Looking up now they see blinding snowfall through those eyes, snow driving through the huge sockets in whirling shift about them. The old Chief's gaping mouth is heaped with snow, above which gleams a row of teeth, each as long as an arm.

"See Crazy Horse dance," the New Indian says. "See him on a war party, see him scalping Whitey."

For reasons Joyel has yet to extricate, the nice New Indian seems intent or sticking close to them.

"Amber," he asks, "is she your daughter?"

Amber is across the way, folded inside a lobby chair, engrossed in a science text.

"She's my other daughter."

"Dearborne, did you say?"

New inventors, fallen priests, are blowing into the motel by the second, shaking off snow, crowding the desk, raising a stink at the mix-up, shouldering each other, bristling. Reservations are not being honored, no more rooms are to be had, it's a whiteout, you know, we've got a lot of stranded people, back off, would you, get out of my face. The lobby, the bar off the lobby, are packed with guests, with sleepers, with riffraff come in from the cold, inventors and fallen priests in constant stroll, highballs in hand, a boy with a yellow bucket, a yellow mop, running back and forth in eternal maintenance of the bespattered floor. No one wants to hide away in a room during a whiteout.

"My husband, Raoul"—Joyel says to the New Indian.

"Raoul, Ms. Dearborne?"

"—saw Jesus Christ running the bases in a baseball game. It was the year the Toronto Blue Jays beat the Atlanta Braves to win the World Series. It was the sixth game, I believe. There he was, rounding second, dressed in a white flowing robe but with regulation cap and cleats. He was thrown out as he slid into third. That's why the Braves lost that game, because Jesus was such a slowpoke."

She can't imagine why she is telling this nice young Indian this dullest of stories.

"I saw that game," the Indian says. "It wasn't Jesus. It was Crazy Horse, our great warrior. He'd have been safe but for a lucky throw. Plus, it was a questionable call. On all the replays the runner looked safe."

An eavesdropping priest remarks that these stories are our new parables. If the Son of God returned tonight, He'd be talking about ball games, complaining about the billion-dollar salaries, arguing the merits of grass over AstroTurf.

"Fuck you, man," argues an inventor. "That story wasn't a parable, a parable has a lesson, where's the lesson?"

"You're the fucking lesson," replies the priest. These two groups will never get along, but for inventors we'd still be back in the Dark Ages. In the Dark Ages it was a rare priest who fell from heaven, you gave to the temple your fatted calf, you sacrificed your dearest son, you pitched a virgin or witch into the flames, God smiled on you until the next year rolled around.

"An inventor invented fire," the inventor says, "otherwise your god would still be in the dark."

In the Best Western Bison Room that evening, the proceedings under way, one of the men who has fallen from heaven nudges Joyel's shoulder: "I admire the way you listen. You listen good. I am myself a nonlistener. If you want to get down to cases, truth be told, when someone was pouring out his or her grief to me in my cloth days, say at confessional, I was only thinking of myself. I'd say, 'Do ten or so of this and that, do a hundred.' But was I listening, was I paying attention?"

"You guys ought to bone up on your sciences," throws in Amber.

"What are you doing?" the same priest pokes a friend. "You keep wrenching about, looking at the door."

"I'm looking for that guy we met in Anne's Ardor, you know, that gin breath who keeps snatching the mike at all our meetings."

"That loudmouth with the daughter?"

"Yeah, him. Gin Breath."

"I'll say. The man attends more meetings than I do. He's our fucking roving ambassador. Someone said they saw him over in Kidder, South Dakota."

"Son of a bitch. You think he's on the way?"

"It wouldn't surprise me."

"Son of a bitch!"

In bed that night, turning off the lights, the girl says, "Well, it has been altogether a pluperfect day. It has been a day of long mind rot. Good night, dear Mother."

All day, perhaps under influence of the whiteout, they have been speaking so to each other.

"Good night, darling child."

"That is like, so cool."

Amber pecks a kiss onto Joyel's cheek, slides within soft white sheets smelling of bleach, and within the lapse of seconds is on snowy slopes speeding into sleep's oblivion. Periodic rumbles sound overhead, followed by screeches on the sloped roof as massive avalanches of snow tumble by the black window.

Joyel had been asleep no more than half an hour when the phone rings. She is frozen with shock.

"I'm calling from Canada," a voice says. "I want to talk to the governor about this Texas thing."

Joyel says, "Pardon me?"

The voice says, "I figure those Texans don't care who they kill. It doesn't matter to the Texans whether a person is innocent or guilty. The message they give the criminal classes is uppermost on the Texas mind. Frankly, I think the way these Texans think is an out-and-out crime."

Ooot-and-ooot, the voice says. Joyel has forgotten Canadians are afflicted that way.

"Apparently the Texans believe the death of an innocent party now and again is the price civilized people have to pay for law and order. 'Don't cry over spilt milk' is what they say. Do I have that right?"

"Sir?"

"But now I see in the press you Floridians think the same way. I got a winter home in Florida. That's why I'm calling. Aboot this death-row woman you've got scheduled for execution tomorrow. I don't like it."

"Beg pardon?"

"Mind you, I'm not making any claim for the woman's innocence. I am merely saying, as a Canadian Floridian, that it behooves the Pelican State to do a better job of it than those Texans. I've seen the burn pictures of those people in your electric chair. I'd say this chair business is cruel and unusual punishment, unconstitutional, I might take this issue to the Supreme Court. That's what I wanted to say to the governor. Can you put him on the line?"

"The governor?"

"You got it. Say, are you the wife? Do you have any influence? Can you talk to him?"

Hours later Joyel leaves the bed. She looks at the clock, cups her hands to the window, peers through at the whiteout. Her window piled with snow. Nothing to be seen. Wind gusting, roaring; she feels the freeze through the pane. Her young Indian friend will be sleeping in the truck's cab. He might be freezing to death.

She pulls on boots, coat, muffler. What is wrong with this nice young man sharing her and Amber's warm room?

"Are you asleep?"

"The one eye is open."

The three wake in the morning at the very same second. The New Indian is in the middle. He has his clothes on, even his hat, which is over his face.

Amber's cheeks redden. "I knew in my sleep a foreign body was in bed with us. Through my pillow I could hear three hearts beating. I can't believe the heat a man's body puts out."

In the bathroom washing his face the New Indian says, "I'll bring you breakfast. I've got to check up on Crazy Horse—there's this movie *Smoke Signals* he's dying to see. Just tick off the squares on that menu card."

So that morning Joyel had the first breakfast in bed since she'd abandoned her husband, and Amber had her first ever. The whiteout, he says, is whiter than ever. It is the whiteout to end all whiteouts, and more is coming.

"You make a good mother," Amber says. "Have you had practice?"

"Not that much. Not lately."

"I always wished I had braces on my teeth," Amber says. "So no one would, like, want to smooze me. But I see that New Indian in our bed this morning, the first thing I think is I want to kiss him."

Here Joyel and Amber are, enrolling her daughter into university: "Oh, my God," Joyel says, "this is every parent's dream,

"Southwest State," a secretary explains to Amber and Joyel, "is an open university. We turn away practically no one, even high school dropouts. That's to say, we have special programs. Parental consent is required."

"I consent," Joyel states. "I am Amber's mother."

The secretary, a woman with wild bouffantish hair, in a tight black mini riding high up her hips, waits with unblinking eye for this pair's sob story.

"Her father abandoned us," Joyel explains. "Amber was in the recuperative stage a long time."

The secretary eyes both of them with what Joyel believes must be a streak of cruelty. "Why are you telling me this?" the woman asks.

"That's why my daughter dropped out."

"Of high school?"

"Yes."

"The poor baby. Is she well now?"

"We think so."

"She's awfully thin."

"It has been a long winter."

The secretary suffers a bad back; her chair is fitted with a special brace. Your poor back, Joyel thinks. It's your punishment for being so mean, so cold-hearted. A black choker rings the woman's long neck. She constantly blows her nose into tissues. I could be just like you, Joyel thinks. But now I'm a whole person thanks to all the new friends I've made, thanks to Amber.

"You'll have to fill out these forms. These and these and that one and those. Please print. Over there if you don't mind."

Over where?

"And this one. Most important, this one. The billing forms. And this one, if it is Amber's intention to take up residence in dormitory. Does she?"

"Yes."

"We will require, of course, an advance deposit. Will you be paying that today?"

"Yes."

"And cafeteria meals?"

"Well, she will certainly have to eat."

"Then fill out these forms and those and these, sign them in triplicate, and take the whole batch down the hall to one of our financial officers. All our buildings are connected by underground walkways. You never have to go outside if you don't want to. Your daughter could spend four years in this school and never once go up into the outside world. Is it still a whiteout there?"

"Yes," says Joyel, says Amber, they cannot believe all is going so smoothly.

"By God, I'll never get home to my husband," says the secretary, looking at her red fingernails. "Once we were stranded here by whiteout for nineteen days. Oh, the smells, it was awful, you wouldn't believe the pregnancies. But that isn't your worry, is it? Have a happy education."

"Thank you."

Joyel Daggle feels herself to be in a daze of elation as she signs her own and Raoul's name to the many forms. Her face has heated up, she feels hot all over; it is so strange being a mother again, the responsibility is enormous. Amber can't stop hugging her neck. "You're the greatest mom. I can't believe it, I'm going to be a scientist!"

Downtown Marshall is unbelievable. Snowplows thunder up and down. Huge snow mountains line the thoroughfares. The sunlight is blinding. Aside from the driven wind the day is warm and sparkling.

Joyel and Amber have been shopping, Joyel has bought herself a new spring outfit discounted down to practically nothing, a yellow suit, a wide yellow hat, quite stunning. Their arms are loaded down with Amber's new wardrobe. "I will not have a daughter of mine being made fun of because of her clothes, no, young lady, nothing is too good for you, we are going to dress you like a princess. Then there is your dormitory room to furnish, I want you to be the envy of the campus. We will have to work out a liberal monthly stipend to take care of your expenses. Don't worry, darling, I'll scrub floors until you get your diploma, really, it will be a pleasure, my goodness, I can't tell you how splendid it feels to be a mother again."

"Why, gracious me," exclaims the shopkeeper, "look at those deer right out there on Main Street, looking in our window."

Joyel leaves Amber to unravel the mysteries of her new universe. She trudges in mile-high snow across a parking lot, across the slushy road, entering the motel by its rear doors. There's a white Infiniti pulling into the entranceway, heaped with snow and grunge, icicles, sludge, truly a filthy vehicle, somebody ought to take that thing to a car wash.

She finds her room overflowing with Indian paraphernalia—beaded dresses, warbonnets, moccasins, paints, drums.

"Crazy Horse requires Amber and you for the festivities at the Lyon County Fair," the New Indian tells her. "Sit down. I must paint your body. I must fit you for the beaded dress. I must drill you in our songs, teach you the Crazy Horse dance."

"Okay." She has always wanted to be an Indian.

"Look at that snow!" he says.

He's right, here it comes again, another blizzard, what a country.

13

the new indian

"WHAT DO YOU CALL THIS, DADDY? Can you see the road?"

"This is called a whiteout. No, I can't see the road but I see yellow lights which might be a Best Western."

"What is that I see way out there?"

"Where?"

"Way out there."

Way out there: a herd of deer in snow-covered drifts up to their necks with one deer standing apart as though on the look-out for more of his kind, and in fact here they come, a hundred or so deer cresting the nearest slope one by one and others appearing on more distant shifting rises, their bodies leaving a hundred or so paths in the deep snow, which paths a minute from now will be filled by the falling snow, and now it would seem the one deer standing apart from the others is satisfied, it clumsily turns, kicks free of the great accumulation of falling snow that in minutes will hide away any stationary creature on that wide expanse, now the one deer leading the others in graceful trudge across the wind-rippling fields, nothing much now showing of them except their antlers, the occasional thrashing of legs, the occasional tumble as one or another loses footing in the treacherous snow, they sojourn on to a destination of their own devising, we who are not deer cannot know where or why, the deer disappearing one by one from view, and in scarcely the time it takes Raoul and Juliette to draw another breath the expanse out there is unbroken by any known living creature, wind swirls the snow anew, snow falls with renewed fervor, the whiteout is white as an endless cloth, one can barely see beyond one's nose, "My eyelashes are freezing," Juliette says, "let's hurry before we croak," she clutches her father's hand, together in near blindness they fight the drifts, the furious wind, why do intelligent beings insist on living in such a terrible climate, at long last, thank God, what a relief, never again, they are inside out of the numbing cold.

In the lobby while her daddy is registering, three teenage boys pretend to be punching each other out. They are up on their toes, weaving and laughing. They dance over the worn carpet, dodge chairs, jump from sofas, throwing their punches. "Pow!" one says. "Down for the count."

Juliette Daggle feels like crying.

"Hey!" the boy says. He drops to one knee, "I didn't mean it. Holy Christ, so help me I was only kidding."

And suddenly all three boys are like proper gentlemen, they are as tender and obliging as three wise men come from afar.

For unfathomable reasons this makes Juliette cry all the harder.

Her father is jumping a sofa, he is up on his toes, weaving and jabbing. "Pick on little girls, will you?" he shouts. "Try this for size," uncorking a haymaker.

And just like that, all four of these people are dancing and punching and laughing.

Juliette Daggle is so mortified she forgets to cry. Her father is insane, everyone is, she wants to shrink away and die. "Grow up!" she yells to the lot of them. "Goddam all of you!"—of course meaning with utter spear-like precision her father most particularly.

In the room Raoul takes to the phone: "When are those priests meeting? What is their topic? When are these invention people doing their business? I want a full schedule up here immediately. Now would you please put me through to Polly White at the following number."

"Sorry, sir, all lines are down."

"Why are you calling Polly?"

"Why? I'm going to sue your mother for desertion, for alienation of affection, such a beautiful term, don't you think? I'm getting a divorce, I'm going to marry Polly White and Olga the kickboxer, Lavender Blue, and anyone else willing."

"What big eyes you have! What a big mouth!"

Juliette sits by the Best Western window in her pansy dress upbraiding the purple pansies for their gross behavior when she spots in a window across the way a woman trying on a yellow summer dress, a wide yellow hat. Juliette would swear the woman over there is her mother but for the presence of a second party, a gross teenager so clearly the woman's daughter, the pair so clearly belonging to each other that no way in hell could that silly woman in the hat and yellow dress even possibly be anyone else's mother.

The window in the bathroom is a sliding panel of milky glass. The cloudiness exists so bad people can't see a little girl doing her business. Juliette does her business, tinkle, tinkle. The human body is so gross. In another galaxy people without ears or eyes but covered with hair like a dog do not have to experience this primitivism. But they can't sing either. She hears her father singing, *Rat-a-tat-tat went the man in the hat. Rub-a-dub-dub went the girl in the tub*. He knocks on the closed door. "If you think about it," she hears him say, "a man singing is pretty silly. Hey, did I tell you? I've met this great inventor, he's going to bore a hole in my ear, I'm going to wear silver."

Through the open window she looks at the whiteout, miles and miles of heaped-up gusting snow, a white desert, the cottonwoods up to their eyeballs, the sky a great overturned bowl icy-white from top to bottom, pray to God her dear mother is on a beach in Florida.

Jimminy-jimmi-dijingles, that tingles, sang Jimminy Ringles, sings her father.

On a television in the next room a woman cries her junket of tears: "You never take me out to dinner, you never want to be seen with me, you're ashamed of me, you don't love me, you will never know how to love me, why don't you just shoot me," *click*, and there is the Pope's voice detailing the vast crimes committed in the name of God, this one beheaded, that one flayed alive, these thousands burned on the stake, names and dates included, the facts are all there in the secret annals, *click*, "For God's sake," a man says, "can't you find something interesting?"

The Pope's televised apology for the crimes of his faith continue, how many weeks now?

"Sarah Klonswonen, made to walk seventeen miles on nails, 1272.

"Six hundred witches floated downstream at Heath on the Ry, 1387.

"Hazanpot the Infidel pierced by four hundred arrows, 1492.

"Felicity Monde and child pulled apart by dogs, 1561."

"Hreulen Woute the glover and nine hundred heretics dropped from the Nutt Bridge, 1591."

The Pope's tactic is paying off, church rosters are swelling, cathedrals are jammed, other world religious leaders are booking emergency air time, we are encouraged by this sudden urgency of those enthroned on high to come clean, in Naples yesterday a respected Mafia official ran into a police station and said, "I am wounded in my faith, I have been an instrument of torture for ever so many, please arrest me." This is happening everywhere. What cataclysmic force has the Pope unleashed?

Dinner.

"Look at this slop," Juliette Daggle says. "Isn't it disgusting?"

"Is tutti-frutti moody?" asks her father.

Juliette laughs. Raoul Daggle is so amazingly funny. He has no way at all with a wife, a child, he is such a clod, such a heathen. Isn't it strange how much she adores him? She's loved these miles and miles with him. It is almost as good as having a mother. But she's aged some in the process. He can be so tiring. Sober, he's serious and gloomy, preachy, that can be grueling. Why is he sober, anyway? In his place she'd be drowning in sorrow. To offer your love and have that offer rejected, how humiliating. "I wasn't good enough for Joyel," he says. "What a bright woman your mother is. She will only settle for the best, that's your mother. Why else would she have taken to the road? I can see that now. I was ailing, I was a sorry husband, but now I'm in a state of recuperation, I'm onto the path of recovery. I've gone down the Pathways of Truth, braved the Shores of Darkness, I've repented and entered the Corridor of Faith, I'm making myself over. Goddammit, isn't it a shame that all those priests who had fallen from heaven could not assist me one smidgen? You'd think all that gospel, all those enunciations from on high, would have some application to a guy on the road burning rubber. But apparently not. It's taken you and all these people we've met on the road. They've done it. You remember that hitchhiking boy you wanted to marry?"

"I didn't, Papa."

"That boy had his head screwed on right. He let nothing I said dissuade him. How many others? What I'll bet is that Joyel has found the same. She's met people, entered their lives, and those people have rearranged her blood cells, forged her anew, hell, a blacksmith has been pounding the anvil. That's why I'm no longer into the gin. My genes have been rearranged."

"Papa, don't overdramatize."

"Hush up. I'm speaking to you, my beloved daughter, the truth. I've gone through the black hole from which no light escapes, I've escaped those stars collapsing on their own weight, I've entered a new regimen of purpose and said 'Fuck you' to those collapsing stars. What do those stars know or care about you and me? I'm fed up with being sucked into black holes. Now here we gather as buds in spring by ye Hyperion waters."

"Please, Papa, people are looking."

The old alky priest with the purple nose heaves himself down at their table. "You know," he says, "I spent years with the people of Pintou, Guelph province. Each night they leave small offerings to God by their pillows. Cookies on a folded banana leaf, wafers sprinkled with sugar. Each morning they look to see if the leaf is empty. If the offering is untouched, they know God is displeased with them. If empty, then they can go off to work whistling."

Juliette's eyes suddenly go large: "Isn't that Tom the New Indian's rig?"

"Well, by God, yes!"

The New Indian has drawn his huge rig up to the Best Western entryway. There's Crazy Horse on the long trailer, under tons of snow but ready for war. They see the shuddering cab, diesel smoke funneling into the sky. There's Tom leaning across his seat, opening a door. Two shapes ignite from an unseen corridor and here they come, two Indians, a woman and a girl, done up in fancy paints, beaded dresses, mukluks, heaps of fur, bones, scampering over slush for Tom the New Indian's open door.

The waitress comes and clears Raoul and Juliette's table. "That New Indian," she exclaims, "he is so, like, gorgeous, his tips are unbelievable!" She blushes to her roots, oh, doesn't the heart soar when witnessing one so witlessly in love.

"I can't wait for my shift to end so I can go see the New Indian and Crazy Horse at the Lyon County Fair. Are you going? My name is Katarina Eubanks, your new server for the evening, how was your *sopa de dia*? May I say to you, mademoiselle, that I truly adore your pansy dress, I had one much like it when I was a little girl, and my purple pansies were always wanting to stuff themselves with ice cream."

On the way over to the fair in the Infiniti, the Infiniti saying to one and all, "Please close the forward passenger door," her father says to Juliette, "I want to tell you a story that my father told me when I was about your age."

"Not another story," moans Juliette. "My life has been usurped by stories, I am so weary of stories."

"Be polite," her father says.

A man and a woman one day arrived at the end of the world.

The man said, "Where are we?"

The woman said, "I don't know."

The man said, "Go and take a look."

So the woman went and looked. She poked and pried about in every corner, she strode up and down the byways of the end of the world, she looked into every cupboard and corner and there was so much to be seen the task took her a thousand years.

In the meantime, the man waited. He began to think for sure that the woman somehow had tricked him and where they had arrived at was not the end of the world but another place altogether. So he, too, went looking.

For a thousand years he looked, poking and prying about in every cupboard and corner, and finally he and the woman met up.

The man said, "Where are we? Is this the end of the world or isn't it?"

The woman said, "You tell me. For a thousand years I've been here sprucing this place up, giving a good scouring to every bitch corner and crevice, planting our garden and making for us a good home, like, you know, preparing for a family, but all you can say to me is 'where are we?'"

The man knew then that where it was he had come to was either the end of the world or not the end but whatever the case it was a place from which there was no returning.

He began to think about all those other places in the world and all those other people poking and prying into every corner.

"Who got us into this?" he moaned. "Why did no one tell us? Woman, this is all your fault, you had to go and take that first step, didn't you? You had to foolishly strike out into the world's unknown territory and now I must spend my life forever in this hellhole."

Yes, and so they did, eternally moaning and grumbling, and if you put your head on a pillow in the night you can hear their incessant bickering.

"I want to tell a story," Juliette said.

"Get right to it."

"Night fell."

"That's it? That's your story? What happened when night fell?"

"Everybody went home."

"Who is everybody?"

"You and me, Daddy. Us and Joyel."

"Okay. Night fell and everybody went home. What else?"

"I don't know. That's as far as I've got."

"Well, it's a lousy story."

But Raoul laughs. He laughs and laughs. He is such a smart, good, and meant-to-be happy soul, our Raoul, driving along there with a yellow *jiva*-type thing looped around his head, although who can recall his putting it on or can figure where he got it. The silver ring in his left ear is glittery, he constantly fiddles with it. "Okay," he says, "I take it back, 'night fell,' I see now it's a great story either way you read it. I wish I had made up that story, I think it's one I will tell my next child?"

"Pardon me?"

But Juliette Daggle is only momentarily paralyzed.

"Night went clunk," she laughs. "That's another one. Day went splat."

"Daddy went ape-shit."

Right on.

Entering the fairgrounds, Raoul says to his daughter, "You were born in a roomful of screaming babies. Did I tell you that?"

"Maybe you told me, maybe you didn't."

"I'd say a minimum fifty mothers-to-be were in that room. Babies were being born right and left. An open room, no curtains, screaming babies. It was how the hospitals were doing things that year. It was an all-girls' night the mothers were having. I think they set some kind of record, fifty girl babies, not a single boy, nearly all arriving at the stroke of midnight. There you were dripping war paint, all six pounds eight of you. 'Please, sir,' a nurse said to me, 'she must go to her mother now for her nursing.'"

"Are you okay, Papa? You're sounding strange."

"No, honey. I'm withered and broken, irresolute and sodden with misfortune. Grief walks alongside me like a desperate brother. I'm unkempt and dissolute, an unfit father, a failed lover, a—"

"Sorry I asked."

"But despite all that," Raoul says, "I feel great. I feel I'm about to make unprecedented discoveries, that I'm bound for a new world. I've been chatting up those inventors—boy, are they a relief after those dreary priests fallen from heaven. I got through to Polly White. Did you know she's a pilot? We've rented a Piper Cub, she's picking up Olga and Lavender Blue, they are in the sky this minute."

"They won't be able to land in this whiteout, Papa."

"They'll make it, don't you worry. You got to have faith, you got to have vision."

A thousand people are milling about, in drift one way or another, their mouths expelling a blue mist, the snow falling about them but everyone warm and cosy, everybody eating hot dogs, cotton candy, the ground crunchy, a loudspeaker squawking, trumpets blaring, bands marching, mini-skirted baton twirlers strutting, batons ablaze in air, oompah-pah, oompah-pah, cheers, dogs running, and there in the middle of the frozen field under a haze of looping snow is Crazy Horse lit up in radiance within rings of yellow lights, those lights casting a yellow haze high and wide in the night sky, the snow falling heavier now, so much snow, squalls picking up as well, a blizzard, if you please, but the Crazy Horse show minute by minute moving to the nitty-gritty.

"The center bleachers, I think," says Raoul, and wouldn't you know it, there milling to their left is that stark-eyed breed of inventors and to their right a legion of dour priests who have fallen from heaven, each set eyeing each other warily, but let's ignore their childish ways, we have more important business because this minute the child Juliette's face has suddenly been infused with rapture, she sucks in her breath, goes weak in the knees, "Take a look at that!" she says, her voice so quickened by excitement all of us must turn our gaze upon her. Across the way, she means, yes, over there, do you see them? On the far lip of these bleachers and stretching away into the darkness of elevated cascading slopes, in that sea of snow converge score upon score of bewitched deer, deer or antelopes, let's say, though deer it must be, the odd elk, a moose perhaps, the random gazelle, animals which, if we are to believe our eyes, have come to bear witness to these Crazy Horse Days that, presumably, they have heard so much about, *I conjure thee in the seventy-two secret names*, perhaps from their distant cousins the buffalo, from a passing hare, from a trilling bird, from another deer, who knows. Isn't it strange, however, that none among the thousands here, including the happy dogs, none except our pair, father and daughter, apparently are privileged to see this great herd. If others did, we would certainly know about it because this is deer-hunting country, a region whose people take seriously their constitutionally endowed right to own and bear arms, moreover this is the deer-hunting season, during these six weeks a man may slaughter such creatures without being clapped into jail, assessed hefty fines, and you may be sure that if this great flock was to be sighted, the stands would immediately empty, every man worth his salt, any man who was a man, and women, too, would be flying home to arm themselves and return quickly as boots can fly, what better way to fill their freezers than with beautiful venison, my God, and there they were, just standing there, saying, Shoot me. Alas, this is not to be, fairgoers tonight are blind to this most blissful of sights, we are all seated now, lights are lowering, break a leg, Chief, let the show begin.

Tom-toms. The faint beat of tom-toms, in the long distance as if from the folds of history then these tom-toms slowly nearing as if arriving simultaneously with the progress of untold numbers in steady foot march from the folds of dark history then these tom-toms everywhere beneath your shoes in the throbbing bleachers the pulsing air as close to you as your seated partner, such a throbbing, please would someone go and ask those in charge to lower the volume. Great explosions down on the field, enfilade arriving wave upon wave and in the instant the first echoes respond volleys of thick sea-green smoke are seen rising from the huge moccasins of the great Indian Crazy Horse that crazy redskin, look at that, it's climbing his legs smoke is firing from his every orifice and appendage, look up there, his nose his eyes and ears his butthole how do they do that it must cost a fortune yes I'm telling you this is some sight, yahoo! In the belly of the great warrior massive gears grind under Tom the New Indian's skilled hands pull this push that crank this and the eyes open the mouth flares wide the head snaps about the eyes swivel they glare in stern appraisal of the massive army arrayed in defeat of him his tomahawk grinding aloft in the one hand the spear in another look Dad he's going to throw that spear oh that axe is so scary but have you seen his belt do you see the skulls all lit up the blood dripping from those scalp pieces now that's history honey you got to admit it was let's say common practice them doing it to us and us to them but that's history for you oh that Crazy Horse he gives a fine show, yahoo, bravo, bravo! But what's this? From within those very same moccasins must be some kind of trapdoor down there dash two squaws in beaded long dress befeathered heads aglitter with light as they leap about within renewed streams of billowing smoke explosions a dazzlement of lights their every inch of flesh painted you would think in celebration of the old warrior's victory over that shitball George Armstrong Custer maybe that's why these two figures pawing the earth hip-hopping dancing all that toe stuff in whooping spins fluttering headdress the weave of hands tom-toms well it's good I'm enjoying it but I wouldn't say it was the Winnipeg Ballet the Bolshoi it ain't Broadway. And just as first Juliette is rising from her seat spellbound into speechlessness her face gone ghastly white and her breathing shallow her father beside her one heartbeat later rising in utter astonishment with silent gaping mouth here comes snow what a snow the entire expanse of all that might at another time be seen all in the one second the one second only or so it seems to all present becomes a sea of undulating whiteness and in the minute these two lifted as though by magic from their seats the priests who have fallen from heaven have lifted from theirs the inventors have risen even a bespectacled gentleman in a brown suit who has pursued a woman through the continent that pretty girl over there just now getting to her feet is that the nice Eubanks couple's runaway kid whose name I forget what a blessing that she has not perished on the road just behind the bespectacled gentleman in the brown suit I see Solly the detective Allah will protect the nasty bespectacled son of a bitch no longer if we had eyes to penetrate this incredible snow likely we might find Jane Dearborne on padded crutches down there by the livestock area by God sight of her gives me a lift she's experienced a miraculous recovery from her ex-husband's beating I'm pleased to inform you that asshole has walked his last mile but as to how and why Jane has come to be at the fair what can be said except that much has yet to be unraveled about this strange gravity business, surely you can't expect every little act transpiring on this continent to have been reported upon, for instance your own acts of the previous evening which some might question and others praise we have omitted out of respect for your privacy, likewise apply this respect to our characters, be reasonable, let's pause and collect ourselves, sit down if you're tired, I know some of you are old.

Everyone along every row is white as white can be as is the awestruck herd of deer what's this what are they about now as is Crazy Horse the great warrior these dancing women who is that singing, in fact the whole of the fairgrounds as far as eye can see this entire geographical entity is wiped clean by the falling snow and nothing but wind the fall of snow is to be witnessed or heard excusing the droning putt-putt of a small airplane up there dropping from the heavens, holy smokes, what idiots are flying in this whiteout do they mean to land right here on our fairgrounds are those women out of their minds?

That wind and snow ever reforming into startling arrangements so beautiful there can be no end, or such at any rate the New Indian would tell you, yes it was something like that the wind the snow and me in there among the Old Indian's guts watching it transpire not a wheel turning my every pulley silent and the snow silent too of course the deer silent the whole fairgrounds so silent you could hear your breath drop though certainly not that falling snow and me there with a look of grand satisfaction on my face as if I had created it with my own two hands and all for the greater good, I might say, the ultimate whiteout, let's call it, my heart in there lifting, let's say, if you will allow me to put it that way, and soon enough, sooner than you might think all those beneath that great billowing snow to find their loved ones by scent by touch and by shoeleather by the compounding of elements for the sweetest of reasons one way or another in all the varieties available eventually to slip and slide their way home, oh my brothers and sisters oh my daughter oh my father and my mother oh all of you in sunlight and in peril we are past Eden we are past the Gates of Hell past the Shores of Darkness every act is crucial including the least of them the elixir is within us shake vigorously and apply daily do not use in conjunction with other medicines we are New Indians fallen priests old lovers warriors afoot over hard trails now coming home.

acknowledgements

My thanks to the Canada Council for a grant which was of vital assistance in the writing of this novel. Thanks to Jenny Kitson for valuable criticism, to Nigel and Irene Guilford for courier service, to my wife Constance, always the loyal, fearless, and astute critic, and to my editor Patrick Crean for the demonstration of faith, not to mention an editorial acumen vastly advantageous to this novel.